GLIMPSE
INTO THE DARKNESS

a novel by Lauren Somerton

BOOK II

 FriesenPress

Suite 300 - 990 Fort St
Victoria, BC, Canada, V8V 3K2
www.friesenpress.com

www.authorlaurensomerton.com

ISBN
978-1-4602-7600-6 (Hardcover)
978-1-4602-7601-3 (Paperback)
978-1-4602-7602-0 (eBook)

1. Fiction, Science Fiction

Distributed to the trade by The Ingram Book Company

For my father,
Ian

With your enthusiasm for conspiracy and mystery,
you encouraged my own obsession.

CHAPTER ONE

"You know..." Emily hesitated. "I'm starting to think none of it was real," she whispered, staring blankly at the blackened crack along the handle of her favorite coffee mug.

"What do you mean?" Mark spoke to Emily while trying to get Sophie to swallow what was left of the pomegranate and apple puree, with which she much preferred to decorate the overly plain, vinyl kitchen floor.

It had been six weeks since the Jarly had abruptly departed from James and Julia's wedding. Though Amadeus had insisted that it was simply protocol and time for them to leave, it felt like a lie to Emily. Something else was definitely going on.

"The Jarly, the attack on that building, the rescue..." She stopped and grinned, as Sophie finally swallowed the last spoonful with a satisfied look on her face. "Don't you think it was odd? We went through so much with them. Accomplished so much together, supposedly for a brighter future, and now all we get is interview requests from gossip magazines and the occasional paparazzo." Pointing at a large stack of white- and cream-colored papers at the end of the table, currently being held down by a SpongeBob doll, she said, "It's just starting to feel less and less real to me. Like one of these days, I'll wake up and be in our old bed. Sophie won't be born, and Amy will still be nagging me about what shoes I plan to wear to her wedding."

Mark smirked, lifting Sophie from her highchair, then walking over to a corner of the living room, which was surrounded by fluffy and brightly colored toys. He kissed her crown, as she became enthralled by her Barbie in a rainbow dress and swatted away her father's affection. Emily arose from the table, placing her dish and mug in the sink.

1

Hugging Emily from behind, Mark brushed his lips from her temple down her neck, gently tugging the back of her robe to reveal more warm skin. Nuzzling into the soft dark locks of hair behind her ear and inhaling deeply, he whispered, "Baby, if none of this is real, if nothing happened, could I do this?" He reached around and grabbed the side of her mug. With a small flash of light, it reformed and rejuvenated until the angry crack began to fade, and the mug looked good as new.

Emily laughed in a single huff. "I don't think that's what Amadeus had in mind, when they gave us these abilities."

Mark rolled his eyes, slowly turning Emily around in his embrace. Gently, he brushed her cheek with the pad of his thumb. "What's this all about? A couple weeks ago you couldn't stop talking about them; what they had done for us, that we needed them."

"Yes, well the lack of news and appearances has made me question what is really going on."

Sophie's overjoyed wail turned their heads. There, standing on the edge of the living room, were Riley and Selene. Riley bent, then rose with Sophie in his arms and a wide, toothy smile on his face. Mark returned their welcoming gesture.

"Ears burning?" he asked, with an accusatory, yet joking tone. "See," he whispered, so only his frowning wife could hear.

Riley and Selene glanced at each other, matching right brows raised. "Miss us?" They finally joined Mark and Emily in the kitchen.

Emily hugged Selene. "Just a little," she said with a grin. "Would you like a drink?"

"Please, sit." Mark gestured towards the dark leather couch behind them.

"Actually, this isn't a simple visit," Riley remarked, all attention on the giggling baby in his arms.

"Oh?" Mark reached for Sophie and Riley returned her without as much as a blink.

"Amadeus has called a meeting and has asked that you be there as well." Selene lightly brushed Sophie's bare feet, before turning to Emily. "He has requested that the six of you accompany Earth's ambassadors." She paused, clearly wanting to say more, but simply added, "He trusts you."

"The six of us?" Mark emphasized the word six.

"We will explain more, soon. The meeting starts shortly; can you come now?" Riley appeared to be getting antsy, though he hid it well. He noticed Emily's accusative stare, then he let out an exasperated breath, his shoulders relaxing, as he covered his left earlobe. "Sorry, I'm getting a constant transmission from the station and the conversation is getting out of hand. Anyway..." He focused back on the couple. "Are you available?"

Before the words had even resonated, the word "Sure" was out of Emily's mouth and the scenery had changed.

"Good." Riley grabbed the back of a plush desk chair, and directed Mark to sit. Selene and Riley smirked, as Emily and Mark glanced around, confused at their new surroundings. A large, brightly lit room had taken over their living room. Twelve matching black chairs surrounded a large oval table. The only decoration appeared to be an overblown aerial view of the entire globe on the right side of the room, and on the left, a similar landscape. However, the landmasses were oddly shaped and much larger.

"Nona," Selene answered their unspoken questions. She took three long strides and pointed to a red patch on the top right hand side of the map. "That's Meanip, the city where Amelia and I were born."

Mark examined the map more closely, as Emily scanned the room. Bare, would be her first assessment. "This is where we are meeting?"

Selene looked as if she was about to answer, but two bright lights appeared at the other end of the room, as Damon and Caleb transported Amy and Rick. Amelia and Isobel arrived seconds later, with Julia tightly clutching the hand of James. It was only now that Emily noticed they were all wearing solid black clothing. Amelia wore an exquisite lace blouse, but it was still equally black. Emily loved how calm she felt when in their company.

The silent awe of the room was broken by Sophie's giggles and frequent hand-clapping.

"Em?" Amy looked half asleep, as she made her way around the large table and into the arms of her sister.

"Oh right, it's only nine a.m. You must have been in bed still," Emily sarcastically stated, as she engulfed her sister into a large bear hug. Rick and Amy had recently returned from a vacation in the Caribbean, which had left them both nicely tanned. Amy's hair had lightened further, bleached by the sun, while Rick had buzzed the majority of his light brown hair, emphasizing his facial features. Where Amy was petite and slender, Rick boasted broad shoulders and a solid physique. Standing over a foot taller than his wife, they looked like the perfect couple.

"Shut up! We had a late night." A small yawn completed her sentence.

One by one they greeted each other. It hadn't been easy to get together since the world had become so interested in their everyday lives. Emily shuddered every time she saw the latest titles on the odd magazine, usually referencing some form of conspiracy, alien heritage, or their new nicknames as "The Chosen Ones." Sophie loved it whenever James was near; he always used his light to play and entertain.

"Please have a seat," Amelia gestured towards the table after her final embrace of Mark. "Amadeus will be joining us shortly."

"You could have given us a minute to get changed." Mark glanced around the room at the barely decent group.

Riley shrugged, "You're clothed, aren't you?" He grinned at their disheveled appearances, rolling his eyes. "Here," with a wave of his hand, the room filled with light again. A slight tugging on their clothing faded along with the light, revealing that their individual clothing had been replaced with matching grey shirts and black slacks.

"How?" Rick tugged at the cotton shirt.

"Hey, I liked that camisole," Julia began to complain.

"Relax, your clothes were sent home," Riley said, now drumming his fingers along the tabletop.

"Is there anything you guys can't do?" James asked, noting that they were all still barefoot.

"Hmm, can't hold my breath for very long." Riley mocked the question, scratching his chin with his index finger.

Selene cleared her throat. "Emily, I think it would be better if Sophie left the room. We will be covering some graphic topics and it's no place for a child." Emily glanced over at Mark, as Selene reached for Sophie. He gave her a reassuring smile and quick nod.

"I won't let her out of my sight." Selene winked, as Sophie willingly went into her open arms. A door just behind them silently swept open as Selene whispered in her best baby voice that they had a large selection of toys on board, and took Sophie out. Emily nervously watched the door close behind them.

Glancing around the room, Emily's mind drifted back to the year before. Unaware of her early pregnancy, Sophie was only a nearby dream. Amy and Rick were blooming with excitement over their upcoming nuptials, while James was cracking every flirtatious joke that he could around the reception tables, dancing with every attractive woman in sight, until his true desires landed on and stayed with Amy's best friend and maid-of-honor, Julia. Smirking to herself as she watched them whisper playfully to one another across the room, Emily wondered why it had taken so long for them to reach out to one another, given that James and Rick had been best friends since they were young boys. After the horrific events of the previous year, James and Julia's marriage grew stronger every day.

The night that the wedding reception was struck by the Jarly-Biron invasion changed a lot of things. Those who had been taken and studied by the military still lived with crippling nightmares, post-traumatic stress, frustrated outbursts, and general alienation from others; some were still afraid to leave their own homes. Though the Jarly took complete responsibility and offered to help in any way to assist those that survived, their help was mostly met with outright fear and disgust.

Those that were once good friends of the Chosen Ones had all but disappeared into a presence of occasional text messages and brief emails. Though it had never been spoken aloud, the continued contact with their Jarly friends and the bonding of their light left a feeling of betrayal in those who had been taken and tormented. As the months went by, the multiple thanks that had erupted from those rescued by the Chosen Ones, with the assistance of Amadeus and his Jarly team, seemed to be the last of the intended communication. Losing good friends hurt everyone involved, but Emily and the others knew why it had come to be this way. The six had to accept it for what it was; helping the Jarly in rescuing their friends' lives had left them labeled as co-contributors to the invasion and continued fear, which in turn cost them their friendships.

Taking a deep breath and distracting herself with happier thoughts, Emily turned to her husband Mark, who was pleasantly distracted by something Rick had mentioned. She studied the side of his face, his dark hair short and hinting at a deep natural wave. His cheeks and jaw covered in a light dusting of facial hair, he looked the picture of health and vitality at the age of thirty-three. They had met during her early years at the Kindred Hospital of Tucson, Arizona. Flustered by her new position, Mark, who was a doctor within the hospital, had really made her feel at home and encouraged her to stick with the overly stressful unit. As the daily visits, accompanied by her favorite coffee and the occasional bouquet of flowers, turned into weeks and months, she knew he would be the one. Mark glanced in her direction, noticing her stare he smiled. Taking her left hand he gently squeezed, bringing Emily's attention back to the table and the current situation.

"So, why are we here?" Mark asked Amelia directly.

"Need us to beat up some more people?" James asked, almost comically. "I'm ready for Round Two." He cracked his knuckles loudly, stretching his neck from side to side, and smirking as Julia elbowed him in the ribs.

"Thanks, but that won't be necessary this time," Isobel chimed in, with humor.

"We have asked the six of you here today as we have agreed to your government's requests to view our space station and report back to their leaders."

The mood in the room took a nosedive into the Arctic waters. "Are you sure that's such a good idea? Giving them access to everything?" Rick blurted, before anyone else could comment. "I mean, let's face it, they weren't very sensitive the last time you tried to show them what you're capable of."

"And that is why Amadeus has asked you to join the team. He is only allowing a few representatives on board at a time." Amelia pointed to the table, which distracted the group.

"On board?" Rick asked, as realization hit. "Here?" He pointed down in general. "Are we...?"

"Yes, this is our space station."

Two illuminated fingers waved at the wall to Amelia's right. The map of Earth slowly faded, replaced by a starry night sky. "Please." Amelia got to her feet, encouraging the others to join her along the wall. A strange light covered the bottom, flickering majestically. As Amy reached the window and looked down, a sudden gasp escaped her lips and she covered her mouth, staring wildly.

Not so much a wall, but a solid window, kept back the invading space. Emily grasped Mark's shoulder, as the group looked down at the tranquil Earth, spinning softly below them.

"Is that..." Julia started.

"Earth," Riley interrupted, staring blankly out the window. He blinked a few times, then turned, focusing on Julia. "We're twelve thousand miles above the surface, to be exact."

Amelia made her way back to her seat at the end of the table. "As I was saying, Amadeus has asked that you accompany the teams that will be shown around the base. Just keep an eye out. Make sure that nothing goes wrong. You are fortunate to have your own light, while having the Human emotions and correct reactions to the new surroundings."

"We just want to make sure everyone is comfortable, while watching for any mischief," Riley added. "There is a reason why we waited so long to allow Human evaluation and review of our technology."

"We understand," Rick stated, after silent thought. "But seriously, you guys must know they're going to be up to something?"

Without another word, everyone slowly made his or her way back to the chairs; some fidgeting uncontrollably, while others seemed to stare off into space. Riley and Amelia suddenly cupped their left ears and listened to an unheard transmission, as if they were answering a call. The others simply stared in silent confusion. Eventually, Amelia nodded, and then they both lowered their hands. Apart from Amelia, the Jarly suddenly stood in a formal line along the edge of the glass, at ease with the apparent lack of protection. Emily couldn't help but feel a pinch in her stomach, as the glass could not have been thicker than an inch or two.

Amelia steepled her hands on the table in front of her, as she spoke in a low and calming voice. "The others will be joining us shortly. Please, follow our cues. We only ask that you observe the others and advise if something doesn't feel right. As part of your initial light transfer, you are able to communicate speechlessly with one another."

The seated group all looked around in shock.

Isobel wordlessly drew Emily's attention to where she was standing at the glass wall.

"How d..."

Isobel shushed her with a single finger to the lips. *It's best if we communicate this way. There's no need to create alarm.* Isobel didn't even make eye contact, as she scanned the room.

"As I was saying…" Amelia drew their attention back to the table. The shocked and excited faces around the room indicated that Isobel and Emily's telepathic conversation was not the only one.

"Wait," Mark lightly smacked the table with a confused look on his face. "If you can communicate like this, why didn't you tell us about this before? We could have used the extra encouragement and g…" Mark stopped abruptly, as he listened to whatever Riley was advising him.

"Mark," Amelia calmly called his attention to her. "As we had explained, we were only allowed limited influence and assistance. Please believe me when I say we wish there was more we could have done, but I must repeat one of your Human expressions." Her eyes widened and her face contorted in sympathy. "Our hands were tied. There is much more about us that you are still unaware of, and with time you will learn much more. Beginning today, I would imagine."

Only Emily was accustomed to the expression on Mark's face. To everyone else, he would have appeared to be placated and quiet, as he nodded and looked away, but under that skin there was frustration and anger brewing. Reaching over, she returned his reassuring squeeze, brushing her thumb over his rough skin. Instantly, as their eyes met, his shoulders began to relax and he took a deep breath.

Amelia touched her ear again, quickly, then gestured to the others. Before anyone could ask, she silently stood and watched the empty space at the end of the room. As all eyes turned, a beam of light flashed, and within seconds Amadeus and three large Jarly soldiers materialized, accompanied by at least ten Humans. Four women in military-style uniform of various colors were scattered within the group of men; two of whom looked as if they were on the verge of throwing up. Some whispers suggested a Russian background; a few others were clearly North Korean and Japanese. The majority of the group appeared to speak with muttered American and British accents.

Here we go, Isobel muttered, for only Emily to hear...which made Emily grin and Mark look confused.

The group beamed, as Amadeus stepped forward. "Friends," he said. Previous frustration seemed to simmer, as his smile grew with sincerity. "I thank you for joining us."

As he continued, a brooding American with a strong Texan accent rudely interrupted him. His long crooked nose and large bushy brows gave him a severe expression. "What are they doing here?" he spat with blatant outrage. "This is not a civilian mission; they do not have the clearance or approval."

Amadeus stopped his rant with a simple raise of his hand. "General Clay, these men and women have every right to be at this meeting. They know our kind better than any. We have a history and shared abilities. If their presence upsets you, I will be more than happy to escort you back to your base and continue our tour with them, alone." His comment, though in response to Clay, was clearly addressing the whole group. His voice appeared calm and collected, but even the broody Texan took an unsteady step back. It was easy to see why Amadeus was in charge.

Amy's girlish snicker and glance towards a smirking Amelia suggested an unspoken joke or snide remark.

Obviously chastised, the general mumbled something to his subordinates, and then grumbled directly to Amadeus, "Please, continue."

Amadeus turned towards the table. "If you'd follow me?" He gestured to the door, which was being opened by another of the unnamed Jarly guards.

Who are they? Emily glanced, one by one, at each and every official who insisted on exiting the room before her family and friends.

Isobel was silent and Emily glanced at her from the corner of her eye.

These are the selected representatives of your planet. You didn't think we were only contacting Americans, did you? She caught Emily's eye and gave her a knowing smirk. *After your team had successfully proven your place among our people, we called various meetings with our old contacts, much like Thomas, which led to more prominent leaders of Earth, and we arranged this. A number of nations have chosen to either have the Americans research on their behalves, or to avoid us all together. We knew the early stages of awareness of us would not be easy ones.*

She continued, as everyone filed down a long narrow corridor. Everything was extremely bright and clinically clean. Very little color covered any of the walls or high ceilings. After two rights and a left, a heavy metallic wall, easily wide enough to fit three people through at once, confronted the group.

"The first room we are going to show you is our communications center." Amelia took the lead. A previously invisible line split the door in two, and with a sudden swoosh the room was accessible.

Hundreds of blinking screens covered almost every surface of the room. Four Jarly jumped, standing to Amadeus' attention. With a single nod, one stepped forward to describe the purpose and functionality of the room. Emily noted that only the women appeared to be writing anything down, and furiously fast at that. As the Jarly, who introduced himself as Trick, finished his speech, the room was slowly depleted of prying eyes when everyone continued to the next room.

So far, little had truly interested Emily's group as much as it should have. They had been guided though the information deck, the lunch-rooms, sleeping quarters, and additional bathing and recreation rooms. Mark, for obvious reasons, had much more interest in their medical bay, while Rick and James couldn't contain their excitement for the fitness and rejuvenation areas.

As the group entered the next room, they found the walls were shiny and highly reflective. As a short, dark-skinned man with a severe limp in his left leg stepped forward to ask Amelia what this room was used for, the room itself appeared to move and descend in a slow rotating motion. It was the closest thing to an elevator the ship could command. Every once in a while, a man or woman would lazily walk onto the platform and exit out of the opening spaces as each floor became visible. Emily watched with fascination, noting at least eight different floors before they were slowly ushered off. This floor was darker than the others; the space was all but deserted.

So, they're all scientists? Emily continued silently with Isobel.

Most of them, yes. A few are men of power, who insisted that they had to see this first hand, before they would allow others to do so. General Clay, for instance, only cares about a few key components of our weaponry and defensive capabilities. Isobel clearly rolled her eyes, then became distracted by something Riley whispered.

A frisson of frustration crossed her features, as she bit down on her lip and glanced at Emily, who was clearly confused. *It would appear that a few members of this group have already tried placing devices along our controls and are attempting to gain access to our systems.*

Anger spiked within Emily. *Why would they even attempt such secrecy and deception, when all this information is being given up willingly?*

Don't fret, we have already scanned and immobilized their devices. This will all be addressed at the end of the tour. Isobel continued walking past Emily, to the front of the line.

They all stopped at the end of a wide hallway. Another set of doors, three times as large as the last, concealed the room ahead. The hallway was so dark, at this point, that Emily was only able to see Mark to her right and Amy to her left. The others were faint outlines.

As she engaged her inner light, Isobel's flames consumed her legs, illuminating her features. Mesmerizing the group before clearing her throat, she spoke loudly and clearly. "Ladies and gentlemen, we are about to enter one of the most important rooms on this station." The entire group seemed to lean forward, listening more intensely. "As the medical lead on this base, I must advise, do not touch anything. Please, stay together. There will be points where we will be able to answer any questions you may have. You will notice that the room is significantly louder, and may seem unstable. Rest assured, you are in no danger-- if you stick together and follow my rules." She glanced at Caleb, and he again took the lead.

With a nod to his brother, Caleb and Damon both raised their lit arms, commanding the heavy doors to open. A sudden gust of wind and heavy air shot a shiver down Emily's spine. Amy gripped her left hand as Emily leant into Mark, who wrapped his arm protectively around her shoulders. Slowly, the doors slid away to reveal a blackened room, illuminated by a shimmering, blue orb. Almost everyone's jaws fell, as they took in the view. The orb was easily ten stories tall and equally as wide. It sat on a narrow metallic stand. The wind whipped violently through their hair, as Emily tucked herself more tightly under Mark's shoulder, gripping his opposite hip from behind. His lips were moving, but the noise was so overwhelming, she could only nod and continue to glance around the room.

Something small and disc-shaped fell out of the pocket of the scientist in front of Emily. Glancing down, she noticed what appeared to be a small flashing light and rotating camera. This must have been what Isobel had been telling her about. It was no accident that this is where the scanner had dropped.

"This way," Isobel summoned the group. She was not yelling, but somehow everyone was able to hear her clearly. To the left, there was a glass room and the others in front of Emily appeared to be excited, pushing forward. Instead of purposefully stepping over the device at her feet, Emily raised her bent leg high, slamming down on it, crushing it under her heel.

Got one for ya!

Isobel grinned at Emily's enthusiasm. Gradually, the room was filled and the doors closed behind them. The noise of the room all but disappeared, fading to a light, buzzing sound.

"This is our core." Caleb then gestured to the orb behind him, "This device powers the station, and all our technologies. It can be created in a number of sizes, to manipulate the smallest of devices." As he finished, a serpent-like spiral of blue shimmer-light traveled in a wide circle at the center of the orb.

"What was that?" The question escaped the lips of a cowering Japanese scientist, before the others apparently scolded her.

"Please," Caleb encouraged her with a toothy smile. "Now is the time for questions." He winked at the embarrassed woman. "That was Calobie, an essence of our home world, Nona. A chemical reaction, with a number of living and non-living components and elements, drives to create a form of energy. Calobie is a form of living material that, in essence, sparks the other compounds and continually rejuvenates the system."

"What specific materials make up this reactor, then?" A white-haired, pointy-nosed man, with a thick British accent, interrupted.

"Obviously, there are a number of elements only found on Nona and localized planets. Along with Sulphate, Magnesium, Calcium, Potassium..."

Caleb continued naming at least thirteen different elements. "But the main Earthly equivalent would be water-diluted Sodium Chloride."

A few of the scientists glanced nervously at one another, and even Mark stiffened.

"What?" Emily whispered.

Mark turned to Riley, who silently nodded, then looked down at his wife. "Em, everything they need to power all this technology makes up over 70% of Earth's surface."

It was as if a light bulb went off, exploding uncomfortably in Emily's skull. "Ocean? Sea water can do all this?"

Mark was clearly distracted by his own thoughts; he simply pulled her closer, kissing her temple as they both turned to witness another passing of Calobie.

CHAPTER TWO

Thirty minutes later and the tour was over. The small group returned to the mapped room, while the additional scientists had been returned to their bases on Earth. Now alone, Amy and Julia played with Sophie in the corner, as the others sat around the table, waiting for more explanation.

"So, that's why," Rick blurted cryptically, then elaborated as he was faced with blank stares. "Think about it, they came to Earth thousands of years ago, when we were nothing special. Well, now we know why they stuck around; they wanted our ocean water resources, nothing more."

"That's not true." Amadeus' voice surprised everyone, so much that they were stunned into silence, staring as he, Amelia, and Riley took to their seats.

Amadeus looked angry; everyone seemed to tense. Slowly, he let out a long sigh, relaxing into his chair, and the room calmed. "I'm sorry. I know this very confusing."

"When we were at Thomas' compound, you told us…" Rick started.

"I told you the truth. We were interested in the natural inhabitants of your planet and vowed that we would observe, with minimal interference." Amadeus stared, as if the group was supposed to get some hidden message from his words. "You see - you are very similar to us both physically and mentally. You are just a younger species and we are proud at how far you have come." He stopped, sighed, and then continued. "I do admit - once initial samples were taken - our added visits were not entirely focused on the life forms, but on your resources. The very fact that the majority of our people, after learning of your many global species, chose to leave you to your own devises and not strip your world created the corrupt and unyielding arguments between what was once the Jarly and now Biron people."

"Why?" Julia asked, as she and Amy joined the discussion at the table; Sophie now breathing heavy with sleep into the crook of her mother's neck.

"When the separation took place, many like-minded Jarly could not justify the destruction of your planet for the advancements of our own. Those who now align with the Biron believe our kind to be superior and deserving." Amadeus' gaze darkened, remembering something; the wrinkling around his eyes appeared to age his face. "You have no idea what wars we have seen, and are still waging, over the status of your planet alone."

"That is another reason why your previous mission was so important; why we needed your kind to join in this alliance and become aware of your own dangers. We hope your people can stop bickering amongst yourselves and unite. Even as we speak, representatives of Nona and the Biron wastelands are communing in attempt to keep what peace we have managed for the last few decades," Riley added, solemnly.

"Sadly, the Biron people are becoming desperate; using far more of their own resources than they can replenish. They are growing in numbers and soon even the Jarly and allies will not be able to stop them, no matter how hard we draw from Nona's light," Amelia numbly stated, as she stared out at the still-starry wall.

"So, this is it? This is what it all comes down to? War is coming?" Mark asked, directly of Amadeus.

"I cannot say how long, but yes, I believe it is inevitable."

"Okay, hold up." James raised both his hands in front of his face. "This is all happening thousands of light-years away. Aren't there other planets nearby or other uninhabited places with the stuff they need?"

Riley huffed with exasperation, while Amelia and Amadeus shook their heads. "Don't you think we would have thought of that?" Riley's words felt like nails on a chalkboard. "We have been fighting for your people, defending you for thousands of years. The Biron don't care who inhabits a planet. If you have what they want, they will ruthlessly take it, and move on. They have already destroyed and killed hundreds of planets and life forms, made countless species extinct..."

Riley had thumped his fist so hard on the table that Julia gasped, and Sophie stirred in her mother's arms.

"Riley." Amadeus spoke sternly.

Riley stopped and glanced over to his leader, straightened in his seat, and turned back to the group. Clearly frustrated, he said, "I'm sorry. You just have to understand...." His hands gestured wide, "We have been fighting this battle since before your ancestors learned to walk on two feet." He let out another sigh. "Now, it's time to get your people ready for what is coming."

* * *

Emily and her group had been returned to their homes, with the promise of another meeting in two days. Amadeus and his team were waiting on further news from their home world on the status of the latest conference between the two nations. Once there was a better understanding of what was going on, there would be a clearer definition of what action to take.

"I think we should ask your parents to take Sophie for a few days," Emily mentioned, as she dried her hair and Mark brushed his teeth.

He looked thoughtful for a few seconds, his brows creased, then spat out a mouthful of paste. "Maybe you should sit this one out?" Emily began to protest, but Mark continued, "Em, there's no use both of us running around up there, with no direction. I'll go to the conference with Amadeus and once we have a better understanding of what is really going on, we can speak to my parents, but..." he pressed his forehead to hers, "Sophie needs her mother, not a warrior."

That made Emily laugh. "Warrior? Yeah. Sure. She needs her father, too."

"Yes," and then a sly grin pulled at the side of his mouth, as he pulled her against his front and they caught each other's eyes in the bathroom mirror. "But if given a choice to miss one or the other, these win every time." Mark gently caressed her engorged breasts.

Emily giggled. "That is true. No one can pass up a walking buffet."

Mark grinned into her neck, kissed her shoulder, and then turned, heading into the bedroom. "Tomorrow, I'll return to the ship and get some worthwhile news... You'll be the first to know."

* * *

"I'm staying here." Emily finally came downstairs, as the other five caught up around the dinner table with an assortment of flavored coffees.

"I've asked Em to stay with Soph, just until we get a better understanding of what's going on and what we are really expected to do about... well, any of it," Mark explained.

Amy stared at her sister and niece, then turned to her husband. "I'm going to stay here, with them."

Rick wrapped his free arm around her shoulders, kissing her temple. "It would definitely be a worry off my chest."

James reached for Julia's hand; before he could speak she bumped his shoulder. "Don't even think of ditching me. I'm coming up there too." She then looked around the table at the other reactions. "As always, there needs to be a woman's..." Stopping, she quickly corrected herself, "A Human woman's touch."

They smiled.

Not twenty minutes later, the living room filled with light, as Riley and Isobel entered the kitchen.

"You're not coming?" Isobel pouted, before anything was said. The others looked confused until Emily grinned and tapped the side of her head.

"We just think it would be better if Amy and I stay with Sophie. Just until we have a game plan," Emily spoke for the room.

Riley agreed. "Fair enough, but the rest of us should get going. The meeting is about to start." The others arose from their seats, silently.

"How long are we talking about, here?" Amy innocently asked.

"These meetings can be anywhere from a long day to two weeks," Isobel replied. "Unfortunately, we wont be able to send anyone home in the meantime."

Emily tensed. "That's longer than I thought." She looked at Mark, who was also uncomfortable with the idea of being separated from his girls for two weeks.

Isobel shrugged apologetically. "It's our policy, but if anything were to happen, I'll make sure you all get back swiftly." Then she continued, for only Emily to hear. *Our bonds are stronger when our emotions are high. I'll still be able to communicate with you, from the station, if anything is wrong, you'll know.*

Emily slowly nodded. *I want a daily update.*

Isobel simply smiled in response.

Amy gave Rick an overly affectionate sloppy kiss, while Mark kissed the top of Sophie's head, embracing the two of them in a large hug.

After a swift yet sweet kiss, Mark whispered, "Catch ya later!" before a light engulfed him and the rest of the group; leaving Emily and Amy staring and Sophie slashing her hands at the empty space where her father had just stood.

* * *

"This waiting around is driving me nuts!" Amy smacked her hands on the leather couch below her, as Emily gently lulled her daughter to sleep on the opposite couch.

"I know," Emily's eyes looked sad, "but it's only been three days. Isobel says they're fine and just deep in discussion." She sighed heavily, brushing her lips against Sophie's forehead. "I'm sure it will be over soon." Though she said the words, it was obvious that even she didn't really believe them. Sadly, Amy could tell.

Three loud knocks sounded on the front door. After some confused glances, the two sisters – with Sophie now asleep in her mother's arms - headed towards the front of the house.

"Expecting someone?" Amy asked over her shoulder. Though having a visitor shouldn't be such a strange occurrence, given the current circumstances the last thing Emily wanted to do was entertain. When they reached the door their moods lifted almost instantly. Abel stood, weakly waving on the other side of the half glass door.

"Abel!" Amy gushed as the door opened and they embraced each other.

"Amy, you look great," he smiled down at her.

Emily carefully passed Sophie to her sister, as she too embraced Abel in a warm and welcoming hug.

"Em, stunning as usual." She laughed, gripping tight as she smacked him hard on the back.

Leaning back, "What are you doing here?" she asked, confused, scanning his face for any bad news. She quickly added, "Not that you aren't always welcome. It's just been so long."

"Amadeus." Abel's face fell slightly at the mention of the Jarly commander's name. "He visited me a few days ago and asked that I visit you. He didn't stay long or give me any details. He just said that you might need my help?" He looked quizzically at the sisters. "I got some things taken care of at work, and someone to look in on Tess... I came as soon as I could."

Emily smiled, "Well, you better come in then."

As she and Amy led Abel through the house and back into the living room, Emily smiled with fondness. Of all those rescued from the hidden military base the year before, Abel was the most enthusiastic and encouraging. Not among the guests of Amy and Rick's wedding, Abel gained his entry into the base through secrecy and cunning deception, which unfortunately did not save him from being captured and tortured far worse than most. As a chemical engineer, Abel had worked on his fair share of top secret government files and knew the telling signs of a cover up was when he saw it. So when his workspace was overrun by military command, Abel knew his own work would act as a perfect cover up when a strange occurrence riddled the news and the military needed a nearby base of operations. With a string of unrealistic accusations and a sudden influx of money and attention, and the understanding that he was not to return to the site, Abel knew there was more to the story and he couldn't keep away.

Thankfully, Amadeus' team had named Abel's best friend and office co-inhabitant, John Stark, in assisting the rescue mission and gaining entrance into the building. At first, Abel wondered why he himself had not been sought out first, given his military involvement and history. John was not privy to any military files, and only shared the workspace out of convenience as he continued his research into his fields of Archaeology and Linguistic Anthropology. Later having asked Amadeus for an explanation, it came to light that John had unknowingly stumbled onto some vital history of Jarly involvement on Earth in his research into Early Sumerian development, he was already on their watch-list for potential friendly contact.

Like Abel, John had kept in contact with Emily and the others after risking his own life to help gain entrance into the military base and later fighting for the freedom of the victims held within. In recent months, John had embraced the Jarly presence with open arms, admittedly hitting the historical jackpot with the wealth of knowledge that the Jarly could offer into early Human development and explanations of rapid technological advancements throughout history.

* * *

Mark and the others arrived into what appeared to be a shiny metallic and white covered room; painfully dull, with large sharp objects neatly displayed in each corner. The group would have had a frisson of fear had they not recognized the room as part of the medical bay. Amadeus was patiently waiting; to his left Thomas smiled, and Isobel stepped to his right. Four guards appeared frustrated; glancing at the new arrivals, then back to the small crack in the door, either watching for those passing by, or waiting to be caught doing something wrong.

Amadeus' smile welcomed the group, but it didn't touch the corners of his eyes, as he was clearly distracted by something. "Good morning." He spoke with his arms spread wide as if to hug those nearest. His face fell. "Please forgive me, but we don't have time for pleasantries." One guard with flawlessly dark skin and bare feet exited the room. He barely opened the door enough to fit his whole body through, allowing it to silently slide shut without allowing anyone to view inside. As Mark glanced down he noticed that not one of them were wearing shoes.

Amadeus continued, "We must prepare you for this meeting. I hope that all of you are brave enough to join and smart enough to observe without interruption." Rick was about to add a sarcastic comment, but thought better of it.

"If you'll turn around," Isobel asked, "before we start, I'll ask that you change into our customary meeting attire." After a few confused looks, Isobel spoke with a persistent pressure, "Please. Quickly."

Everyone mechanically and silently removed their shoes, resting them on the tables provided. Rushing with their clothes, James shielded

Julia as she quickly shuffled out of her clothes and into a skintight black one-piece. Much the same appearance and feel of a scuba diving outfit; it was all black, with no pockets to hide anything. Turning back to the group, Thomas held a black tray with four metallic syringes, gesturing towards Isobel. It was only then that the group noticed the simple changes to Thomas' appearance; they made him almost attractive. His hair was shorter and slicked back, darker too. His matching uniform gave him a more updated and younger appeal. Cleanly shaven, and with his false Jarly markings, he could easily be mistaken for a much younger man than the one they met on his farm.

Amadeus commanded their attention as Isobel picked up the first syringe. "These are complete with an auditory translator and a mild form of adrenaline. I want you all alert." His eyes passed over each one with a steady glare. "I cannot stress the importance of this meeting and your hidden identity. As custom dictates, the entire meeting will be held in the Jarly ancient tongue. These translators will sit just inside your temporal lobe," he absently brushed the side of his forehead, "and they will translate every spoken word into English. Obviously, you will not be able to com-municate back. If a question is asked of you, I will field your response."

Isobel took her syringe and walked towards Rick, who took one invol-untary step back. She noticed and raised her hands, saying, "It will only hurt for a second as the device settles." She gently cradled the left side of his head, positioning the short needle point just behind his right ear. Her eyes found his. "Deep breath." With a weak smile she forced the syringe below the skin. Rick's face contorted with pain. His sudden gasp, while reaching for the nearest table for support, made Julia grasp James' arm. After shaking his head a few times, Rick eventually straightened up and felt the injection spot.

Isobel stepped back. Her words were now foreign and peculiar to the others, but after a second Rick began to nod and turned, eyes wide, to his friends. "It worked. I understood what she said." His voice came more breathy than usual, his eyes slightly dilating with the added adrenaline.

As Isobel injected the others and marked their faces with the trade-mark Jarly freckles Amadeus smiled, softly clapping his hands together, satisfied with the results. "Okay, now I want you all to show me your light."

They look momentarily confused. "Now," he encouraged, more emphatically. "All over. I want to see." Julia took a step forward into the center of their semi-circle and without moving another muscle, a bright and vibrant flame started at the tip of her toes, working its way up her feet, around her waist to her shoulders, eventually consuming her entire body.

"Beautiful." James' eyes reflected the glowing flames that escaped his wife's form.

Mark minutely spread his legs and held his hands a few inches from his face. Closing his eyes his light ignited and he too, followed by James and Rick, was engulfed in harmless flame.

"Perfect. That will do." Amadeus' words doused their flames. He continued with severe hand gestures, "I am breaking countless rules by allowing you into that room. Many believe you are still too weak of a species to have a say, or even be heard, but I believe otherwise. As this meeting determines the fate of your people, you have every right to know what is going on."

"Our fate?" Mark interrupted.

"Yes. " Amadeus looked distracted; taking in a deep breath he explained, "This meeting will determine if we, the Jarly that is, will continue to defend your world from the invading Biron. They wish to strip you of your natural resources and have your kind join the Jarly home world. The Biron are at the brink of desperation and believe - in order to preserve their current way of life - that it is their right to go about and take whatever they wish." He grew angrier with each word. Staring at a dot on the floor, his rant got louder. Eventually, Thomas placed a gentle hand on his shoulder, which drew Amadeus out of his outburst.

The large guard reentered the room. "Five minutes, Commander."

"Thank you, Bates." He nodded once, turning back to the group. "As I was saying, this is a very delicate subject. No one is to speak. You will follow the lead of my team. You are to stand in a row behind me, with your hands crossed behind your back. There are a few customary traditions that you will have to observe and quickly duplicate. The most significant would be covering your feet in flame as the leaders enter the room, until all are seated." Mark and the others nodded as he continued their preparation.

Amadeus appeared satisfied with the group. As he made his way to the door he stopped abruptly, turning on the spot to the line up of Human and Jarly representatives behind him. "One last thing... This is a meeting with a number of representatives. The majority will be Jarly and Biron, whom you have already witnessed in their natural form, but there may be a few other representatives of other colonies and alliances. Though this is all new, please do not stare or draw any form of attention to yourselves. Not everyone and everything is as systematically generic and smooth as our own forms. Though fascinating to you, rude behavior is understood universally. Agreed?" Their Human heads bowed, eyes wider than normal as they attempted to conceal the shock and fear bubbling in each of their empty stomachs.

Slowly the guards led Amadeus and his team to the conference room, if you could call it that; it was closer to the size of a gymnasium. The walls reached as high as a five-storied building, or more. The air in the room felt denser, oddly sweeter, and it took much more of an effort to breathe. Already filled with at least one hundred individuals lining the walls, Mark and his group tried to keep their eyes on the person in front, as they were led through the growing masses towards the center on the room.

A long rectangular table filled the open space. Julia's eyes strayed fractionally and her body became stiff as she took in the group of Birons casually standing in the far right corner of the room. Roughly eight or nine were either filled with absent stares or angered expressions. A few continued conversations amongst themselves, occasionally cheering or smacking each other on the shoulders, oblivious to the attention the were getting from many of the quieter - seemingly Jarly - viewers.

A small gasp escaped her lips as her eyes fell next on a new race of beings. Their skin appeared to be a shimmering blue, almost translucent. Their eyes were larger than that of a Human, and solid black. Their skulls displayed a thick sagittal keel, creating a boney Mohawk. Julia grew fascinated by their slick black and white fur, which started at the front of their skulls, traveling down their spine to the small of their backs. Oddly, they too had the overall feel of a Human structure; bipedal, with two legs, two arms, and a wide torso. In general, they were roughly half a foot shorter than the nearest Jarly, but their most menacing aspect was the overly generous jaw. With wide smiles and small pointed teeth shown clearly as they appeared to laugh and talk amongst one another, one could also see two extra rows of teeth, top and bottom; quite menacing with an absent tongue.

Julia touched the back of her teeth with the tip of her tongue, distracted. Out of sync with her group, she didn't notice when the line had stopped, and she walked straight into the back of James. Quickly stepping back and finding her place, her cheeks reddened as the group abruptly turned, forming a line parallel to the length of the table. Amadeus gracefully walked around the large feature, reaching for an elderly figure sitting alone at the opposite side of the table taking a sip of a blood red liquid. He smiled fondly as Amadeus clasped his shoulder; they talked freely with one another.

Taking their cue from their companions, the Human impostors clasped their hands behind their backs, lowering their heads so that only the table could be seen clearly from their gazes. Gradually, the conversation died down; a bird-like screech silenced the remaining conversations and the room stilled, as everyone then stood to attention. The large doors at the empty end of the room slowly opened to reveal at least twenty more Biron representatives. Fear spiked in the group. Julia forced her hands into fists to prevent them from shaking.

A number of short, child-like, Biron rush into the room, weaving themselves into the larger scattered group. Three representatives of the blue race stepped up to the table and stood behind their seats. These seats were definitely not of Human design; no two matched. Standing twice as wide as the average office chair with backs that came all the way up past the heads of their occupants, they curved and illuminated as the individual sat. Each chair felt like a personal throne, focusing on the individual and drawing others' attention. Eventually, a group of five Biron stepped up to the table and stood directly in front of the Human row. Luckily their backs were to the Human group, leaving their growing discomfort unseen.

"Sit," one exceptionally deep voiced Biron commanded the room. His voice echoed and vibrated through those nearest. Flames spiked around the feet of the guards, followed by most among the Jarly in the room, then by Mark and his team; those still standing around the table grabbed the backs of their chairs, dragging them back as they nestled into place. As each seat became occupied the room grew brighter with each glowing chair. Once all had been seated, and the crowd had taken to their own, only those bordering the table remain standing. Fourteen beings completed the large table. The flames went out and the room fell silent.

CHAPTER THREE

The elderly man that Amadeus had greeted earlier leant forward in his seat, resting his hands on the table. His olive skin was much more wrinkled than any other in the room. Each line on his face appeared to pull down his eyes and collect at his chin. The large brown freckles on the side of his eye were all but faded and appeared worn. His clothes were different to the other Jarly in the room. His fell, loose fitted, and uncharacteristically grey with pale feather-like shapes and designs.

Amadeus and the others looked almost ridiculous in their solid black, skin-tight outfits. The blue men were wearing similar garments to the masses - black and form fitting – however, theirs did not show their hands and feet; in fact their hands appeared to be solid, like that of a small fin. Their feet, if visible, would have been twice as wide of that of a Human or Jarly.

Clearing his throat, the elderly man spoke; loud enough for the whole room to hear, though his words were slowly formed and breathy. "Welcome." It was hard to tell if he truly struggled to speak or the translation syringe faltered. Much like watching a foreign sitcom with English translation, his lips oddly moved and formed contrary to the words escaping his lips. "Thank you all for coming to this peace conference. Before we get to any specifics, I would like to direct you all to the documents provided." He waved his hand over a small green light situated within the table in front of him. A panel moved to the left and a shelf began to rise, holding a few unrecognizable devices. With shaking hands he reached for a silver rod that would fit perfectly in any Human hand. The others around the table did the same. Slowly pulling at its sides, he twisted one half away from him 180 degrees until a small click was heard by all. Placing it down on the flat surface, the rod fully split in two like opposing magnets. They spread at least a foot apart and a translucent film covered the gap between each end. An image of earth appeared with a legend to the right, with flashing objects and non-legible writing.

Mark craned his neck to the left, trying to get a better look at the page in front of one of the Biron representatives, until Bates lightly stepped on his foot. With a sharp glance in his direction, Mark followed his gaze up roughly fifteen meters above the table; the very same image was displayed, large enough for the whole room to view and regard. Circular units that worked together to create the detailed images had replaced the plain black walls. Upon further review, Mark could make out cities and prominent landmarks on the map. Landmasses near large bodies of water with exploding populations appeared in a darker shade of red; mainly encompassing China, Japan, India, South America, and parts of the United States and Canada. At random spots in the Pacific and Indian Oceans, bright flashing green dots drew more attention.

The Biron who had spoken previously pointed a large dark green finger at one of the flashing lights just below Alaska. "Here," his voice once again echoed and rumbled through the crowd. "The population is minimal in comparison and has one of the highest concentration of Nairi we have ever seen."

The elderly man nodded, not taking his eyes from the screen in front of him, "Yes." He spoke again, slowly, "But those living in that area rely heavily on the marine life for their sustenance and..."

"Ah! Velo." The Biron commander slammed his fist on the table. "We are here to negotiate the safest and more remote areas of this planet. Any area we touch will be affected. Simple marine life will be the least of their worries."

Velo continued, untaxed by the outburst. "We will only agree on an area that is less prominent to the Human species and their way of life."

The frustration in the room was almost palpable. The discussion continued for another two hours with next to no agreements formed. The blue men did not utter a single word during the entire meeting, but simply nodded or shook their heads at random remarks. Julia wondered if the head gestures for 'yes' and 'no' were truly universal or something that had been adopted by the Human race. When another bird-like shriek sounded, those at the table stood, the feet of their guards flamed, and food was announced. After being led to a common room filled with over-plush couches and Human food, Mark walked up to a pile of their clothing on a small table near the end of the room, checked his watch, and noted that it was just after noon.

He turned back to the door as Thomas accompanied Amadeus and his team. "Well, that seemed like a waste of time. What kind of agreements can you ever come to if there are so many different opinions, and everyone talks over each other?" Rick asked as he sat at the nearest table, grabbing a sandwich from the large pile in front of him.

Mark leant against the back of one of the couches, letting the others crowd around the table. Amadeus and Amelia remained standing, "I understand that this process may seem like a waste of time, but there is progress being made. Only last year the Birons and the Jarly couldn't even be in the same room without violence taking place." He turned to Mark, saying, "I apologize, but I do believe this conference will last a few more days. Unfortunately, you will not be able to return home to Emily and Sophie until it is all complete."

Mark agreed. "I know. We've already been told about the protocols on leaving. To be honest, I don't want them anywhere near this whole thing." He stopped, reaching across the table for half of a tuna sandwich.

"Amy is with them too," Rick added between bites.

"I have contacted Abel, as well. I believe he will be on his way to your house, shortly." Mark looked confused as Amadeus continued, "I just felt that he too should be involved in this process, and his protective presence may give you peace of mind."

Mark considered the idea. He did like Abel; the two had emailed frequently over the last few months, and he also knew Abel would do anything to protect the girls. He nodded to Amadeus, as he chewed over the idea of why they would need protecting, especially by someone so newly introduced to the light himself.

Isobel distracted Mark's reveries. "Also, I thought you would like to know, Emily and I are able to communicate at this distance. I have advised her of the status in the conference and she wanted you to know that everything is fine, other than the basement toilet has apparently exploded," her eyes grew with exaggeration, "and flooded the room." Isobel grinned at the last comment.

The group laughed as Mark smirked and rolled his eyes. "Well, good to know the house is still standing," he glanced down as his wrist, " four hours later." He laughed, shaking his head as he took another large bite.

"It was probably Amy," Rick joked. "She's always breaking things."

Together the group nodded, then laughed at their unified agreement of Amy's clumsiness.

That night the four were ushered into their living quarters. A narrow hallway just off of the common room led to four bedrooms. James and Julia took the largest room at the very end and called it a night. Mark laughed at the size of his assigned room. Not much bigger than his college dorm room, the back wall was consumed by another window open to the stars. Walking to the end, he pressed his forehead to the clear material, ignoring the small circular fog created by his near breath. He looked down upon Earth, spinning in its tranquility. Everything was so calm and quiet at that moment. It was very easy for him to forget about tomorrow's morbid agenda. Eventually, as the invading hallway lamps dimmed, he tossed and turned uncomfortably, trying to find a moment of mental rest. Mesmerized by the shimmering lights created by Earth's atmosphere, he watched as a mirage of color danced and touched the room's sharp corners. Mark attempted to control his breathing, finally drifting into sleep.

* * *

The following morning a heavy fist pounded on each of their doors. With sleepy eyes they quickly dressed, eventually making their way to the common room. The food table was now covered in an arrangement of fruits, vegetables, eggs, and meat. At one end, Riley and Amelia were whispering to one another, laughing every now and then. Isobel was creating a large plate of fruit for herself, as Amadeus was in a very animated conversation with two of the four guards at the other end of the room. Thomas entered behind the others with a silent nod; he seemed cheerful with a bounce in his step. He made his way around the others, grabbing handfuls of fruit, mixing it with his bacon and eggs.

"Help yourself," Isobel smiled at the frozen group. The atmosphere was oddly relaxed, yet excited at the same time. Given the severity of the day ahead, the group couldn't seem to lift their suspicious and sour moods. Sluggishly, they filled their plates, found their seats, and ate in silence.

After a few minutes, Amadeus made his way towards the table, settling in next to Rick, grasping his shoulder. "Sleep well?" His eyes probed those around him.

"Yes, thank you." Julia smiled, reaching across the table for the large jar of orange juice.

"Given the situation it's kind of hard to truly relax... As I'm sure you know," Rick added.

Amadeus agreed. "I am sorry for the predicament we are putting you through. You never asked for any of this. I can only hope that today we are able to agree on more terms and this whole thing will be over." He paused, looking around the room confronted by the large and interested eyes of not only the Humans, but of his Jarly team. "I don't doubt that some form of invasion will take place. The Birons are too powerful and large in numbers to be completely thwarted and dissatisfied with the meeting's outcome. I just pray that resources can be taken in reasonable sums, with little to no impact on you Humans." Absentminded, he pulled at a loose thread on the corner of his placemat.

"What happens if that's not good enough?" James squared his shoulders. "What happens if they won't agree to anything other than complete drilling rights and free reign over Earth? What then?"

Amadeus took a deep breath, but Riley was the first to respond. "Then you should pray to whatever God you believe in, because we can only protect you for so long before the Earth you know and love will become a barren wasteland."

Julia stopped mid-chew as Mark turned to Amadeus, waiting for him to ague against Riley's words, but no argument came.

"So, that's it?" All eyes fell on Mark. "This conference is really about dictating the Biron's invasion plans, and how hard the Jarly want to push back, or continuing the war?" He stopped to think for a second or two before his voice got slightly louder. "Last year when you picked us for your wild goose chase, if we had failed, you would have been ordered back and the Birons would have free reign over earth. Right?" He prodded.

Amadeus went to answer, but Julia interjected. "But they helped you. They were the ones that made contact at their wedding." She gestured towards Rick without taking her eyes away from Amadeus.

He raised his hands in a gesture of defeat, slowly nodding his head. "There are a few, still loyal to the Jarly way of life. You have to remember, the Birons were once our kind. A few millennia have led to their change in appearance and that very exile has led them to the destitution and desperation their entire race is living in. Even to this day, those still loyal will do anything to survive, even if that means fighting against their own kind."

"So what are we talking about here... Numbers wise?" James asked, his mouth half full with melon. "You guys have your light, the technology, the mental influences and manipulations."

Amelia shook her head with her elbows propped on the table, silently blowing at the hot tea in her hands. "They outnumber us ten to one. Even with some of theirs on our side," she glanced at her Commander, "whom I suspect would change sides to suit their own survival." Turning back to James, she said, "The Jarly are explorers and scientists. Our flames enlighten us, but over half of our population are either young children or elderly peacekeepers. Yes, we have technology that is both useful and affective." She put down her tea, "But my point is, no matter the outcome of this conference, the Human species can no longer be ignorant to the expanding universe around them. If war is sprouted in your system, then mankind will have to play their part in protecting their world, just as the Jarly will be spread thin protecting Nona and Earth."

Isobel continued, her calming voice evident. "You have already proven your worth and right to protection. You have a vast history that deserves its recognition and growth. I don't doubt your future global involvement in peaceful proceedings and conferences." Isobel then added, almost embarrassed, "I don't mean to be so blunt, but you as a species are intelligent and are nowhere near as pathetically inept as the Birons would suggest."

"Gee, thanks!" Julia added sarcastically, popping a strawberry in her mouth.

"What I mean to say is, you are now on the universal map as an equal," Isobel finished.

"You have something... a lot of things actually, that they want," Riley prompted. "A bargaining chip or two that you can fight with."

Mark wished he could take his words back the minute they escaped his lips. Staring at the table, he said, "Unfortunately, if this conference falls in the Biron's favor, I can almost guarantee we Humans will do anything to prevent the raping of our own planet for the preservation of your own. We'll blow ourselves up and destroy our oceans before the second ship lands."

The room gasped as one, staring at Mark's growingly apologetic face.

After a minute Amadeus whispered, "Then let us pray for a better outcome."

Bates entered the room then, announcing that the conference would continue in fifteen minutes. As they got to their feet Amadeus concluded, "One day at a time," before they got in line and made their way to the giant hall.

This time Amelia joined Amadeus at the table. The same blue men appeared, later described as the Ventari, who inhabited a water-based planet in the Tadpole Galaxy. As the room filled, Mark noted that Velo never stood and was never reprimanded for his lack of traditional proceedings.

Riley? Mark silently spoke to his bonded Jarly.

Riley seemed surprised, standing just behind Amelia on the opposite side of the table. Their eyes met for a few seconds.

Mark, now is the time to focus. His words were stern and chastising.

I just want to know who Velo is? Why is he so important? Mark quickly questioned.

As the hall doors were still open and no discussion had begun, Riley's eyes drifted to the elderly man at the end of the table.

Velo is the eldest Jarly leader still active. He is famous among all of my people. He is respected to the point where... Well, lets just say, not too many men argue with his final word.

As the Biron leaders entered the room and all eyes watched them take their seats, Mark added, *Well, that's good, having someone so respected on our side! How old is he?*

A proud grin pulled on the corner of Riley's face as he straightened up, clutched his hands behind his back, and concluded, *Three thousand earth years.*

Mark's jaw dropped open as Velo began his opening statement.

*   *   *

It took approximately three hours for the discourse to turn tempestuous. The Humans had separately come to the conclusion that Velo and the others were insistent on compromise and stalling, while over-exaggerating Earth's defensive abilities and the likeliness of Humans destroying themselves and their planet before allowing an alien presence to invade and dictate. At first the Biron leaders appeared understanding, even willing to cooperate, but as the day continued tempers ran wild and the conversation led more towards the Biron's need for resources and their lack of empathy for the Human way of life.

"You cannot guarantee the safety and survival of the Human race and we cannot stand by and allow you to pillage their lands without supervision," Amadeus chimed in.

"We do not need to be watched by the Jarly. Enough of our kind is under your command as it is," another Biron leader roared, with a tattooed face and numerous metal piercing along his forearms that almost distracted from his green and black leather-like skin and awful stench. A violent scar covered his right shoulder, barely concealed by his garments, reemerging at his left shoulder and heading down the back of his left arm.

"We do not force any of your kind to work for, or with, us. It is done so by their own free will," Amelia added.

A second Biron slammed his fists on the table across from Amelia, making many in the room jump uncomfortably. A split down the side of his tongue made his speech slurred, "They are forced to take such pathetic jobs to survive in what little you have allotted our kind." His words spat from his lips. Amelia stood her ground, but Mark noted Riley's growing temper, his stance inching forward.

The slow slurred speech continued, "Enough of this!" All Birons had the ability to command the room, much like Velo did. Each of their unique voices vibrated through the walls and those near. "We are Biron," he slowly stood, "and we will take what we wish. Enough of this useless banter." He glanced down at his two seated kin. "We will no longer be dictated to by these Jarly scum." His last word felt like a cheer.

The room erupted with hurried discussion, some louder than others. Many stood as the crowd's discussion turned into an angry mob of pushing and shoving. The Biron at the table stood slowly, as the remaining Biron in the crowds began to fight and argue with their Jarly counterparts.

Suddenly, Velo's words sound out louder than all others and those in the room abruptly stopped in their stances. "I move for a Causeer!"

Gasps filled the room. Riley's uncertain eyes fell on Mark's. *This is highly irregular. We've been trying to avoid it.*

"Agreed," the Biron leader and his two companions concurred, taking to their seats as the main hall doors spread wide.

What does this mean? Mark hurriedly asked as the men and women in his row turned, making to leave the hall.

Riley stepped up to the table with Isobel, whispering something between Amadeus and Amelia's heads. They waited for Amadeus' response before Riley solemnly agreed. Isobel took a seat next to Amelia, as Riley and Amelia glanced at each other longingly before he turned and joined his exiting row. Riley's brows were creased as he focused on the individual in front of him.

Riley! Mark spoke more insistently. *What the fuck is going on?*

The conclusion of this conference will be made in the sole presence of those around the table. A decision must be made within three hours. No witnesses, no guards... No protection. Riley eventually added with a mental sigh.

The small group convened back at the common room. The attached halls filled with Jarly and a few loyal Biron deep in discussion. The group sat around the table as the others further discussed what was going on.

Riley sat down opposite Mark and as their eyes met he added, *The fate of mankind will be decided in the next three hours, and from the looks and sounds of things, the result doesn't look good.*

"So what happens if Amadeus and the others can't convince these Biron leaders that Earth and our resources are not just things that they can help themselves to? That we have a right to our own planet?" Julia asked aloud to the room.

Riley was about to answer, but the words were out of Mark's mouth before he was even aware of their merit. "Then they take Earth by force."

Thomas added, "And Earth's next war begins." In its finality, the room went silent.

CHAPTER FOUR

Not one hour had passed before Riley was pacing the room, chewing on his thumbnail. James and Julia had disappeared to their room, while Rick and Mark waited silently at the table. Thomas had managed to find a pack of cards and after the others kindly declined a game he spread the cards, beginning to play solitaire at the opposite end of the table. Mark watched every step Riley made as his stance got more and more paranoid, continuously glancing at the exit, and then back to his feet.

"Will you calm down?" Mark startled the room as he stared at Riley.

Riley stopped mid-stride, letting out a loud huff. "I should be in there!" he responded too loudly, gesturing to the door. "I don't trust those Biron leaders. I can feel Isobel's distress." He gestured to his chest as if to make his point. "She's nervous and panicked. Not to mention my mate is locked in that room." He trailed off as Mark got a mental image of Riley and Amelia's overly affectionate discussion at the breakfast table.

Mark rose from his seat and filled a large clear glass with cold water, passing it to Riley. "Drink this. You need to breathe and try to relax. You need to give Isobel the strength she needs to fight for us. Calm her." Riley reluctantly took the glass and after a long sip, took a seat in the nearest chair. Mark sat across from him and they continued to wait.

Roughly another hour had passed when there was a commotion in the hallway as a number of individuals fled to the halls and rushed towards the conference room. Riley was the first to his feet and out into their path. Julia and James caught up to the others, rushing to keep up with Riley. Turning the final corner towards the hall, they could see smiles on Velo and the others' faces. Even the Birons appeared in good spirits. Slowing to a brisk walk, the group made their way through the crowds of people. Only feet from the group, Velo raised a weak arm and called for silence.

"We have reached a verdict and would like to share with our friends and loved ones." Resting his raised arm on the shoulder of the nearest Biron, he continued, "We have agreed on large scale elemental mining, supervised by the Human and Jarly representatives. If any Human or wildlife is endangered or poorly influenced by any initiation, they shall either be compensated for their losses, relocated of their own volition, or mining will cease. Before any drilling begins, we will hold meetings with the affected leaders and proceed amicably. No war will come of this!" His final sentence was met with joyful cheers and long drawn out sighs of relief.

Mark's beaming smile, at his family and friends, dropped suddenly when he saw the expression on Amadeus' face. His false smile had been replaced by the true fear and calculated shock as something rattled in his mind. At that moment, Mark knew the conclusion of the meeting was not as flowery as the mood around him would suggest.

"As per tradition, the feast shall begin within the hour. Return now to your quarters and prepare for a night of celebration." Velo didn't appear to be affected in the same way Amadeus was. He genuinely seemed pleased with himself, even striking up small talk with the Ventari and the odd Biron nearby. Amadeus excused himself, along with the others, as they made their way back to their common room.

"So what really happened?" Mark's accusing tone surprised the others.

"Just as Velo said. The Biron leaders agreed to our terms and the alliance can now begin." Amadeus didn't seem convinced by his own words. He could see the others were now confused and he continued. " I..." Turning to Isobel and Amelia who sat silent and thoughtful on a near couch, he said, "*We* just thought the agreement came too swiftly and easily for it to be believable."

"What are you saying?" Rick joined in the discussion.

"Well, you heard how they were when the Causeer was first called. They were angry, almost violent, in their demands to get their full drilling rights; then, behind closed doors, they completely changed." Amadeus sat at the table.

"In less than an hour the Birons went from demanding free reign over earth and limited Jarly involvement, to full blown agreement and appeasement," Amelia said.

"Well, maybe they just realized that their demands were too unreason-able… and this is the best way to get what they want?" Julia fumbled with her words.

"Or they were just agreeing to whatever we were suggesting because they secretly have no intention of sticking to any agreement." Isobel weakly added, "Their minds were made up before they even entered that conference room, on day one."

"So that's it? This has all been for nothing," Rick angrily interjected.

"Not necessarily. They have signed upon our arrangement." Amelia ignored their surprised faces as she sat on Riley's lap at the other end of the table. He wrapped his arms protectively around her waist as she contin-ued. "We can only hope and pray that our assessment of the situation was wrong. And like you said," gesturing to Julia, "maybe they finally saw the error in their thinking and will stick to our terms. After all, they cannot afford a full blown war, losing precious resources, any more than we can."

* * *

The feast that night was extravagant to say the least. After being led through a maze of crowded hallways and down deep into the spiral eleva-tor, Mark and his small group couldn't believe the vibrant, explosive colors that decorated the hall. Much like the conference room in its ceiling height and boxy construction, this room was twice as long; its ceiling cut in half with a metallic grating with white and purple twinkling lights much like a Christmas tree's, but brighter. On the walls, sheer fabric clung to every corner, intermixing, as if a silky tapestry. Down the center of the room, a long - apparently floating - green table overflowed with fine foods, some noticeably Human in their display and preparation, while others drew their own attention. The festive Ventari appeared to focus around the center of the long table.

"What are they doing?" Julia whispered to Riley.

After a close look he smiled and ushered her closer. A few feet away, a foot or so space separated the Ventari cuisine from all others. Six large, clear containers held a mixture of colored liquids with a number of small fish filling each bowl. Some shimmered as they passed the lining. Julia smiled simply at the array of color, but took a sudden step back into James' front as two Ventari hastily dunked their entire heads into their separate bowls. From a distance it looked as it they were bobbing for apples; now it was clear that they were simply taking a bite out of their preferred meal.

Grinning, Riley turned her around, facing away as he whispered to those nearest. "The Ventari are an aquatic being. They have adapted to both life on land and submerged." Julia utilized her peripheral vision to discreetly stare. The two men were still completely submerged, up to their shoulders; the clear containers allowed for an even clearer view. Though many of the fish rushed to the corners of the bowl, a select few were greeted with the sudden thrashing of the Ventari jaw. Julia turned, fully mesmerized; much like that of the ocean's Great White shark, each row of the Ventari's teeth moved of their own accord. Their lower jaws drew back as the rows of teeth pushed forward. Small bursts of blue blood created bubbles in the water. The Ventari seemingly sniffed, enjoying themselves to the point of closing their eyes and relishing the taste. The bubbles were pulled into their nostrils as they withdrew their heads, still chewing with their mouths full as fluid sloshed onto the floor below and another Ventari took their place.

Julia turned back as Riley continued, "They still prefer their fresh aquatic diet."

Wrinkling her nose, Julia nodded once, letting James pull her towards the display at the other end of the table. Her mouth watered at the abundance of juicy chicken breast, roasted beef, and a vibrant array of fruits and vegetables. Mark and Thomas enjoyed small talk as the others found them in the crowd, picking at their food together. Riley, Amelia, Isobel, and Amadeus were laughing and filling their mouths with circular chunks of meat, using their fingers to pinch small amounts of blue rice.

Rick looked around to ensure enough privacy. "When do you think they will send us back?" he asked the group, but his question was directed at Thomas.

"Shortly, I would assume. If all goes as planned, I'm sure they will either return us tonight or in the morning. I honestly don't know what more is expected at these things. This is the first one I have witnessed, myself."

Thomas stopped and smiled as Amadeus and the others joined their growing group.

"How is my old friend doing, today?" Amadeus gripped Thomas' shoulder. His other hand grasped a heavy glass of black liquid. The way his speech was slurred, the others could only deduce it was a strong inebriant. Isobel took two large gulps of her matching drink before passing it to Rick.

"Try some!" she almost giggled. At that moment none of the Jarly acted much older than excited teenagers. Grasping Caleb's arm, he and his brother Damon joined the group. Isobel used her free hand to rest on her knee, slightly hunched over.

"Are you okay?" Rick loudly whispered as the room was now filled with rambunctious discussion, laughter, and a strange repetitive beat.

"Of course!" Isobel's brow creased as she stood up straight and then hiccupped, followed by a giggle, and reddened cheeks.

Looking around, Mark grinned as he took in the group. "You're all drunk."

"Well, it is a party," Amadeus slurred, passing Mark his drink. "Given the last few days and the severity of what has just been avoided, I'm surprised any of you are still sober." Reaching behind him he grabbed four more drinks, two in each hand, then passed them to the empty hands in the group. "Drink!" he cheered.

Three more glasses each and the personalities came out. Amadeus, Thomas, Rick, and James were huddled in one corner playing an odd game involving two cups, four straws, and a ball. Mark and Caleb were arm wrestling, both engulfed in flames, with Riley and Amelia cheering them on while banging the table. Julia and Isobel sat against one wall; their legs spread out in front of them, comparing each other's clothes and manicured fingernails.

"After everything, I feel silly asking, but how did the four of you meet?" Isobel slurred, taking a large gulp of blue-tinted liquid and gesturing to her Human companions around the room.

Taking in a deep breath and blinking past the alcohol-fueled exhaustion, Julia smiled and welcomed the pre-offered goblet. After taking another sip she wiped her lips with the back of her hand. "James and Rick grew up together since they were five years old; they lived just down the street from each other." Taking another sip of the warming liquid, she continued, "Amy and I went to high school together." She hiccupped and began to laugh a bit too loudly, drawing the attention of those nearby before blushing with embarrassment. "We actually hated each other at first."

"Really?" Isobel asked, acting surprised, fully turning her body towards Julia.

She nodded, "Yep. We were both competing for lead cheerleader in our first year. We were always butting heads and could never agree on anything. It was pretty bad. I'm ashamed to say I was a bully to her... No, I was a downright bitch, with a capital B." Her hands now moved, as she became more animated. "But by second year, when Stacy Collins joined the team, she became the queen bee. She totally worked the group and pitted everyone against us."

"So what happened?"

"Amy and I found ourselves bonding over our hatred of Stacy." She glanced sideways at Isobel, whose confusion was evident. Julia laughed, "I know, it sounds terrible... We bonded over mutual bitchiness. But once we really got to know each other, we found we had a lot in common." Julia took another swig of liquid courage, saying, "Then when Amy's parents died in that car accident, I was all she really had; outside of Emily, of course. Amy went through a time of not leaving the house at all. She barely spoke, lost a ton of weight, and just cried all the time. So I started going over to her house on a daily basis; I practically lived on her bedroom floor."

Not knowing what more to say, Isobel asked, "So how did you meet James and Rick?"

"College," Julia smirked, remembering. "Amy actually met them both our first year. She had taken a history course as one of her options and they were in it. I think they fought over her attention at first-"

"James too?" Isobel blurted, interrupting.

"Yeah! Some of the things they would do to get her attention..." Julia shook her head, then laughed louder when James glanced their way with an eyebrow raised after hearing his name, not knowing what was being discussed. "I'm not sure if Rick purposefully failed his exams, but he played the 'Oh I need a hot little tutor' card very well." Isobel shook her head, watching Rick as Julia continued, "Either way, he got Amy's full attention. They started dating nearer to the end of the first semester and have been inseparable ever since."

"So why did it take until their wedding for you and James to get together?" Isobel asked, scanning the room and smiling at the celebrations as they unfolded. She continued, whispering, "They were together for almost four years. You must have met each other before then?"

"Oh we did. You know my husband; he's definitely a charmer. We hung out quite a bit before." Julia shrugged, draining the rest of the blue liquid that Isobel had offered. "Timing I guess. It just never seemed to work out. Whenever I was single, he wasn't, and vise versa. We had made out a few times, and often gravitated towards each other at parties and events, but I guess nothing really pulls two people together like a terrifying alien invasion."

Isobel's eyes were wide and her face tried to remain still, before her face split in two and her head fell back with laughter.

"Hey!" Julia chastised before joining her, bumping their shoulders.

"Well, from one terrifying alien to another," she winked, "you're welcome."

Julia shook her head, smirking as she turned back to the others.

It must have been late as the crowd had greatly dispersed and spread into nearby hallways and other floors, but with no Earthly clocks on board time came and went as it pleased. After a short while, Amadeus and Thomas said goodnight and left. Rick replaced Riley and Amelia as the cheering squad, as Celeb and Damon now played a fisted tug-of-war, attempting to pull one another across the table. James almost tripped twice as he made his way over to his wife. Without a single word he stooped down, grabbed her by the hips, and tossed her over his shoulder.

With a weak, "Put me down!" and a giggle, Julia waved at Isobel as James smacked her backside and they left the hall.

Using the wall to support herself, Isobel dragged her tired body to its feet, slowly making to leave. Passing the remaining others, she weakly waved, and yawned. Shuffling towards the revolving elevator, she only passed two Jarly and three Ventari, who had passed out during their attempt to leave and were now sprawled along the walls. Finally, she managed to enter the ascending elevator, after two awkward attempts.

Now leaning against the cold solid wall, knowing there were at least twelve floors before her own, she let her head fall back and eyelids droop.

A loud scream sobered her instantly. Looking around frantically, she got her bearings and noted that she was still alone in the dimly lit elevator. Another scream jerked her head upright just as a loud thud hit the echoing rooftop. Gasping and throwing herself low against the wall, her senses came back and her hands ignited with flame. The elevator slowed to an eventual stop and her flame dissipated. Partially shaking, she slid along the wall around the corner into the brightly lit, deserted hallway. With as much courage as she could muster, she took to the short, barred stairs, which allowed maintenance to reach the top of each elevator. Slowly peeking over the top, at first the only visible light came from the circular cut outs each exit offered. Then slowly a dark figure sprawled out on the roof of the elevator in an unnatural display came into view as her eyes adjusted. Peeking her head over the edge and looking directly up, no one else appeared to have heard the loud noise or had come to the aid of the screams.

High-kicking her nearest leg over the edge, Isobel managed to pull her body over the side and roll onto the top with a simple elegance. Drawing herself to her hands and knees, she slowly made her way towards the figure. Her hands moved forward and were met by a warm slick substance. It didn't require her extensive medical training to know that one whole side of the elevator roof was now covered in blood. Taking a deep calculated breath, she ignored the splashing sound and moved forward until she grasped the shoulder of the unknown body, positioning herself to get a better look.

Placing her left hand for support on the elevator roof near the head of the person, Isobel ignited her flame and brushed the side of the individual's face. At first the blood smeared across the features and the disfiguration from the fall made the victim hard to recognize. Hovering her hand closer to the person's cheek, Isobel screamed loudly, pulling Velo's lifeless body to her own. Rocking back and forth, she held him tightly.

"Help me!" she cried up at the open hallways. "Please," tears fill her eyes, "someone, help me!"

CHAPTER FIVE

A number of faces appeared at the elevator entrances, peering down. Isobel continued to rock on the spot as Riley, her bonded protector, appeared at the top of the elevator stairs.

"Isobel!" he yelled, panic evident in his voice.

He dragged himself up onto the elevator top, attempting to run while slipping towards a hysterical Isobel. Amelia's head popped over the top and she quickly ordered someone behind her to lower the elevator. As Riley reached Isobel, he gripped her shoulders and with concerned confusion, pulled her away from the body.

"No!" she screamed, gripping Velo with renewed determination.

Slowly the elevator began to descend and curve towards the opening. Those on the elevator came into view. As the light filled the elevator shaft, Amelia and the others gasped and a few covered their mouths, sobbing at the sight of Velo's distorted body. Anguish filled them, unable to pry their eyes from their beloved leader lying limply against Isobel. As Riley got a full view of the victim, he too fell to his knees, reaching for Velo's hand.

More people followed the growing cries, crowding around, as Amadeus forced his way to the front of the group to see what was going on. Joined by Mark and Rick, the three came to a sudden stop, as they took in the large amount of blood now spilling onto the hallway floor. After a few seconds, Amadeus remembered his place and turned to the distraught crowd.

Spreading his arms wide, he tried to shield as many from the tragic view as possible. "Please return to your rooms. Clear this hallway." At first no one moved, but as he repeated his request a few helped, turning more away. After a few drawn out minutes the area was almost completely cleared.

Cautiously, Amadeus made his way over to the three in the shaft, kneeling by Velo's head.

"Who did this?" he whispered to Isobel. She appeared shaken and unresponsive. "Who did this?" he repeated, grasping her shoulders.

His touch pulled her out of her trance. Staring into his kind eyes, she whispered, "I don't know." It was a quick response, but she continued louder, "I was in the elevator when I heard him scream and fall."

"Fall?" Amadeus looked directly above and into the prying eyes of a few spectators. Looking from hall to hall, only one entrance six floors up didn't appear to have an audience.

"Damon." Amadeus found his crewmate standing beside Rick. "I want this shaft closed off and surveillance reviewed." He looked up again and focused his eyes on the sixth floor entrance, "Starting with the sixth floor."

"Sir," Damon nodded, turning as he left swiftly.

"Isobel," Amadeus gently raised her chin, drawing her eyes to his. "I need you to place Velo back on the surface and take a step back." She looked surprised by his request; her bloodied fingernails tightened on Velo's arm. Amadeus urged Riley, getting to his feet and taking Isobel by her shoulders, helping her to stand. They took a couple steps back and watched as Amadeus ignited his light and briefly examined the body.

In this state and location it was next to impossible to see anything. Mark had to squint to even make out the true color of Velo's torn clothing. A team of men and women in matching purple uniforms rushed past the others and formed an expandable stretcher on one side of Velo's body. After transferring his body and lifting it to standing height, Amadeus ordered them away. Three men stayed behind to start removing the remaining blood.

"I'll be right there," Isobel called behind them.

"No," Amadeus stopped her, "you're too involved in this situation." Her jaw clenched in protest, but he continued, raising his palm. "Isobel, Velo was closer to you than any of us. I won't put you through the torment of his autopsy, and besides... you've had too much to drink and need rest."

New tears filled her wide eyes. "Amadeus..." She trailed off, walking over to him, as he pulled her into his strong arms. She then let go; big tears violently broke through her usually reserved demeanor, and she wept into his shoulder. He gently ushered her out of the elevator shaft and released her into Amelia's arms. She slowly walked her down the hall and around the corner, out of sight.

"Sir," Riley turned to Amadeus, "what do we do now?" Amadeus stared down at his red-covered hands, then into each of the eyes of those remaining. It was clear that he was on the verge of a breakdown, as well.

"We need to find whoever is responsible and bring them to justice," he commanded, as his eyes darkened with each word.

"How can we help?" Mark was adamant, taking a step forward.

Amadeus glanced back at the men working in the shaft. "The sixth floor," he said, wiping his hand absently across his shirt. He turned back to the group. "I think this all started on the sixth floor. We should start there," he finished as his hands ignited and fisted.

"Who occupies the six floor?" Rick asked as the group turned and walked to the nearest staircase.

Just before they reached the door, Amadeus spoke over his shoulder, "The Ventari and Biron delegates."

* * *

To no one's surprise the sixth floor hallway was completely deserted, but there were signs of a struggle. The walls were streaked with red and blue liquids, furniture was broken and tipped over, and a number of lights were flickering near one of the living quarter entrances. A wheezing sound drew their attention, with a tapping noise faintly heard in the distance. Staying close to the walls, Amadeus took the lead. Reaching the edge of the nearest hallway, the wheezing got louder. Amadeus slowly peeked his head around the corner.

"Help me!" A strained whisper escaped the lips of one of two Ventari, as he lay in a pool of blue blood.

The others rushed into the hallway, crouching at their injured sides, as Amadeus placed his hand to a white scanner near the end of the hall. The scanner lit up and he spoke directly into it. "Get a medical team to the sixth floor east elevator entrance now!" he ordered.

"Yes, Sir," Damon's voice rang from the glowing pad. "Two more Biron ships are heading towards the station. Their docked ship is attempting to detach."

"Shut them down!" Amadeus yelled back. "They are not to leave. I want them under guard until we figure this all out. No communication is to take place without my approval."

He withdrew his hand and rushed to check the life signs of the nearest Ventari.

"Who did this?" Riley demanded, holding the Ventari's head in his lap.

Struggling to take in any breath, the labored reply was, "Birons." He coughed up a sticky dark substance, managing, "And Jarly."

Riley's eyes shot up to Amadeus, who now stood at the Ventari's feet. "Did you recognize them?" Riley tried to raise the man's head higher so that his coughing would subside.

"One." He looked up at Amadeus and in his final breath he whispered, "Bates."

His wide eyes glazed over and a third eyelid, previously unused, drew outwards from the inside corners of his eyes. His body went limp and the gargling noises ceased, filling the hallway with silence.

The short silence broke with Damon's clear voice emanating from a near speaker. "Sir, I think you need to get down here right away. I have the video footage available."

Amadeus returned his hand to the white pad. "I'll be right down." His shoulders hunched, defeated, and he hung his head. Another purple-clad medical team rushed down the hallway, seeing to the two lifeless bodies.

The group then followed Amadeus' lead as they made their way back down the staircase, heading deep into the bowels of the space station. The hallways became less lit and more mechanical. Eventually, Amadeus forced himself through a near exit, marching towards a guarded room. The room looked similar to the observation room they witnessed on their tour, but this was much smaller with half as many screens.

Isobel, freshly showered with dripping wet hair, sat quietly in between Caleb and Amelia. The others crowded around them as Amadeus turned to the large screen to the right.

Without even glancing in their direction, he commanded, "Show me."

The screen came to life as a colorful display of lights and movements showed the sixth floor earlier in the evening, as people returned from the feast. Eventually, Velo is seen entering the hallway accompanied by the two Ventari and a single Jarly. They appeared happy and deep in discussion. The Jarly stepped forward, opening one of the rooms and allowing the others to go ahead of him. Before he joined them, he discreetly slapped his hand to the wall near the doorframe. His hand lit up and then faded quickly as he entered the room, closing the door behind him, leaving a very evident seared handprint near the door.

Amadeus clearly stiffened, as he tightened his arms across his chest, inching closer to the screen. Damon sped up the footage until some time had passed and the lighting in the recorded hallway had already dimmed. Slowing the footage again, they watched as two unidentified Birons entered, along with Bates and two other Jarly. They searched around until they found the marked door. Knocking on the two other doors in the hallway, they said something to the surprised individuals, who appeared shocked and hurried out and down the hall. Waiting until the space was cleared, Bates took the lead and kicked in the door, causing it to split and the frame to crack. As the others rushed into the room, unfortunately, the cameras only seemed to take footage outside the vital scene. Nothing could be seen until one of the Ventari tried to escape and was met with a crippling shot to the back.

"That was a Biron weapon. I thought they had all been searched before entering the station?" Riley asked.

Amadeus' eyes never left the screen. "Unfortunately, Bates was the lead security on the Biron arrival."

The Ventari man fell to the floor, beginning to convulse. One of the Biron soldiers exited the room, and then hovered over his weakened victim before shooting two more blasts into his back. The two Jarly exited as well, with the second Ventari man in their grasp. He was already coughing blood, as they deposited him just outside the doorway. Making room, Bates exited with a vicious grin, taking the time to address the camera directly. He dramatically gestured to the room and stepped aside, as the final Biron exited with an ill-looking Velo. His face was too pale compared to the others. There was blood already dripping from the side of his face as he stumbled over the fallen Ventari.

Velo paused and muttered something to Bates, and then was met with a swift backhand to the face, knocking him towards the doorframe. The Biron appeared to laugh as he drew Velo to his feet and further into the open hallway, dragging him to the open edge of the elevator entrance. Bates was clearly speaking, as he gestured for the nearest Biron to proceed. Taking two steps forward, it could be seen that he was easily three feet taller than Velo, and twice as wide. The Biron gripped the old man's left shoulder, causing his head to jerk backwards as he screamed in agony. His face contorted in the most unpleasant manor.

Without warning the second Biron lunged forward and a blade sliced through Velo's abdomen. Isobel let out a short wail and rushed from the room, with a glance at Riley, Amelia quickly followed. As the blade withdrew, a patch of violent red began to spread over his torso. The Biron still gripping his shoulder laughed and used his free hand to grip around Velo's neck. Squeezing tightly, he raised Velo two feet into the air, holding his body over the empty shaft. A light wind made his feet sway uselessly.

In a final attempt at revolt, Velo ignited his flesh, using it as a weapon; burning the outstretched arm of his Biron attacker. The Biron yelled, releasing Velo to plummet to his death. Grabbing his wounded arm to his chest, the Biron charged past Bates, almost knocking him over the edge as well, then through the exit doors. Bates and the others quickly followed, with the door closing behind them. The recording then stopped and the screen went blank.

The room remained silent as all eyes fell from the blank screen. Slowly, Amadeus turn to the others. "Have you tracked them down?"

"They snuck into a crowded hall of party goers. We lost them, but I have my team working on it now," Damon responded, turning back to the footage he was previously reviewing.

"Sir, the Biron commanders are demanding your presence in the conference room," an unnamed Jarly announced with his left hand to his ear.

Amadeus looked around. "All of you, with me." He headed towards the door. "Damon, have five of your men meet us there too."

On the short trip back to the conference room the silence of the station grew strange, drawing them in. It was now the middle of the night and the hundreds of people who had filled the halls were now fast asleep. As two guards ahead of Amadeus opened the grand doors, their group was met with an eruption of angered discussion, then accusatory interrogation.

"How dare you restrict us from leaving!" one yelled from behind two seated Biron.

"You have no right to dictate our movements and communications," another spat.

Another was about to begin, but Amadeus responded, "Enough!" His voice grew menacing. "Our beloved Ambassador Velonarious Kital has just been murdered." The room fell silent and the majority of the Birons in the room had enough grace to look shocked and surprised.

He continued, "We have viewed the security footage and found two Biron, as well as traitor Jarly to be the culprits." More cries of outrage sound from the back of the room at the reference of Biron influence. "Until such time as the murderers have been caught, no one leaves this station. You are more than welcome to return to your own ships, but they will remain neutral and immobilized until I give the order for release, is that understood?"

After a brief staredown, one Biron stepped forward and silently acknowledged the command. Turning, he marched from the room, pushing the doors so hard that they swung wide, banging at their hinges. Gradually the room filtered out and Amadeus turned back to his group.

Amadeus turned to a few of the Jarly known to be under Damon's command. "Find those men. I want their images plastered all over this station. We will find them," Amadeus ordered, almost placating himself. "Riley, check on Isobel and have Amelia meet me in my office within the hour." He turned slowly towards the remaining Human company. "The rest of you return to your rooms. We will collect you in the morning and return you home." Without another word he left the hall, leaving the others frozen where they stood.

* * *

When Mark reached his room, he flopped onto the bed with a large huff. He was too wired to sleep given the present situation; he couldn't rest his mind. After an hour or so he began to drift off, his mind freeing from the current concerns. Turning on his side he gently caressed the silk sheets that would hold Emily if she were there. As his breathing steadied and his eyelids drooped, he was whisked away to a time before contact. A pleasant evening that he and Emily shared. He could feel the cool breeze cover his face as he lay still next to her, their eyes drawn up to the night's sky. Their bright red picnic blanket was spread wide, held down by four jagged rocks. Their summer trip to Alaska, five years ago, led them to witness an evening of Northern Lights and the brightest stars either had ever seen.

Suddenly the memory blurred and became sinister. Unlike the true events, the scene had changed. Mark turned his head to see the near tree in flames; the night's sky was alight with graphic detail. Meteors struck the ground in growing numbers. Emily screamed and started to run, abandoning Mark in his shocked state. Eventually, he got to his feet and followed his love over a nearby hill, overlooking the oceanfront. Emily was no longer running, but stopped facing away a few feet ahead.

"Em?" Mark called out, his dream voice slow and mechanical.

He reached for her as a silver spike pierced through her chest and out towards her spine. 'NO!' He tried to scream, but no sound escaped his lips. He was forced to watch, frozen to the ground, as her body lifted and turned. An overly ferocious Biron now stood before her. His hand gripping the end of the blade, he turned her convulsing body towards the cliff line, blood spewing from her lips. Her arm reached for Mark, but it was too late; the Biron let go of his grip and she plummeted into the abyss.

"No!" Mark screamed, waking himself from his own nightmare. A thick layer of sweat covered his skin as he frantically searched his surroundings. Calming his heart, his head fell back onto the pillow and he covered his face.

Two rapid knocks pulled him back to reality as he slid off the bed to answer his door.

"Are you alright?" Julia stood with James and Rick behind her. At first he looked confused, so she continued, "You were yelling pretty loud."

"Oh..." He relaxed, his cheeks lightly flushed as he shook his head. "Yeah, sorry. Just a stupid nightmare."

Julia's brows creased and she continued with her accusatory stare.

"Well, Riley just said we will be leaving in an hour so pack whatever you need and we'll meet you in the common room for some breakfast." Rick smacked his brother-in-law on the shoulder in the only form of manly affection he could muster before turning back down the hallway.

"Let's get the hell outta here," James added in a loud whisper.

"Yeah. Thanks." Mark hurried to organize his things.

Back in the common room everyone seemed to be alert and moving. No one could have got more than two hours sleep, but everyone seemed to be functioning just fine. Julia was pouring drinks for all those at the table, and James was passing around the toast just as Rick and Thomas scooped large amounts of scrambled eggs onto their plates.

"Where are the Jarlys?" Mark asked, rubbing his eyes as he took his seat.

Rick shrugged as James muttered something unintelligible with his mouth full, and Julia simply said, "No idea. They should be here soon." She smiled as she poured him a glass of juice.

Forty minutes later and there were still no Jarly escorts in sight. Mark popped his head outside of the common room, quickly scanning the halls. He noted that this was the quietest he had ever heard the station throughout his stay. How could hundreds of people make such little noise?

Another twenty minutes passed before the group got restless and decided to wander. Julia and Thomas stayed behind in case anyone came looking. Mark, Rick, and James stuck together as they roamed the deserted hallways.

"This is weird, right?" James muttered, as they turned yet another hallway. "I mean, I'm not the only one that thinks that we should have run into at least one alien by now?"

Mark and Rick nodded in unison. Taking the now functioning elevator to the floor above, there was still no sign of anyone. On the third floor they started airing their theories.

"Maybe they're still sleeping," Rick suggested.

"The entire station?" Mark answered, skeptically.

Turning the corner, the group slowed as they saw an open hallway with flickering light coming from an unseen entrance.

"Should we just go in?" James asked, popping his head around the hallway entrance. Two tall men in traditional conference uniform were guarding the door, though their eyes were drawn into the room. Before James took a step closer, Rick grabbed his shoulder yanking him back.

"Rick," he huffed too loudly, "What the f.." Mark covered his mouth as they all pushed against the wall, thankfully shaded away from a near light. Four Jarly and two Birons exited into the hallway, accompanied by their guards.

"Bates." Mark spat the whispered name, recognizing the traitor.

Each Jarly and Biron carried a multitude of weaponry and firearms; one had a sickle shaped blade spanning from one shoulder to the other. After they had passed out of sight, Mark released James.

"We need to get back and explain what we've seen to the others," he suggested, as they slowly made their way back to the revolving elevator.

Two floors down, they began to run back to their common room. Bursting through the doors, James had to fight against Rick and Mark's grip, as Bates stood behind Julia. One bloody hand was gripping her shoulder and his left was lit, gripping the side of her face. Her gaze grew distant as her body harbored a new wound, spilling blood onto her shirt. From the looks of it, it was a deep wound; jaggedly slicing from her right shoulder, down across her breast, and ending just above her heart. Her face grew paler as Bates held her still.

"Did you really think we couldn't sniff out a few Human spies?" Bates muttered, as a sickening grin spread wide across his face.

James was about to explode as Mark responded, "You've known we were here all along, why now?" He gestured to Julia's tear-soaked face. "Why this? We were just leaving."

Bates laughed; the two Birons joined from the corner of the room. His face pulled down, becoming serious as if the very point of his presence should be already clear. "You really are a pathetic excuse for a species. Leverage, my dear boy." He then pulled Julia back and onto her feet. In doing so her chair was knocked backwards and only then the cold body of Thomas became visible.

James went to take a step, but was held back my Mark's strong arm. "Don't."

Just then the adjoining doors burst open with Amadeus and Isobel at the lead of a Jarly squad. This seemed to surprise Bates, who had backed himself and Julia into a corner, backed by his Biron cohorts.

"Bates!" Amadeus' voice rang loud and clear. "Don't do this."

Anger flared in Bates' eyes; his light grew brighter as the two Biron raised their guns.

Bates jerked Julia out of her sagging stoop. Her eyes suddenly became alert and a cry of sheer pain escaped her lips. Where his hand grasped at her chest, more blood soaked his skin along his forearm. Already weak, now Julia's pale skin appeared slick with sweat.

"Take one more step and I will rip the life from her," Bates growled through clenched teeth. "Changes are going to happen around here, start-ing with the end of your pathetic little reign."

Amadeus raised both hands in a show of defeat. Extinguishing his light, he pleaded, "Whatever issues you have with me, let me be the one to take your aggression. Let the girl go."

As if to solidify his words, Julia began to shake, little more than a shiver, but evident to the room. Bates glanced down at his victim and grinned. His free hand began to caress her face as if to show affection. "Oh, I don't know," Bates squeezed her closer to his body, brushing his cheek along her hairline. "This particular Human does excite me."

James' light grew ever brighter while the veins in his arms bulged forward.

Isobel spoke with a bland, if medical, voice. "Whatever it is that you want, if you don't let me heal her your leverage will cease to be within a matter of minutes." She eased a foot forwarded, but halted as the Birons moved to aim at her.

"James," Julia's frantic whisper could only be heard by a few.

Mark still held James as best as he could. "What is it that you want? Why are you still here?" Mark added after a pause.

"Just buying some time. But you're right," Bates now looked at Julia with disgust, "you Humans are far too weak to withstand anything worthwhile."

He paused, mulling something over, and then his eyes shot to Mark's. "So I propose a trade."

"Take me." James demanded, pulling his arm from his friends' grip.

Bates shook his head, while laughter escaped his lips. "No, no, you are far too brutish to entertain me. I will allow you to take your wife back in return for Amadeus and Rick's surrender."

The room burst into howls of chatter, but Rick pushed past his best friend and brother-in-law, only a few steps away. "Done. Hand her over."

"Rick!" James and Mark protested.

Bates grinned, turning to Amadeus who was stood in the grips of his team fiercely whispering to him. "Enough," he practically swatted them away. Stepping forward, he stated, "Agreed. Release her."

"You two. Over here. Get behind me," Bates ordered, frustration mixed with boredom now etched into his features. "You," he directed towards Mark with his chin.

Mark slowly edged forward as if cornering a wild animal. Julia had lost consciousness seconds before and was now little more than flesh and bones, upright only by Bates' will. As Mark reached for her Bates laughed, removing his grip, forcing Mark down with her sudden weight.

A flash of light filled the room and within a blink of an eye the others were gone. Bates had escaped.

"Julia!" James and Isobel were at Mark's side instantly.

Isobel went to work as quickly as she could. "Lend her your light!" she screamed, not taking her eyes or hands from Julia's limp body. Both seemed confused until three silent Jarly stepped up and placed their glowing hands on Isobel's back and her own flames brightened to blistering heights. Quickly, the Humans obeyed, clutching at the first piece of flesh they could find.

As their lights expanded and grew, Julia's eyes burst open, frantically gasping for breath. Her eyes bounced around the room, not settling until they found her panicked husband's. "James," her trembling lips formed the word in a rasp, as her eyes brimmed with tears.

He squeezed her hand tightly, while brushing a few blood-soaked strands of hair from her face. "Hush, baby. I'm right here." As Isobel peeled away the remains of her ruined top, a scream escaped Julia's lips as she squeezed her eyes shut. More blood spread from her wound into her red-soaked bra.

While attending to Julia, three Jarly wearing only purple made their way over to Thomas. Mark knew he was dead simply from the way his body was distorted and sickly still. Though they had not known him for long, Mark couldn't bring himself to look at his fallen comrade. For whatever reason, Thomas' relaxed involvement and help last year solidified the group's continued involvement and pursuit of the truth. He put a Human face to the extreme situation; in a way, Thomas felt like a piece of home while on the space station.

Voices grew louder in the halls now; the group could hear running and commotion. The door flew open to reveal Amelia, and Riley who had a severe gash across his left eyebrow. Both seemed dazed and confused.

"Mark!" Riley exclaimed as he reached the others. "I've been looking for you, what ha..." He was cut off by another cry from Julia, who was now squirming uncontrollable as her skin slowly, yet visibly, knit together before their eyes.

"Where were you?" Isobel demanded, not taking her eyes from her patient.

Riley made his way around the crowding Jarly to drop to his knees next to the others. He placed his hand on her working arm. "Amelia and I just woke up on the floor in the sub-engineering hallway. We don't know what happened."

Isobel nodded to herself, finally glancing up at her protector. Her brows grew together and she quickly placed her hand above his eyebrow long enough to heal the skin, and then turned her attention back to Julia. "It was Bates. He must have released some kind of airborne sleep-aid. A few of us were in the vault when we heard cries of shock. We ran out but the air was clear."

Julia, now still and breathing deep, seemed to have calmed. Her wound had laced back together into an angry red line. James smiled down at her, softly kissing her forehead as the conversation continued.

Glancing around, Riley's eyes dropped onto Thomas' face, his body already placed on the stretcher and being covered by a dark blanket. "No!"

His words were forced around the lump in his throat. "Where's Amadeus?" He asked no one in particular.

Mark cleared his throat. "Bates offered a trade," he stated, matter-of-factly, "Julia, for Amadeus and Rick."

"And you agreed?!" Riley blurted, anger flaring in his eyes. James' swift glare and stiffened stance made him continue. "James, I understand that we needed to save Julia, but this station and this conference is lost without Amadeus."

"Well, don't worry -- the minute Julia can move I'm taking her home. The rest of us will help in any way we can," James paused as Julia went to sit up. "Stay still." He held his wife down gently as he continued directly speaking to Riley, "They have Rick, too."

Amelia, who had remained silently stunned in the corner, seemed to come to life. She began barking orders at the nearby Jarly. Stepping forward, she spoke clearly to those crowded in the center of the room. "In Amadeus' absence, I am in command." She paused, placing her hand gently on Isobel's back. "Can she be moved?"

Isobel nodded, her light already extinguished. She seemed to be checking Julia over for more injuries. Turning to James, she said, "She must not walk for the next twenty-four hours. She needs food and water."

Without a word James pulled his wife into his arms and rose. Amelia continued, "Good. Riley, Isobel... I want you to take them home now, then meet me in my quarters."

"I'm staying," Mark said, surprising the others. Turning to Amelia, he continued, "My brother is out there. I want to work with your team and create a plan."

Amelia was already shaking her head. "And you will, but right now I need to convene with my people, and you need to check in with Emily and Sophie." Mark grumbled in disagreement, but she continued, placing her hand supportively on his shoulder. "Mark, I give you my word, as soon as we have any news or decide on a course of action, we will collect your team. In the meantime, be with your family." She continued, speaking to Riley, "Ri, please." She directed her chin towards the group.

Isobel and Riley went to embrace the three remaining. Their lights filled the room, and then in a single blink they were in a familiar living room.

CHAPTER SIX

Emily woke from her slumber with a scream, followed by free-flowing tears. Surprised by the sudden outburst, Sophie cried from her nearby crib. Emily continued to scream, clutching at her chest in agony; her body so overcome with anguish it shook. One swift knock to the bedroom door had Amy rushing into the room to see what was wrong. She joined her sister on the bed, pulling her close and cradling Emily's head in her lap. Abel rushed in then; having slept on the foldout couch downstairs, he was out of breath from running up the stairs.

"Emily," Amy tried to calm her inconsolable sister. "Emily, what is it? What's wrong?" She reassuringly rubbed Emily's arm as Abel reached for Sophie.

"Shush," he gently rocked the distressed child up and down, trying to get her to quiet. "You're okay."

"Emily?" Tears filled Amy's eyes blurring her vision. Shaking her sister, "Emily, tell me what's wrong? Has something happened?"

Emily tried hard to focus, to calm herself, but nothing seemed to be working. Her body remained stiff and aching as she recognized the feeling of shock and dread. Her words came in a slur of hiccups and pain.

"Not me." Frantically, she shook her head. Her wide eyes focused on her sister's, she managed to say, "I think something terrible is happening to Isobel. She's hurt. She's in pain."

A new wave of tears and cries escaped her lips as her stomach cramped and pain rippled through her. Emily curled around her sister like a small child clutching its mother.

Abel and Amy sat silently, staring blankly at each other, unsure what action was needed.

"I'll take Sophie downstairs. I'll make some tea," Abel offered as he stepped from the room.

Amy held her sister for ten minutes before the tears seemed to slow and her body began to relax. Brushing the clinging tendrils of hair from her face, "Better?" she asked, when Emily finally reopened her eyes, pulling herself together as she sat up.

Taking a deep breath, Emily nodded. "Amy, something is seriously wrong."

Amy blinked in agreement. "Come," she slowly rose from the bed, offering her hand. "We'll get you some tea and sit for a bit."

Slowly they made their way downstairs and into the kitchen. Sophie began to wail for her mother as soon as she entered the room. Brushing her eyes, Emily reached for her daughter. "Thanks, I'm sorry I woke you." She spoke directly to a concerned Abel, who was busying himself around the kitchen trying to prepare their drinks.

"Nonsense. It's why I'm here." He weakly smiled, giving her an awkward side hug as she cradled her daughter. He returned to the cupboard containing the coffee cups, adding, "You okay?"

Emily nodded as she absently kissed Sophie's forehead. Sophie had a handful of her mother's hair, twisting it throughout her fingers, and a rapidly moving pacifier seemingly indicated she was placated by her presence.

"Yes," she joined Amy at the dining room table. "It was so strange. I was fast asleep when this wave of emotion hit me. The shock of it woke me up, but then it felt like my heart was ripping from my chest." She recounted the events, not taking her eyes off her daughter. "Amy, she's hungry, could you pass me that blanket?" Abel respectfully turned and finished pouring the hot water as Emily positioned Sophie for a feed, covering herself with the provided blanket.

"Do you think they were attacked?" Shock and fear filled Amy's shaky voice.

Emily had to think about it before she could truly answer. "I don't think so. The pain felt more like heartbreak and loss. Something major has happened, but I don't think she was physically harmed. I still feel the ache but it's not as intense."

Abel joined the girls at the table. "Do you have any way of contacting them?"

"I've tried," Emily blurted. "Isobel and I can communicate telepathically, but she's not responding." She turned to her sister, "Have you tried Amelia?"

"Yeah, she isn't replying either, but it's late, she could just be sleeping."

Ten minutes passed as Emily and the others sat in silence, sipping their tea. A sudden gasp from Amy pulled the others' attention.

"Amy?" Emily squeezed her sister's hand.

Amy cried out again; this time tears consumed her as well, as she buried her face in her hands, resting her elbows on the table. After a minute, she began rocking back and forth.

Emily reached over, gently rubbed her sister's back. "It will pass soon. Hang in there."

"I. Feel. Sick," she sputtered, not removing her hands.

"This is crazy. There has to be some way to turn it off," Abel said, but Emily was already shaking her head.

"It's part of our bonds. It's what allows us to still use our light. It's a protective mechanism. It will gradually fade as we grow stronger and use our own light more… Kind of like we are weaning off the strong stuff."

Sophie was fed, burped, and returned to her crib. Emily brought down some extra blankets for Amy, who was now sprawled out on one of the couches, exhausted. Abel was positioned across from her, his pullout bed now returned into a seat.

"So what can we do? What can I do to help?" Emily could tell Abel was out of his element.

She smiled reassuringly. "Just being here helps." She glanced over at her sister, who seemed to be returning to herself. "The pain is slowly calming. Amy, how do you feel?" She sat at the end of her sister's couch, taking her head into her lap.

"Better," she said with her eyes closed. "It felt like I was still me, with a rational mind and my own thoughts, but my body was elsewhere completely out of my control."

Emily merely nodded.

"Just keep trying to contact her and I'll do the same. Hopefully, we get an explanation soon," Emily finished.

Two hours later, still nothing. They had turned on the TV an hour ago, simply for some kind of distraction.

Five minutes before 4AM, a bright light filled their living room. Abel quickly turned off the TV.

"Mark!" Emily leapt up from her seat into Mark's arms as James discreetly laid Julia on a second, nearby couch. Riley and Isobel had not joined the others.

Concern crept onto Mark's face, as he took in his wife's distraught appearance. Her eyes were still red and puffy, her cheeks tear-stained. "What is it? What's wrong?" He looked around the room, alarmed. "Where's Sophie?" He gently cradled her face in his hands.

She shook her head, understanding his panic. "Sophie's asleep," she paused before continuing, while gesturing towards her own face. "Isobel," she stated, as if that were to explain her appearance. She wiped her nose with a heavily used tissue. "What happened? One minute I was asleep, the next I was uncontrollably screaming and shaking with these extreme emotions. Pain, fear, anger... More pain," Emily recounted.

Before Mark could answer, Amy blurted, "Where's Rick?" She continued to scan the room over and over, even though it was evident he wasn't there.

Mark took a deep breath, leading the two women over to the couch. Abel stood then and silently shook Mark's hand, while clearly making room.

"Mark, what is going on? Where is Rick?" she repeated.

He slowly began recounting the events of the peace conference. Explaining in detail about Velo's horrific death, Bates' involvement, Thomas' death, and finally the trade for Julia. Amy's eyes filled with tears as she pushed past her brother-in-law towards her best friend, only realizing now how close she was to losing her.

"Julia?" Amy knelt on the floor by her head. Julia was fast asleep, weakened from the blood loss.

"She'll be okay," James muttered, not taking his eyes off his wife. "She just needs to rest."

"Yes she does." Mark's medical training finally resurfaced. "James, take her up to the spare room. I'll make an IV, then double check her wound."

James already had his wife in his arms as Amy spoke, "I have some spare clothes. I'll bring them up in a minute."

"I'll get you a wash cloth and warm bowl of water. She needs to get cleaned up, but I don't think a bath will work," Emily added.

James made his way up the stairs and out of sight, leaving the four remaining motionless. Amy's attention was brought back to her absent husband. "So now what? What's the plan? When are we getting Rick back?" she asked in rapid succession.

Mark shook his head, placing both hands gently on Amy's shoulders. "The Jarly are strategizing as we speak. The minute they make a decision they are coming to get us." He paused, seeing that his words did very little to nullify her. "Amy, look at me." Her tear-filled gaze met his. "We're gonna get him back. He's strong. He's smart. And he has an entire species of power-wielding aliens at his rescue. He'll be fine." Mark idly wondered if he believed his own words; he was there, he saw the hate and darkness in Bates' eyes.

CHAPTER SEVEN

Rick awoke with his hands tied above him, his head fallen back. He tried to free himself, but found even his light to be ineffective. Glancing around, he noted the room was dark, and felt his toes dangling two feet from the grated flooring. Below, he could see Birons working furiously, paying no attention to him. Oddly, it was as if whatever craft they were in was fashioned after a narrow tower. Blocks of steel-crated rooms stacked on top of one another, though the walls were solid metal. He watched, mesmerized, as one particularly deformed and grotesque-looking Biron bonded some form of shield to the bloated chests of two others. One seemed to notice his gawking and banged on the above grating, startling Rick, pulling him back into his room.

Next to him, Amadeus was heavily strapped to an oddly shaped leather seat. Much like a dentist's chair, his arms were painfully bound to the armrests, which were riddled with rusted spikes. Clearly this chair was used to restrain anyone intended for torture and interrogation. Rick whispered Amadeus' name though he didn't even stir, clearly still unconscious. Having been dangling for so long, Rick's arms already felt numb as he continued his meek attempts at freedom.

Roughly two hours later a loud bang drew his attention to the far wall; the only wall with nothing attached. Clicking noises filled the room, joints and hinges whined, as a door slid into the roof, exposing Bates with an overly arrogant grin on his face. With a long metallic tool in hand, dragging across the grating, he made his way into the room, followed by two more Jarly that Rick didn't recognize.

"What do you pricks want?" Rick spat as he tried to steady himself, angling himself towards their path.

Without a single word uttered, Bates ignited his flame, which extended into the rod, turning it an electric shade of blue. He swung, striking Rick just below his chest. A sickeningly sharp pain laced throughout Rick's body, as his breathing grew ragged and his whole body began to vibrate and burn. Every tiny hair felt ignited as a sizzling noise filled the room. He absently wondered what the overwhelming noise was until he realized it was his own screams, mixed with a sort of static zapping.

"Enough!" Amadeus had resurfaced.

The pain ceased as Bates and the others turned their attention to their former leader. Rick found it hard to gain his breath as his head flopped lazily onto his chest. Paralysis seemed to overcome him, forcing him to look down at his body as his head drooped. Where the rod had hit his torso his clothing had all but melted away to reveal a harsh purple lash covering his skin from left to right hip. Blue veins surrounded the line, which was now growing darker and spreading. Rick's skin was still stinging and violently twitching, but he knew he had to hold on and pay attention. He had been ignoring the current conversation until now.

"...thing will come of this. You have started a war against your own kind." Amadeus was already full of his speech, looking much weaker than before. Rick had never seen him so pale. More anger ignited as Bates seemed to laugh at every other word.

"My people," Bates paused and added just enough disdain in his voice to portray his true hatred, "have done nothing but enslave me and my family for generations. All we do is what we are told. We live on bare minimum rations." Anger grew in his voice until he finished by touching the slight tip of the glowing rod to Amadeus' chest. Only now could Rick see first hand what had happened to him. Amadeus' eyes began to glow blue as the rod touched him. The sizzling noise filled the air again, as the rod melted away his shirt, sparking the skin with harsh bruises. Luckily this was just a taste; the rod was away from his burning flesh before Rick could count to five. Amadeus' eyes no longer glowed, but closed as his head drooped.

"What do you want?" Rick practically whispered, with not enough energy to raise his head.

A quick burst to his ribs from the rod gained his attention. "What I *want*," Bates growled and emphasized the last word, "is for you to stay quiet. The only reason you are here is for backup." Bates turned back to Amadeus. "What I want is for Amadeus to renounce his leadership and involvement in the treaty. Not before convincing the other members to change their minds about Earth. I want all the remaining Jarly in this Galaxy to return to Nona. The Birons will then take what they are entitled to and strip Earth of all and anything they can."

He stopped then as Amadeus began to chuckle, sounding just the right side of crazy. "Bates, that will never happen." He paused, gaining what strength he could muster to lock eyes with his capturer. "And what of you? What do you get out of this little deal? Do you really think the Birons will leave you anything?"

Face serious and determined, Bates inched forward. "You fool." Passing the rod onto one of his cohorts, he firmly placed both hands on Amadeus' shoulders, ignoring the protest and clear revulsion. Leaning in for only Amadeus to hear, he whispered, "I've had this plan in the works long before I joined your ranks. I was born in the Biron wastelands, raised by a exiled Jarly mother and half Biron father." Amadeus' eyes widened with each revelation. "When my parents were killed by a Jarly raid, I was taken and raised in the mud of a Biron orphanage. When I was of age, I returned to Jarly territory, falsified my records, and swore to gain the revenge my parents deserved. I gained experience with Jarly tools and controls, passcodes, air travel authorization..." He paused, pulling back and focusing on his next words. "When Earth falls, and it will, I will eventually become commander of the planet and remaining resources. I will be a God to ants." He spat his last words, turning to Rick. "Your people will bow at my feet and beg for the scraps I toss at them." He then gripped Rick's bruised ribs, pulling his body downward, causing the wrist restraints to bite and trickle blood down his forearms. Rick cringed as Bates pulled him to eye level, "Your people will learn to be nothing but my puppets for entertainment. I will gain power among the Jarly and Biron populations as a savior. Respected and loved; saving our kind from the plague that is the wasteful Human."

Rick couldn't resist. Entrapping Bates with his free legs, he pulled him close and forced his head forward. The satisfying crunch of Bates' broken nose was almost worth the extended beating he received from all three Jarly traitors.

* * *

"So what's the plan?" Abel asked those around the kitchen table, deep in thought. "What do we know?"

"I think it's best to wait and hear from Amelia and the others, before we make any rash decisions." Emily spoke over the rim of her coffee cup. Amy could not stand waiting around; she pulled back from the table, loudly screeching her chair across the tiled floor. Forcing herself into the other room, she headed for the stairs. "Amy, wait!" Emily followed close behind, reaching for her sister's arm, pulling her to an abrupt stop.

"Wait around all you want, I've got to do something." Amy tried to free her arm.

"Like what?" Emily utilized her patented big-sister voice. "You're going to go off on your own? You're no good to Rick distraught and getting yourself in unnecessary trouble."

Amy freed her arm then, taking a step back, "Well I'm no good to him sat around here," she forced out almost as a scream. "If it were Mark?" She paused with a raised eyebrow, "Would you be sat here, twiddling your thumbs, and drinking coffee?"

Emily took a deep breath, "I would be making a plan, but I wouldn't go storming off with no direction or help. We're all in this together. The best thing to do is wait for the others to contact us and see what can be done." Her tone weakened at the swell of fresh tears in her sister's eyes. Cupping Amy's face, Emily spoke slowly in her most calming voice. "We're gonna get him back. We're all worried and scared, but we are also a team of fighters and we will get him back. Just give the others some more time. This isn't just about a building we can attack and save him. This is space, which we know nothing about. Extraterrestrial spaceships and aliens with God-knows what abilities, which we can't even comprehend. We're out of our depth here, Amy, but that doesn't mean any one of us are giving up or slowing down. We just need some more answers."

"I just... I can't." Tears freely fell down her cheeks as Amy tried to find her words.

"I know," Emily pulled her close. "We know. Go lie down. I know you didn't sleep last night. I'll wake you as soon as we know more."

Amy only nod, turning towards the stairs, her shoulders slumped in utter defeat. Emily angrily brushed at her betraying tears, turning back to the kitchen. Heading to the stovetop, Emily retrieved a warming bottle of milk from the saucepan, wiping it down before passing it to Mark, who had Sophie wide-awake and fidgeting on his lap. Sophie took long and slow sips as her hands gripped wildly, her father lightly rocked her back and forth.

"How's Julia?" Emily asked James, who had spent the better part of the morning running back and forth from their room to the kitchen. He looked exhausted and drawn.

"She's going to be okay. She's fully healed, but the loss of blood really drained her." He paused and winced at his choice of words. Scrubbing his face with his free hand, he settled his coffee back on the table. "She just needs rest, fluids, and she will be fine." He then seemed to sober up, locking eyes with Emily, "I don't care what the plan is, Julia doesn't leave this house."

"Of course," Emily supported his decision to save his wife from the ensuing danger.

"I'll stay with her," Abel piped up, drawing the attention of the room. Turning to James, "I assume you will be going on the rescue mission, so I'll stay here with Julia and Sophie." James was already nodding as he turned to Emily and Mark, saying, "If that works for you?"

"I was going to call my parents, but if I can save them from this mess then it would be one less thing to worry about." Mark turned to his wife for reassurance, "Em?"

Pulling her eyes from her feeding daughter she spoke to the two men, "Yes, I think that would work. We will have to figure out some form of communication though."

As if on cue, the kitchen filled with a bright light, and Emily was calling for her sister to join them again.

The room fell silent at the appearance of Amelia, Riley, and Isobel. Their eyes were tired and swollen; their usual sophisticated and prim appearance now disheveled and unkempt. Mark passed Sophie on to her mother as he stood and rounded the table toward the others.

"Are you hurt?" Mark offered a glowing hand, holding his arms wide for Isobel, who shocked him by taking in his gesture and cringing away.

"We're fine," Amelia spoke for the others. "Just tired," she added for good measure.

"Please sit." Mark gestured to the empty chairs near them, returning to his own, showing his concern in a quick glance to Emily.

"So what do you know?" James sat up straight in his chair, businesslike.

When the others did not immediate respond, Riley spoke up first, clearing his throat. "We know they were taken on a B-class mining shuttle."

"B-class?" Abel asked before he could stop himself.

"Battle-class. It is a standard mining vessel, but one that is equipped as a second resort battle ship," Amelia explained.

"What does that mean? Don't you have more advanced technology and weaponry? Catch up to it, surround and board it." James thought the solution was obvious.

Sighing, Riley rubbed his face, not looking at anyone in particular. "It's not that simple. The ship is crewed by hundreds of Biron warriors. The layout of this particular ship is unknown."

Isobel added, "They had a small fleet waiting just on the outer limits of our scanners. They reached them within a matter of minutes, both outnumbering our pursuing ships and preventing any ambush."

"So you let them leave?" The outrage that filled Amy's voice pulled everyone's attention. Entering the kitchen with her fists at her sides, her flame igniting, "You abandoned them," she accused.

"Never," Amelia stood with her own outrage. "We managed to get a tracker onto their vessel before we pulled back. We know exactly where they are. Now it just a matter of strategy and patience." Amelia sunk back into her seat, as Amy took the unoccupied spot between her sister and James.

"So lets hear it," Amy demanded, folding her arms across her chest. "What's this great plan that rescues my husband and your leader from their current torment?" Her voice spewed distain as Emily reached for her hand, giving it a reassuring squeeze.

"We've come to ask you how far you are willing to take this?" Riley asked, already knowing the answer.

"What do you mean?" Amy's frustration and anger brewed. "We're in this 100%, you tell us what to do and we'll do it!"

"Be that as it may, Amy," Amelia started before turning to the others, "I need to hear this from everyone. This isn't some small town rescue mission we're talking about. This is all out war. I cannot guarantee there will not be further casualty or losses."

The room fell silent as the others contemplated her warning.

"I can't speak for anyone else," James spoke past the growing lump in his throat, "But Rick is my best friend and he saved my wife's life. There isn't anything I wouldn't do to get him back."

"You already know my answer," Amy blurted, her eyes trained on the table.

"Em?" Mark whispered ignoring the others, his eyes trained on his wife.

A single silent tear traveled down her cheek, reaching the tip of her chin before dropping inoffensively onto her daughter's pajama top. Sophie's eyes followed the tear, staring down at the darkened material; her free hand brushing at it, mesmerized.

"Emily?" Mark's hand rose to her near shoulder.

Her head whipped up and focused on Amelia. "We'll do whatever it takes." She spoke for herself and her husband. Mark followed her gaze and concluded with a nod.

"Very well," Amelia sighed, turning to Riley to continue as she rested back into her chair.

Steeling himself, Riley leant his elbows on the table, interlocking his fingers. "We do have a plan. A good one," he reassured with a faint smile. "We have already made contact with some of Earth's leaders who are more than happy to help in the rescue mission. Of course with their own demands, but that is none of your concern. As we speak, some of your best warriors are preparing and being transported to our station; being given the same instruction as you are now."

"So spit it out," James muttered in frustration, "What exactly is the plan, and where do we fit in?"

"Given the nature of the mining vessel, they will only be able to travel so far and so fast. I am positive, from their current position, they are attempting to reach one of our supply planets. We call it Kalepti. They will either switch ships or simply regroup in numbers. We're going to lead a wave of assault ships, tracking their movement, staying just out of their known radar capabilities. We'll take another route and try to head them off. It will take roughly three days to reach the post, but I am confident that we will beat them there with enough time to set up a decent perimeter."

James clapped and rubbed his hands together, getting to his feet. The others watched, slightly confused. "Sounds like a great start, three days... Probably best that we get going. You can fill us in on the way." He left the room, heading upstairs.

The others watched after him. Finally Emily stood, shifting Sophie onto her hip. "He's right, we have three days to fill in all the details. Lets take a few minutes to prep, then get going."

Amelia nodded, offering a slight smile of reassurance.

Turning to Mark and Abel, she said, "Can I speak to you both upstairs?" Emily turned and left the room, the men swiftly following after her.

Taking two steps at a time, Emily didn't bother to knock as she walked into James and Julia's borrowed room. Biting the inside of her cheek, she tried to prevent the wide grin forming as they quickly pulled apart; both blushing, as if they were caught completely naked and in the throes of passion.

"Sorry," Emily looked down momentarily, as she took to the plush seat in the corner of the room. Turning to James she asked, "Did you explain?" as Mark and Abel entered the room. Mark went straight to his wife, half sitting on the armrest of her chair as Abel leant against the near wall.

"Pretty much," Julia answered, not sounding too impressed as she crossed her arms over her freshly healed chest. "Not that I agree or approve of it."

"Julia..." James started, sitting next to his wife, propping himself up against the white overly carved headboard.

"No," Julia pulled the covers up, tucking them just under her arms, before turning to Emily. "Em, I should be there with you." Lifting her far arm without turning back to see, she pressed her hand softly over James' mouth, preventing his protest, making Abel cough to cover his light laughter.

"You need my light and my abilities. I can help!" Though the others were no longer bonded to her decisions, Emily was consulted as the pseudo-family leader.

Before she could continue, Emily raised her free hand, speaking with said authority. "We do need your help... I need your help." She took a shaky breath, looking down at her daughter. "I need you to stay here and protect this little one." She tried to plaster a large smile on her face as she bounced Sophie on her upper thighs. "Abel is going to stay here too." Turning towards him, she returned his genuine smile. "I know he has the light now too, but he's still getting used to it. I also need someone that we are bonded with for contact." She could tell Julia was readying her argument, so she continued with more emphasis. "Julia, like it or not, you are still not 100%. We don't know what using too much of your light will do to you. We need you to stay here and if needs be, protect them."

Confusion covered Julia's features. "Protect them... From what?" She looked back and forth between her two charges.

"Nothing yet," Emily reassured. "But with everything going on, we really don't know who to trust and who will be targeting us on Earth. We need to be cautious and cover all of our bases." Emily could see Julia almost visibly deflate as her head sunk back, resting on James' shoulder. "We'll get Amelia to come bond us, maybe both of us" - she quickly glanced at James -"so I can check in as much as needed and you can know what's going on."

Julia nodded, still not completely comfortable with the current plan.

"Abel," Emily began. He pushed away from the wall, giving her his full attention. "I need you to watch both of them. I don't think Julia should leave the house, Sophie either, so if you could just ensure they have everything they need and watch over the house. We'll keep in contact as much as possible, but it would really give me peace of mind if you stuck around until we got back."

"Of course, I'm not going anywhere," he offered with enthusiasm. "I'm here to help in any way that I can."

That soothed her nerves slightly. "Babe, anything you want to add?" Emily looked up lovingly at her husband.

He thought for a long minute, his brows pulling together. Eventually his face smoothed and he shook his head. "No. As long as we have contact, I'll be happy." Turning to Abel, "You do everything in your power to protect them." There was a stern undercurrent that was both domineering and a plea.

Abel took two strides, thrusting out a newly acquired flaming hand in a gesture to shake. "I'll protect them with my life. Don't worry about that." They shook as Mark left the room. Shortly after, he returned with Amy and the three patient Jarly, crowding into the small space.

"Please. Can you bond us again so we can communicate? Then we can leave," Mark requested.

The Jarly looked somewhat surprised as their eyes passed over the room. Amelia stepped forward towards the bed, as James and Julia made no effort to move; the others crowded around. Emily quickly passed Sophie into Abel's arms as she joined the group.

"There is a bond not like our worrier bonds." Amelia took a deep breath. She held her hand out, palm up in the middle of the bed, suspended a few feet over the sheets. "Place you hands over mine, palms up, not touching."

The others quickly complied enthusiastically. Isobel then spoke slowly, "You all need to try and clear your minds. Try not to think of anything but this room."

A lavender light erupted from Amelia's lit hand. A slight sizzling sound filled the small space. "Ignite your flames," she encouraged calmly, though the tension on her face betrayed the ease of the transaction.

One by one, their hands erupted in varying shades of orange and yellow flame. Then to their amazement, in ascending order, the palms changed to a matching shade of purple. Mark's hand, at the very top, changed and his fingers moved, almost toying with the light.

"Now, in order, lower your palms onto the hand below. You will feel a strange expanding sensation. Nothing to worry about," Riley chimed in, his lit hand resting between Amelia's shoulder blades.

The others did as they were told. Emily lowered her palm onto Amelia's, gasping as a surging pressure pushed from the back of her hand with a pin-pointed concentration at the very center. Not quite painful, but not pleasant, her fingers and joints felt bloated and expanded from within. Amy too gasped as the back of her palm pressed into Emily's. By the time Mark's palm rested on James', the stack of flesh looked solidified, as one.

The others turned their gaze onto Amelia whose head had fallen backwards, her eyes squeezed shut; the Humans gazed in confusion around the room at one another, but Isobel and Riley raised a single finger to their lips, silently encouraging the others to be quiet and patient.

Amelia's eyes returned to the group. The others watched, frozen at the sight of purple light consuming her pupils, sparking with small bolts of electricity that dashed across her sight. That light left her eyes, traveling down her outstretched arm as if it traveled only by her pumping veins, entering her hand in a rush.

"Brace yourselves," Riley offered, shortly before the light surrounding their palms ignited brighter than ever seen, then went out, dissipating throughout each of their arms. A small surge of energy pushed the group back, though none were forced off their feet.

"Whoa." James took a deep breath.

"Shush," Amelia muttered, her eyes squeezed shut, both palms still raised. Slowly she opened her eyes and glanced around the room. A growing ache filled each of their heads, a couple even rubbing at their temples.

"Listen to me," Amelia was emphatic. "As I speak your neurons are firing much quicker than they are used to. They are trying to understand the new material." The growing ache was blurring the group's collective vision. "It may seem painful, but it will shortly subside. The five of you are now bonded by speech only. No emotion or abilities have been transferred, but the connections alone are not usually so large. Give it a couple minutes and I'll explain further." The room fell silent as Emily and the others lounged on whatever surface they could reach. Most either with their eyes squeezed shut or gripping their heads. Julia went so far as to rock back and forth, trying to ease the worst migraine she had ever experienced. Breathing heavily and feeling uncomfortable, they waited as the pressure ebbed.

Sophie let out a slight screech, reaching with concern towards her tormented parents. Emily raised her hands, barely squinting in their direction, muttering, "Mommy's okay, baby." She tried to smile, ignoring the growing dark spots in the corner of her vision.

"Abel, can you take her downstairs and distract her? Please," Mark whispered from the opposite corner of the room, eyes squeezed shut.

Without uttering a word Abel took Sophie away. As the door clicked behind them the pain drastically lessoned, until their breathing returned to normal and eyes opened wide.

"Good." Amelia stood with her back to Riley, his hands resting on her hips, with a kind smile on his face. Isobel leant against the wall; she too had a knowing smile. "I've completed the bond, but I didn't choose to bond with you so I can't join the conversation," Amelia added.

"Okay, so the five of you should now have the ability to communicate, much like we had before." Riley spoke, and then added for only Mark to hear, *Those bonds are still intact, by the way.*

"I would suggest speaking to each other, one at a time; it's much easier to begin with," Amelia offered.

"It worked," James grinned, turning away from Julia.

Em? Mark spoke silently to his wife across the room.

She smiled and turned to her husband. *Hey there, sexy.* She winked.

He laughed out loud.

They each shared a quick connection before Amelia interrupted. "Good. Now let's try as a group. James, Julia, and Amy, I want you to concentrate on each other simultaneously and speak." The others waited as the three looked at one another.

"I can hear them separated, but not in one conversation." Amy blurted, turning to Amelia for advice.

"Relax your mind. Start with something simple. James, starting counting; Julia, you start reading off the alphabet." Turning her attention to Amy, "Now listen. What do you hear?"

Amy focused, her head bobbing back and forth. Julia and James started laughing together, causing the others to turn with raised brows.

Feeling the need to explain, Julia spoke. "I've got James counting in one ear and Amy's random cursing in the other."

James nodded, in agreement. "And I've got: A, B, C, Fuck, F, G, H, Damn it, I, J, for fuck sake... Going in my head."

Amy visibly bristled. "And I've just got 1,2,3,4, when I look at Julia and A, B, C, D from James, but I have to shut out one to hear the other."

"Amy, I think you'll be able to hear both once you settle down a little. You've got a lot on your mind, a lot of panic and something like this isn't going to come easily." Isobel offered, not moving from her spot near the door.

"Mark, Emily, James. Now you try," Riley ordered.

The room fell silent as they concentrated.

Eventually, they each nodded. Emily turned a sympathetic gaze to her sister. "You'll get the hang of it soon."

"Great, let's get going," Mark said.

The room moved in an organized frenzy as it emptied.

CHAPTER EIGHT

Ten minutes later and the kitchen table was surrounded with random bags thrown across its length, and the group had changed in preparation. Emily had just finished showing Abel where everything Sophie-related was. He was now fully prepared; from her food and drink supply, diapers, to her favorite blanket and children's channels.

She kissed her daughter with force between her little brows, then quickly on the cheeks, before turning her attention back to Abel. "We will be in constant contact with Julia if you need anything." Emily turned to her friend then, "Don't leave anything out. I want to know exactly what is going on around here. Hopefully, we will only be gone for a few days, but we can't say for sure."

"Hey," Abel whispered, pulling her attention back to him and her daughter in his arms. He held her gaze, "Don't you worry about a thing. We've got everything covered here. Don't be stressing about us, while you have much bigger things to worry about."

His eyes quickly pointed to Amy, who was in an apparent daze staring down at the table. Her slight frame looked weighed down and weakened by the heavy black backpack and training gear.

Emily nodded, understanding, and kissed her daughter's forehead one last time. She then surprised Abel by kissing his cheek and engulfing both of them in a bear hug. "Thank you," she whispered before pulling away.

Mark kissed his daughter's crown and then lightly patted Abel on the back. "I really appreciate what you're doing. I'm sure you have a million other things to do, rather than babysit."

Abel laughed, shaking his head. "Nowhere I'd rather be," he reassured.

Mark smiled, joining the others at the end of the table. Julia had her arms tightly wrapped around her husband's neck, just off to the side, in the living room.

"Don't even THINK about being a hero and putting yourself in some macho bullshit danger." She held his gaze and emphatically continued, "You're coming back to me."

James smiled, rubbing his hands along her upper arms. "Baby, crazed diabolic aliens couldn't keep me away from you." He tilted her head up, their lips brushing tenderly, before she pushed up onto her tiptoes, sealing her lips with his.

Pulling back, her light eyes bore into her husband's. "I'm serious, James! I hear of you pulling any unnecessary crap... It won't be crazed aliens you'll have to worry about!"

He kissed the tip of her nose, unable to hide his sheer amusement, and whispered, "Is that a promise?"

She couldn't help but grin back, nodding as he turned, joining the group.

"Ready?" Amelia asked, her hand absently seeking and finding Riley's.

"Ready as we'll ever be," Emily answered for the group, not taking their eyes off of the remaining three.

Excitement grew in Abel's chest as their light ignited and filled the room. Taking an involuntary step back, the flames were too bright and vibrant. Within a blink of an eye the light disappeared, along with the anxious travellers. Abel turned to Julia, who could not hide the swelling of tears at what was to come. Sophie, now accustomed to a house of light shows, merely looked up at the both of them for her next trick and form of entertainment.

∗ ∗ ∗

When Rick woke again, the room was much brighter than the last. He was fastened to a chair similar to the one Amadeus had inhabited, however this one was newer; no sickly stains or grotesque gouges covered this seat. The lights flickered above, calling his attention. Much like the familiar hum of a florescent light, the entire ceiling was solid and alive with luminosity.

Glancing around the open space, Rick noted that his chair was the sole piece of furniture. The walls appeared to transition from a clinical white, as they met the lighted ceiling, changing to a deep shimmering pearl, as they touched the dark tiled floors. A familiar click had Rick straighten out of his lazy slouch. His head swiveled to the left as the paneling folded in on itself, revealing Bates alone.

He had a seemingly mundane, lightweight metal chair gripped tightly in his left hand. Taking his first steps, the chair legs purposefully dragged across the tile, echoing off of the acoustical walls. Searing pain gripped Rick's ears as he visibly cringed, pulling away. His body tensed until the screeching stopped and Bates had settled, rather smugly, within feet of Rick.

"What the fuck do you want?" Rick spat, his body beginning to loosen. He idly wondered how long he had slept. His mouth was dry and tasted long overdue for nourishment.

Bates leant forward, leaning onto his elbows, eyes squinting in concentration, as he appeared to examine his captive without touch.

"What?" Rick leaned forward, jaw clenched, as his bottom lip split from the fierce dryness.

Bates took a deep breath, shaking his head and leaning back. "I see some potential in you, but you really must evolve from your caveman tendencies." He watched the first trickle of blood trail down Rick's chin. Eyes focusing, he continued, "It's quite comical really." Bates even began to chuckle.

Rick brimmed with anger. With no saliva, he pulled back and spat what he could. The defiant display left blood spattered across Bates' face and maroon shirt. Bates had already attempted to escape the spray, standing inhumanly fast, kicking the chair out from under him. Now standing in shock, much to Rick's amused pleasure, he lunged and his rough right knuckles collided with Rick's jaw. Rick dramatically wiggled his jaw though the pain was acute and exhausting. He managed to keep his smile as he turned back to face his assailant.

Raising his head, Rick spoke slowly, ensuring his clarity. Feeling the swell pull at his jawline, with one eyebrow raised, he remarked, "I guess cavemen tendencies are truly a universal thing." He now chuckled, but cut off as the venomous grip of Bates' left hand surrounded his throat, cutting off his airways. Bates pushed forward as Rick's head was forced back into the metal headrest. He tried to resist, his arms attempting to wrench from the restraining armrests.

"Enough!" an overpowering deep voice came from the previously vacant doorway.

Bates quickly pulled away, pure hatred diluting his pupils as he took another two steps back. Rick gasped for breath, as his heavy head began to droop and bob under its own weight. As his chin rested on his chest, his eyes drew to the left; a dark figure entered his blurred vision. Given the lack of food and water, Rick knew exhaustion would claim him again too soon. He tried with all his might to pull his eyes wide open and focus.

The blurred figure came closer, stopping directly in front of the solid chair. Reaching down, a thick black hand lifted Rick's chin with force. The rough pads of each fingertip scraped across the swollen, sensitive flesh. Rick's eyes drew up and froze to note an impressively scarred Biron. His charred flesh appeared mangled and misshapen. His left eye must have been damaged as the eyelid only allowed for so much movement. A chunk was missing from the back of his right lower jaw; with little help from whatever medical support he was offered, the wound had healed with only a slight covering of flesh.

The Biron watched Rick's examining stare, his head easily twice the size and thickness of any Human or Jarly. He tilted his head, a movement that too felt labored and unnatural. His voice was loud and heavy in the air, "Do your Human eyes find my appearance displeasing?" There was a sarcastic bite to the end of his sentence.

Rick's eyes bounced from the Biron to the stonefaced Bates, and then back again. "Who are you?" His heavy brows pulled together, "What do you want from us?"

"Ah," the Biron managed a wide smile. Letting go of Rick's chin, he pulled back and straightened. "My name is Kavar Trone." He turned, glancing at Bates, whose head now drooped in a sign of submission. Kavar's face fell, seriousness and intensity covering his features. Turning back to Rick, he said, "I am the commander of this vessel... Well, the whole fleet.

From you, I plan to utilize your weak Human mind. Gain knowledge…" A mangled hand stroked at the air.

Rick pulled at his restraints, "I'd never betray my…" He halted as a deep chuckle built in Kavar's chest. Bates grinned in response, his eyes never leaving Rick's.

Bates took the opportunity to step forward, his left hand resting at the top of Rick's chair. Leaning down whispering into Rick's near ear, "Do you really think you would have a choice in the matter?"

Kavar's chuckle now escaped his lips as he turned and walked towards the exit. Rick had intended to call after him, to demand his attention, but fell short as the glowing left palm of Bate consumed his face and the bright light consumed his consciousness.

* * *

Amadeus awoke in a violent shiver. Stripped of his shirt, Amadeus now lay unbound on a cold rusted metallic floor covered in a vile smelling liquid. In his weakened state he could barely raise his head. Slowly he managed to crawl to a nearby wall, propping himself up so his outstretched arms rested on his knees. His head had fallen back, scraping along the rough wall as his eyelids began to fall rather than remain wide and focused.

Frustration bloomed as any and all communicating with the distant members of his team fell silent.

Estimating that another two hours had passed, Amadeus watched mindlessly as liquid was poured from above, trickling through the grated ceiling and splashing onto the solid floor below. In his declining state he couldn't ignite his light long enough to heal any of his wounds. He knew his natural healing abilities would have all injuries sewn and lessoned within days, but any strength could not go wasted.

The slopping of new liquids distracted Amadeus enough to not notice the movement in his peripheral vision until it was close enough to touch. Strong arms wrenched him to his bare feet, his body relying on their grip to hold him upright.

The sight before him shocked him and held his attention as his jaw weakened, hanging open.

"Kavar?" Amadeus slurred, his body attempting to drag him back down.

"Always a pleasure, Amadeus. Especially when I get the privilege of seeing you so weak and broken like this. It truly brings tears of joy to my good eye," Kavar mocked.

His initial surprise subsided. "Broken?" Amadeus offered by way of confusion. "I may be weak, but I have not and will never be broken."

"We shall see," Kavar's grin further corrupted his features. Turning, he barked his order to the men at Amadeus' sides. "Bring him."

Amadeus couldn't muster the energy to walk so he settled for the uncomfortable scraping of his bloodied feet, dragging across the harsh surface that made for relatively unstable footing. Only a short distance brought the group to a stop as they waited for a loudly banging and beaten elevator to except them. The elevator spiraled like that of the space station's; however this one was a quarter of the size and much older, needing maintenance.

To Kavar's extreme frustration the elevator froze with more than a foot at the bottom, forcing the group to awkwardly climb over the brim and onto the leveled platform of the next corridor. Amadeus was to be dragged out of the elevator last. To his obvious delight, the elevator began to ascend again, leveling out; forcing his wide grin, Amadeus merely shuffled from its hold. Kavar burst past his guards and struck Amadeus with a blinding backhander, forcing him back, hitting the near wall.

"Wipe that smile off your face," he spat as Amadeus hit the floor with a loud thud, causing old dust and dirt to flare into his nostrils. Once again, more hands pulled and pushed at him as he was returned to his feet, before being pulled into yet another dark and crippling room. "There!" Kavar roared as he pointed to the near wall with free-floating shackles protruding from the stained surface.

This room was obviously used for creative brutality and coercion. The ceiling was dimly lit with panels of hanging lights. Barbaric tools hung from different hooks, some swinging and clinking together with the gentle sway of the ship. The walls, once clear and lightly covered, were now charred and dented. Amadeus gave little resistance as he was led over and securely fastened into place. The bite of chains against his delicate flesh did awaken many of his absent senses. His right wrist had been cut in an earlier struggle, leaving the pinching, icy metal too present in his mind. Resigned to his fate, Amadeus slouched back into the wall. The numbness was already beginning to consume his arms as his limbs were fastened above his head, spread wide.

Amadeus heard the room seal behind the other Biron, though he knew from the stench that Kavar was still present. His head now resting on the supporting wall, his eyes trained on the flickering lights above. Something heavy and metallic was retrieved from its designated spot, bouncing once on the hard floor before it began its slow, tormented drag towards its next victim.

Kavar, now only feet from Amadeus, leaned forward with a grin in his speech. "Now, you remember my favorite part."

Unable to utilize Nona's light, Kavar's band of miscreants had manipulated what tools they could to duplicate similar results. Amadeus only had enough time to gasp and squeeze his eyes shut as the sparking rod raised and began tracing across sensitive tissues. Sadly, the sizzle of burned flesh and agonizing pain was not enough to pull Amadeus into his much desired unconsciousness.

CHAPTER NINE

"It's been three hours and I still haven't heard anything." Julia chewed on her cuticles, sat at the end of the oak dinning table as Abel wrestled with Sophie to finish the last few bites of her vegetable puree. Sophie's eyes were trained on the colorful display of mixed fruit at the center of the table, her little hand swatting at the small spoon hovering near her face.

"Come on, Sophie... Two more bites." Abel's persistence was getting him nowhere. Turning, he spoke directly to Julia, pulling her out of her continued trance. "Can you do it again?" his eyes pleading.

Julia dropped her hands onto the table with a playful huff. "Sophie, are you being a little madam?" The pair was awarded with a loud baby gurgle and flailing hands. Julia puffed out her cheeks and crossed her eyes, before igniting her light and focusing it into her already untamed hair.

With the slight drop in Sophie's jaw, Abel managed to coax her into taking the last few bites before calling it a day.

"Thanks," he managed a small smile as he wiped his messy fingers on his already stained t-shirt.

Releasing her light, Julia stood, reaching for the remnants of their meals. "Are you still having a hard time projecting?"

Abel grabbed the remaining dishes, but not before yielding to Sophie's loud demands; her little fingers pointing to the large ripe strawberries. He reached over, carefully placing one in her excited palm and watching as she brought it to her lips, sucking to no avail.

"I just can't seem to focus, calm myself, or whatever is needed to actually maintain anything." Abel displayed his lack of confidence with a soft fizzling of his light that danced over the tops of his hands and dissipated as quickly as it came. "John seems to be getting the hang of it, though."

Julia turned after filling the dishwasher, leaning against the kitchen countertops. "How is John? I haven't seen or heard from him since the wedding."

"He's good. I actually texted him not long ago. He's been in his element working with the Jarly historians. He's really bonded with that one guy, Toby, whose specialty is in early-Sumerian development. Apparently he's opened John's eyes and explained things that have always plagued him." Julia grinned at his heavy sarcasm, laughing when he rolled his eyes at the end.

He stopped. "What?"

"Is somebody a little jealous?" she pouted, pushing out her bottom lip.

This made Abel laugh. "What are you talking about?"

"You're totally jealous of John and Toby's newfound friendship." His only response was to roll his eyes. Julia reached for Sophie, wiping her chin of excess drool before lifting her out of the solid highchair. Laughing, she continued playfully, "You totally are. Your best friend is spending all his time with his new boyfriend and you don't like it."

"Come on. Give me a little more credit. Toby's a nice enough guy and he has a lot in common with John. They talk for hours and he's even helping John control and manipulate his light," Abel argued his case, unconvincingly.

"Yeah, yeah." Julia placed Sophie on a soft blanket in the center of the living room surrounded by her toys. Sitting on the carpet nearby, she continued, "If you want I can..." her soft speech trailed off as her eyes glazed and her head tilted to the side.

Abel waited a moment. "Julia?" He crouched down to her level, his hand reaching out to grip her shoulder.

Blinking rapidly, he felt her shoulders relax and her body sag. "They're doing okay." She spoke cryptically, "That was James. He said they've just been traveling so far. Cooped up in one of the common rooms. I think they're playing darts or something; they're pretty bored at the moment. James just can't wait to get to the training aspect of it. He wants to see all these soldiers and military guys in action."

"Oh, I'm sure what he really wants is to challenge them." Abel chuckled at the thought.

"Yeah, well you know how they are. Always gotta one-up each other. Sounds like they are just gonna grab a bite to eat and then a meeting will be called when they get closer to the other ships. I don't think James really knows when they will get going… You know, in pursuit." Julia's face fell at the end, concern etching into her features.

"Hey, they're all in good hands." Abel tried to comfort her, but her eyes had already glazed once again, as she followed a second conversation.

As he waited for Julia to return to the present, the doorbell rang loud and clear, causing Sophie to drop her fabric dolly and Julia to turn her head towards the door. "Are you expecting someone?"

"No." Abel ambled to his feet, "Stay here with her."

Flicking on more lights as he made his way to the foyer, Abel could only make out the dark silhouette of a single individual on the doorstep. Glancing at the large clock near the entrance he noted it was just after 9:30pm. Stepping closer, he reached for the light switch, illuminating the front porch and revealing John through the wide window smirking at his best friend.

"Ever plan on opening the door?" John spoke through the glass as he took a step or two back.

Turning the knob and yanking the door wide, Abel made room for John to pass through. "John, what are you doing here? It's pretty late."

"Nice to see you too," he tapped Abel's shoulder as he pulled off his light jacket, walking over to the closet and hanging it on the nearest hook, making himself at home. "Well, you texted me that you were on your way over and something had come up. Then you stopped replying, so I decided to come check things out."

Confused, Abel reached in his front pocket retrieving his cellphone to reveal two missed calls and three texts. "Sorry. I guess it was on silent."

John smiled and shrugged. "Hey Julia, how are you feeling?" John made his way back around the corner where Julia had Sophie balanced on her hip as she leant into the open doorframe separating the front and the living room space.

"I'm fine, John, thanks… Just the usual fun and games." She took a step forward and into his half embrace before releasing an ecstatic Sophie into his grip.

"And how are you, missy?" John put on his baby voice as he hugged her close and tickled her lower left side. Her laughter filled the space as she playfully pulled and twisted her body away from his onslaught.

"Do you want a drink?" Abel passed the trio as he entered the kitchen.

"I'll take some coffee if you have any going." John followed quickly behind, returning Sophie to the blanket below.

Taking a seat at the table, John leaned back, crossing his arms as Julia joined him, both waiting for Abel.

"Julia?" Abel asked, reaching for the coffee mugs.

"Yes, please. I take a little bit of sugar and cream," Julia answered before turning to John. "How have you been? How's Kristine and the kids?"

"They're great, thanks. They're visiting her parents in Montana this weekend." John met Abel halfway across the table, reaching for his black coffee. "Thanks."

Julia smiled, adding a single nod, as Abel passed her hers. "You didn't want to go too?"

"Nah, her dad always takes the kids camping and Kristine just likes to spend the time with her mom... Girl stuff and all. Plus, it means I get the house to myself for the weekend." He winked, taking his first sip, "So, tell me what's going on?" He glanced between Julia and Abel, "Abe just said Amadeus got a hold of him and said things had come up, and you and Sophie needed some company. Or in other words, needed some protection."

Julia rolled her eyes at the assumption that she couldn't take care of herself, let alone a small child. Leaning her elbows onto the table, she spent the next forty-five minutes retelling the events of the past couple days.

"Jesus Christ, are you okay?" John reached across, resting his hand over hers as she nursed her cup of coffee.

"I'm fine." She glanced between the men, clearly unconvincing, "Of course it was terrifying and took a lot out of me." She absently touched her chest, covered by her t-shirt; she still felt the agony deep within her bruised muscles and tortured flesh. "The healing saved my life, but it's like I can still feel it here. I guess I'm still a bit shook-up." Once again she touched her chest, this time to add emphasis.

"Of course you are. That's not something that you lightly forget, but we're here now and we won't leave you until this is all figured out," Abel said.

"How's Amy holding up?" John's question was all but whispered.

Now that the attention was away from Julia, she seemed to relax. Taking a deep breath and literally shaking off the relived moments as they changed the subject, she said, "I think she's hanging in there. Obviously, she was a wreck when we found out, but she seemed to pull herself together pretty quickly and has been with us ever since... She hasn't really had a moment to herself either since it all happened, so I don't really know. Usually, we tell each other everything, but right now she's remaining silent."

"Well that's good, it means she's focused and knows what needs to be done to get Rick back. The worst will be at night when she is left alone," Abel added.

"I don't think Emily will leave her if she can avoid it." Julia raised herself from the table, reaching down for Sophie. "I'm gonna put her down for the night, I'll be back in a minute."

CHAPTER TEN

"It's been an entire day," Amy's fist pounded on the Jarly table, "When are we gonna hear about this magnificent plan?" Her sarcasm didn't go unnoticed. They had been traveling as fast as their ship could travel. It took four hours before they were initially met by the Jarly fleet of varying sized assault vessels; both Mark and James were awestruck at the magnitude, but the girls could care less.

"Amy, please…" Exhaustion filled Emily's voice as the ongoing battle for her sister to see reason was failing. "Just take a breath and calm down." She pulled her sister onto the nearby couch. The Jarly had fully equipped the Human living space just like the space station; nothing looked out of the ordinary, not unlike their quarters on Thomas' farm. The current space looked that of a mundane Human kitchen, with dining room table and lounging space; the only reminder that they were currently traveling faster than the speed of light was the giant, sparklingly clear widow, displaying the impressively beautifully depths of deep space.

"I'm sure they will join us soon enough and clue us in. They have an entire ship of Jarly and Earth's soldiers to catch up," Mark reassured from the other side of the room. Emily wrapped her arms around her sister's shoulders, squeezing tightly.

Though the room was abuzz with conversation and strategy, Emily couldn't pull her thoughts from Sophie and the others.

Julia? Emily silently spoke for the tenth time.

Yep, still here. Emily smiled at the exasperation in Julia's voice. *All good still… Nothing's changed in the last fifteen minutes.*

K. Thanks, just making sure the connection's still in place. Emily finished.

The sisters began practicing their light, their silent communication, and eventually their ability throwing the kitchen knives. Luckily the walls seemed to heel by light as easily as flesh. Another three hours had passed as the group gathered around the table, finishing their late lunches. Amelia and Isobel strode though the cafeteria-style swinging doors. They stopped abruptly, both with raised brows, at the three steak knives protruding from the near wall.

The others followed their gaze; Mark barely batted an eye when he shrugged, "Target practice."

Emily quickly followed, "I'll fix that when we're done."

Amelia smiled, "I'm sure you will." They continued their stride, taking the two available chairs.

James passed down the plate containing a variety of sandwiches. "Hungry?"

Isobel enthusiastically nodded and took half a slice, "I just realized, I haven't eaten since the festive dinner."

James forcibly swallowed as he thought aloud, "That was four days ago."

Amelia explained, "We don't need to eat as often as Humans. We can usually go two or three days before any hunger signs emerge." She finished by grabbing her own slice of a ham and cheese sandwich.

The room fell silent for a time before thought returned.

"So what's the plan?" Mark cleared his throat as the others continued to eat.

Amelia licked the last crumb from the corner of her mouth before answering. "We believe we will reach the planet before they can. Our vessels are much faster, so we hope to have at least half a day on them. There has been a recorded fleet of roughly twelve vessels awaiting their arrival. So we'll have to overpower them, take out their communications, and leave them stranded." She reached for the second half of her sandwich as the others froze, listening intently. "We will then fall back and approach the planet from the far side. The planet is five times the size of earth and can easily cover our ascent. It also has a highly metallic cloud layer, which will help distort us from any radar tracking without weakening our own tracking sensors. It's been estimated that their fleet will arrive and attempt to land on the surface. While their ships prepare to land, we will take out their propulsions and board."

Isobel cut her off, staring into the half eaten sandwich raised to her mouth. "Board the ship, get our family, kill the bad guys." The lack of emotion in her voice worried Amelia, though she didn't show it.

James waited to make sure the others didn't have anything immediate to say. "What do you need from us specifically?" He squared his shoulders, leaning onto the table.

"That will be threefold. Emily, you are the healer of your group. I want you to stay at Isobel's side and assist with any injuries." Emily nodded in response.

"Mark, James, I want you on the front line with Caleb, Damon, and Riley. You will coordinate with your Human teams and be our first wave of attack when we board the ships." The men repeated Emily's gesture.

Finally, Amelia turned to Amy. "I'd like you in the command room with me. I'll need your protection if we do get attacked, as my light will be bonded with this vessel. Mainly, I want your connection to the others; you will need to be my eyes and ears. Help me organize our attacks, while keeping our people safe."

Amy couldn't shake the feeling that she was being left behind, babied and coddled, while the others were out their risking their lives, though she knew now wasn't the time to argue. "Okay," she merely whispered.

Isobel loudly clapped her hands together once, brushing off the remaining crumbs as she stood. "Good, lets get moving. Emily, if you'd follow me. Boys…" she grinned and turned to the others, "Caleb and the others are in the ammunitions training room downstairs. Do you remember how to get there?"

They both stood, "Yep."

"Great, Riley and my team will meet you there later." Isobel smiled, turning enthusiastically towards her interim commander. "Let's get ready."

Isobel was out of the room before Emily could catch her thoughts. She placed a reassuring hand on her sister's shoulder as she stood and leant across the table, quickly kissing her husband, before charging out of the room.

The room emptied, leaving a sullen Amy and Amelia, who finally stood. "Ready?" she asked her companion.

"Did you hold me back on purpose or do you really need my protection?" Amy stayed sat at the table.

Amelia sighed and sat back down. After a minute of no response, Amy finally turned to look into the saddened eyes of her friend. "I do need your help, but you're right, it's not the only reason." Taking a deep breath, Amelia continued, "Your husband is out there and no matter how hard you may fight to get him back, I'm not prepared to have you running into a foreign vessel, light blazing, with only your rage to keep you going." Amy went to interject, but Amelia pushed on, "Riley and I have been mated for over two centuries." Amy's jaw fell open at that revelation. "I have been in your position too many times to count. Though you may seem angry and focused to the others, you are anything but that. You will be of more use to him from where we'll be."

Tears burned the back of Amy' eyes as she took in a shaky breath. "I can't just stand around. I'm going insane here."

"I know that," Amelia reached across the table, squeezing Amy's shaking hand. "And you won't be just standing there. Please, trust me. We'll get them back."

* * *

James and Mark couldn't hide their excitement and enthusiasm as they hurriedly made their way to the training bays. With only a quick glance during introduction and tour, they were now barreling through the swing doors, but stopped abruptly at the scene before them. Much like the training room on Thomas' base, this vessel's training space encompassed more than two football fields in length and width. The walls were dark and felt industrial, filled with targets and hanging manikins of various shapes, materials, and sizes. The floor appeared to be sectioned off with a different scenario and unique terrain.

In the far corner, one entire section contained plant life and trees of narrow proportion with sandy coloring. Distant chirping of insects created the full first-hand environment of a foreign landscape neither James nor Mark recognized. Another corner was filled with a muddy rock formation. Steep and jagged, a few soldiers attempted to climb and battle the terrain in overly weighty uniforms and heavy weaponry. James was surprised at the ease with which they moved, after slinging a scout-sniper riffle over their shoulder as if it weight little more than a bag of groceries. Near grunts and groans pulled their attention to the right. Row and row of training mats held various soldiers from a number of countries, gripped in wrestling matches and battling stances.

"Ye." A heavy set Scottish SAS soldier strode towards James wiping sweat off his brow with the hem of his shirt, revealing a collage of battle scars and taught flesh. Though he was easily in his late forties, his stance and frame gave nothing away as a sign of weakness. "Come show me whit ye kin dae, laddie." Walking past the two, he padded over to a vacant mat. Turning back, "Any day now," he goaded.

Caleb appeared next to Mark, a wide smile of encouragement on his face as he gestured James forward. James was slightly taller, but that appeared to be his only physical upperhand. The soldier's muscles were clearly bulging under the red heated flesh, his previous wrestling-match still fresh in his reflexes. The only thing that gave James solace was his light.

As his feet touched the mat, James tore the sweater over his head, turning to his sparring partner. Thrusting out his hand by way of greeting, he said, "James. I have no formal training." He shrugged as they shook hands.

"Reid," the Scot smiled, welcoming. "Just show me whit ye kin dae. Ye dae hae th' bonded light, dinnae ye?"

In response James ignited his flame, the light spiraling up and settling above the knee.

"Wull it burn me?" His head gestured towards the open flame.

James spread his legs, squared his shoulders, and raised his fists. "Not one bit."

At first they seemed to pace in circles around each other, sizing up their prey.

"C'moan, LASSIES! Git a move oan." A second soldier joined the small group of bystanders.

Distracted by the comment, Reid took his opportunity to lunge at James, half knocking him to the ground before he could catch his feet and surge upright. Using his light to enhance his speed and responses, James rounded on Reid. Kicking his leg out, he spun low to the ground, causing Reid to buckle under the weight of his bent knees, falling heavily on his back. The two gripped and pulled at one another. Before he knew it, James was held in a deadly headlock, while Reid struggled to keep his grip. James pushed back, rolling onto his stomach and lifting the both of them up. To the growing crowd, it appeared as if James were attempting an awkward push up with Reid half clinging to his back.

Fully twisting to the left, Reid took an elbow to the stomach as James forced to his feet, bouncing lightly, working the stiffness out of his neck. Scrambling to his feet, James didn't react fast enough, before Reid's solid right fist made contact with James' left cheekbone. Stumbling back a couple paces, his left eye watered, further blurring his vision. James shifted; engulfed by his light he used the momentum to force everything back on Reid ten fold. James' fist forced down on Reid's open chest with such force that he was knocked off his feet; compelled back the five meters needed to reach the solid wall, Reid's head smacked into the dangling feet of the manikin above.

"Shit!" James exclaimed, rushing over to Reid's heaving body. "Reid, you okay?"

His body lay limp as he gasped for breath, but James' concern faded as a wide grin covered Reid's features. One heavy hand came up, gently tapping James' reddened face, "Yer a'right wi' me, laddie."

James pulled back, offering his arm, which was gently brushed aside as Reid gathered his wits and raised of his own strength. A few of the others had stopped, stunned by the blatant show of sheer strength and power. "Yi"ll need tae work oan yer foot work," the second soldier, later introduced as Alistair, preferably Al, offered.

The remainder of the afternoon had both James and Mark wrestling everyone from German Bundeswehre to members of the Israeli Sayeret. Each offered strategic words of wisdom and combat training advice. Damon had left the basic combat training to his brother, while he assisted in the far corners of the training space, educating others on the Biron's current inhabited planets, their chosen hunting techniques, and unique weaknesses.

During a break Mark approached Caleb, discretely gesturing towards the far corners. "Why are they training in Biron environments? I thought this was a rescue mission invading the enemy ships?"

Caleb pulled Mark over to one of the spare mats, changing his stance as he prepared for a spar. "Our ultimate goal is to end this with the invasion on their vessels," Caleb answered, as he made a move to strike Mark with a backhander of his left hand. Mark spun and ducked out of his reach, raising his fists to block future attempts. "But as with any situation, things don't always go as planned." Continuing, he dodged one of Mark's punches. "We need to all be prepared to take this to the end. To take it to their door step," he swung again. "Right?"

Mark managed to block the majority of the blows, but took a graze to his left ribs. Heaving a grunt, he pushed back at Caleb, igniting his flame. "Whatever keeps my family and Earth safe... We'll do everything we can."

Caleb ignited his own flame and then drew on his telekinetic ability to pull one of the metal rods from the near wall. "Good," he took two bounds, and then leapt in Mark's direction. Mark only had a split second to summon his own metallic bar and grip it tightly at each end, the force of Caleb's blow knocking him to the ground below.

Mark's left hand left the bar, spreading out wide in front of him. As Caleb's body fell towards his, Mark's light pushed back, causing Caleb to change direction, falling backwards. With a satisfied laugh both men got to their feet and drew on their light to throw and block various attacks on one another. Roughly ten minutes in, the sparring match left their mat, working its way across the expanse interceding on others'. The room fell silent and still as Mark and Caleb went at each other.

Scorching sweat covered their dampened clothing as they exchanged blow after blow. At one point Mark took a swipe to the face, with a blunt metallic paddle, like that of a short handled shovel. A deep gash along his forehead and bridge of his nose caused blood to trickle down his face and hinder his defensive capabilities. James chose that opportunity to ignite his light again and force Caleb back against the near wall. Damon saw this as an exciting challenge, igniting his light he dragged the basketball-sized cement-boulders up and forward, hitting the unsuspecting James directly in the stomach.

The men got to their feet swiftly. Caleb and his brother dominated the far corners of one large mat as Mark and James occupied the other end. All others stood silently bordering the mats, often pushing the near fights away from their ends and into the center. James and Damon stuck to a blow-to-blow, physical match, while Caleb and Mark, now both growing exhausted, used their various abilities while staying out of one another's physical reach.

James and Damon were evenly matched in their bonded ability and physical traits. Caleb and Mark had called it a draw now sitting on one corner on the mat observing. Mark playfully punched Caleb on the near shoulder, wiping the blood from his forehead and spitting the excess blood onto the mat before him.

Damon and James would have continued if it weren't for the sudden and outraged demand from Isobel.

"Enough!" she roared as Damon loosened his grip on the chokehold he had James in.

Emily looked equally irate, forcing her way through the crowd of fighters and across the mat to where her husband sat. Kneeling down, she ripping away the hand that held a reddened towel to his face. Gasping, she ignited her light and went to work healing him. Mark could tell an argument was brewing under his wife's overpowering silence.

"Em?" he whispered.

"Don't." She couldn't even look him in the eyes. Turning to his attacker, she offered kindly, "Do you need healing?"

Caleb had the grace to cower under her stare, "I think Isobel can take care of me. Thank you." He stiffly rose to his feet, clapping Mark on the back as he did, making him cringe. "Thanks for the warm up."

Mark only muttered a grunt before Emily pulled his face back to hers so she could focus. His forehead now appeared to have a dark red gash, as the flesh bubbled and worked its way back together. The soldiers had taken their cue to get back to their own training, simultaneously working on one another and avoiding the current chastising coming from Isobel as she healed Damon and Caleb. Riley grinned at James' concerned face as he passed him and reached for a bottle of water. Turning away, he chose to join his Human companions.

James' backside had barely reached the mat before Emily threw her hand out to the gash on his near shoulder. A groan of surprise and soreness left his lips, as Emily fumed, working on both men simultaneously.

James glanced in Mark's general direction. *What's her prob...*

"Shut up!" Emily spoke aloud, "I know you two are talking."

"Em?" James' cheek flushed as if caught doing something he shouldn't, "What's wrong? We were only training."

Her hand dropped from Mark as she slapped the second palm against James' chest. His eyes cringed for a short second.

"What's wrong? I've spent all morning training to heal again after how many months? I'm tired and exhausted. My sister is becoming irrational, and I'm worried that she will do something stupid. I haven't heard from Julia about my daughter in over an hour." She could feel the familiar burn at the back of her throat that she knew would lead to tears.

"Emily," Mark leaned forward and rubbed his hand reassuringly down her back.

She angrily brushed it away turning back to him, "Then I come in here and my husband's face is cut up and a mess." She pulled his chin from side to side, examining her work, and then turned back to James. "You two are fighting like idiots, practically killing one another, when you should be learning and working strategically together." She huffed, pushing to her feet, bending over the two men so they couldn't follow. "You both need to take this more seriously. This is so much bigger than before. We all have so much more to lose. Stop screwing around!" She abruptly turned, pacing over to the others.

Firmly chastised, Mark and James shared a look before getting to their feet and heading towards the larger group. Isobel was deep into the topic of unifying each assault team with individual members of the assisting Human group, utilizing an array of talents and abilities. There wasn't enough time to bond the soldiers with any available Jarly while training them to be of any use. The Humans had to fight using their own abilities with the backup of the Jarly assigned to their squad. One medical aid would be stationed within each group, with one solider specifically assigned as their protector.

CHAPTER ELEVEN

Entering the control room, Amy felt the sudden drop in temperature - a light moisture filled the air. Taking a deep breath, she absently pulled at the sleeves of her long shirt, curling her fingers into a tight ball. The entry space was narrow and dark, involving three thin steps, which opened up into an even darker room. Five glowing lights cocooned in purple tubes barely illuminated the room.

"You'll get used to the chill in the air. With these particular monitoring systems, we need to keep our body temperatures under control," Amelia explained as she walked up to the far wall of tinted glass, sliding a flamed finger across one panel, illuminating a holographic control panel. More panels lowered from the high ceiling with various dials and flashing beacons.

"Bodies?" Amy watched from the middle of the room, confusion covering her face, as Amelia flicked switches and touched buttons with practiced ease.

Without a word, Amelia paused before stepping towards one of the cocoons. Placing one lit hand onto the tubing, floor to ceiling the light spread where she had touched it. Amy drew closer, amazed as an inner shield drew into the grated flooring below to reveal an encased Jarly; her caramel-skinned body engulfed in Nona's flame, her eyes wide with the third black eye lid firmly in place. It took Amy a minute to realize that the woman was practically naked, the essentials covered by thin fabric, while the rest of her flesh was caressed by narrow wires that sparked and jolted in random areas.

"Shouray?" Amelia leant into the tubing to support her weight.

"Amelia, I'm so sorry to hear about Amadeus and Thomas." The woman's voice seemed mechanical, vibrating throughout the surroundings. Her eyes remained black, her head unmoving as Amy deduced she was not actually seeing either of the people standing right in front of her.

A pained sigh escaped Amelia's lips as she turned to face away, towards the glowing controls. "Thank you, Shouray. I'd like to introduce Amy Michaels of the Human fighters."

Shouray's body stiffened slightly, her breathing increased as she placed her hand against the internal tubing. "Amy? Oh, Amy it's such an honor. I've heard a lot about you. You're pretty famous around here." Her voice grew shaky and she couldn't help the wide smile spread across her features.

Taken aback by her welcome, Amy's voice seemed to catch at the back of her throat, causing a slight stutter as she spoke. "Thank you. I…Well, I don't really know what to say, but thank you."

Shouray's smile stayed in place as she turned to the general direction of Amelia's stiff stance. "Is there something you need, Ma'am?"

"Amy, ignite your light and place it against the glass." Amelia's tone was stiff as she waited for Amy to comply. "Shouray, I'd like you to give Amy a quick rundown of what you are working on today, show her the defensive capabilities of this room."

Shouray silently nodded as she turned back to focus on Amy. Her external eyelids closed and her head dropped, her chin resting on her chest.

As Amy's hand connected to the plastic–like material, a light tingling was felt in her fingertips, causing her entire body to straighten and her breathing to accelerate. Her body pulsed with every passing second, feeling energized, and overly alert. Her pupils dilated and she drew in another long and shaking breath, flaring her nostrils.

Amelia pulled her hand away slowly. "I'm going to finish preparing. I want you to close your eyes and focus on your breathing. Shouray will do the rest." Turning and stepping back to her control screens, Amy watched her walk away, her brows knitting as she glanced around the room.

"Amelia…" She breathed.

"Just close your eyes."

Shaking her head, Amy turned to look at the frozen Shouray, watching as the wires continued to move and glow of their own accord. Unsure of herself and her direction, Amy allowed her eyes to droop and her shoulders to relax, not letting her hand move from its secured spot.

* * *

"Amy?" A familiar voice caused her to quickly open her eyes. Her head shot up as her breathing began to increase. Overwhelmed by the scene before her, Amy lost her footing, falling backwards onto a smooth marbled floor below.

"Oh, I'm sorry," Shouray reached down and helped Amy back to her feet. Amy couldn't utter a word as she scanned the room. The floors and walls were midnight blue, reflective, sparkling as they shone. The warehouse-like space was filled with rows of paneling; columns with metallic objects that clinked and moved within. The noise grew with each machine working over its capacity, banging against the restrains of the shelving.

The space was overwhelming and Amy found it hard to focus on a single item, though nothing fully distracted from the evidently flaming ceiling. At least twenty feet above the surface, a large-scale layer of Nona's flame moved like molten lava, spiraling and dipping as the odd flare of green and orange sent a surge of energy to the nearest machine. Nearly a foot shorter than Amy's already petite frame, Shouray had to reach up to wrap her arm around Amy's shoulders, guiding her towards the center of the room as Amy's eyes remained glued above.

"I know, the first time is very disorienting," Shouray's girly voice seemed to echo off of the heavy columns.

Amy's attention drew back to her guide, trying to steady her breathing as she was led to a plush chair nestled in the open corner. A table sat in the center of the communal space, with hand-molded glass in all shapes and sizes hanging above. It was only then that Amy recognized the distant silhouettes of others in the near vicinity, their backs facing away as they busied themselves with their task at hand, paying Shouray and her guest no attention.

Sinking back into the seat and enjoying its cocooning comfort, Amy waited for Shouray to sit on the tableside stool, turning to give her attention. Shouray still had the giant smile spread wide across her features; her smooth skin, long heavy hair, and gentle features would easily pass off as a Bollywood star on Earth.

"Where are we?" Amy whispered as her head seemed to dip into her shoulders and her eyes kept falling on the lightshow above.

Shouray surprised Amy with a guttural laugh, swiveling, and gripping the near table. It was then Amy figured Shouray could not be more than fifteen or sixteen in Earth years. She looked young and childlike when she laughed.

Amy couldn't help but grin back at her, "What's so funny?"

Shouray seemed to have a hard time catching her breath as she shook her head with amusement, saying, "You!" She steadied herself before swiveling back, "You don't have to whisper." She reiterated by practically yelling, "As you can tell, it's already pretty loud in here." She paused, and her eyes grew sympathetic. "I'm being rude; I'm sorry, I'm just not used to Humans yet. Your reactions are pretty funny sometimes." Amy stiffened and frowned in response, causing Shouray to continue in a heavy rush, "Sorry." Glancing up at the ceiling, "I'm sure this is very strange and can be unsettling, but let me reassure you that you are in no danger. Nothing and no one can harm you in here, so please relax." Amy slowly settled; her arms loosening their grip on the armrests of her chair as she straightened and further took in the room.

"First of all," Shouray continued, "physically, you are still standing by that tube you found me in. When you touched the casing, Nona's light allowed you to connect with me and the device to simulate what you see here." She spread her arms wide and leant back as if to exaggerate her claim.

"So it's like a game? What I see isn't real?"

"Oh it's real, it's just a little hard to explain. Do you remember that tour your took when you first came here?" Amy nodded, her eyes once again drifting up. "Do you remember the large Orb that was in the engine room?"

Without looking down Amy blurted, "Calobie."

"Right. Yes, exactly! Well, long story short we are currently situated in that orb."

That caused Amy head to jerk back down with a skeptical brow raised. "We're inside that stuff with the dragon thing moving around."

Shouray winced, her features distorted, clearly not explaining properly. "Well, yes and no. As I said, physically we are both in the command room, but as our sub-consciousness has connected to the vessel, our minds were redirected here. That orb may look liquid but is far from it. Think of it as a vast galaxy of information. We are in but a droplet of that…" she used her fingers to mimic quotation marks, a mimicked Human gesture no doubt, "fluid that controls a small portion of this ship." Pointing to the brightness above, she continued, "That is the constant movement of Calobie making this all possible." She then paused, scrutinizing Amy's response. "Are you following me?"

Again, Amy glanced around the room, and then back. "I think so. So none of this is real even though they affect real things." She pushed her chin out towards another individual who passed by, distracted by something large and thick in his hands. "You're kind of like engineers or maintenance crews working on the ship from within?" Amy grinned to herself, "Like the Matrix."

"Matrix?" Shouray looked confused, "I don't think I know that word."

"Never mind. It's just a popular movie on Earth."

"Interesting. Well yes, I guess that would be an accurate assessment. We ensure all systems are working and the vessel is in good shape. We can make changes and alterations from within. If we didn't have this technology to compartmentalize and organize, our vessels would be one hundred times larger than they already are; they would be slower and require much more maintenance."

"So, how many people are down here?" Amy glanced around, though many of the columns sheltered her view.

"Five on this level, six including you. My crew - which you saw in the other tubes - controls the vital features of the control room like navigation, defenses, communications to Nona, and more. But as I said, we are in one small portion of that Orb in engineering. There are hundreds of other sections in this ship that have similar manned tubes, working at any given time."

Amy nodded, trying to comprehend what she was being informed. Shouray stood, smoothing out her black t-shirt and matching formal pants.

"But, you were almost naked in the control room?" Amy noticed the change in attire, only moving enough to lean forward, resting her forearms on her upper thighs. She had already noticed that she too wore a newly pressed black outfit.

Glancing down, surprised by the observation, Shouray explained, "We all have matching clothing down here. When our physical forms are connected to the vessel our body temperature skyrockets and we become dehydrated much faster. The tubes are regulated and have their own environment to ensure our own brains are not fried due to overexposure." Shouray gestured towards her new friend, "You yourself might feel a little light headed when we leave, but as you are only in here for a short while your internal light will heal you within a couple minutes."

Clearly eager to move on, Amy followed Shouray's cue and stood. She turned, talking as she went, passing two columns and down another corridor. "Amelia would like me to show you what I'm working on." She abruptly stopped and turned towards one for the mechanically encased columns, and placing her hand on the surface, the clear panel gave way. Taking a step back, her flaming hand pulled out the inner workings until it was nestled before them; apparently floating, the forest-green block expanded and continued to churn, revealing more controls within.

"I have been tasked with overhauling and enhancing our tracking abilities. I'm sure you have been advised on our plan to take control of the enemy ship." She stopped again, her face growing sad as she turned to Amy, "I was sorry hear… I should have said something before. I'm sorry about your husband's forced involvement in all this."

Amy forcibly swallowed past the lump in her throat, the back of her eyes burned from the unshed tears at the very mention of Rick. Taking a steadying breath, she replied, "I know, and I'm sorry for Amadeus, as well."

Shouray surprised Amy again by engulfing her in a bear hug, her head barely resting on Amy's shoulders. "We'll get them back," she whispered, her own internal struggle evident.

Amy could only offer a weak smile, unsure of what to add.

Turning back to the unfolding panels before them, Shouray went on. "As I was saying, I've been working on enhancing our tracking abilities, while ensuring nothing is lost when we enter the planet's metallic rings. In the past that had all but crippled a large number of our sensors and had left many other systems damaged. I'm almost finished." Amy watched as Shouray's eyes grew large and engrossed in her task at hand. The way she spoke about her work displayed excitement and genuine intrigue. She continued to fiddle with a few dials as she continued, "I'll be done by the end of the day."

GLIMPSE INTO THE DARKNESS 103

Amy leant into the column behind her, watching Shouray work with ease of grace. She busied herself as her right hand dove into the belly of the machine, not concerned by the moving elements around her.

"Um… Shouray, the control room's defenses?" Amy practically whispered, not wanted to startle her.

Quickly withdrawing her hand from the machine, she resumed speaking. "Right, I got a bit carried away." Touching the base of the hovering machine, it began to collapse in on itself until it was safely nestled back within the column and the protective barrier set back into place. Turning back, she said, "Follow me." Shouray nodded towards the end of the corridor, taking another left onto a wide path.

"I hope Amelia isn't planning on me remembering much of what you have shown me. I'd get lost after a single minute down here, alone. I'd never be able to find these units again."

Shouray genuinely smiled. "Don't worry. Amelia just wants you to get a better understanding of what we all do on a daily basis. How the ship works, where to find certain people, why your work here is so vital…"

"Or you're distracting me, keeping me out of the way while she gets ready for today." Amy smirked as realization hit.

"Not exactly," Shouray said straight-faced, before glancing up at Amy with a grin. "Maybe a little."

What felt like half a mile of columns and corridors eventually led to an open circular room, not much larger than a master bedroom. The flame of Calobie did not fill this particular space; as a result the room remained dark with nothing visible. Amy, already in the center of the room, turned to Shouray who had yet to pass the threshold. Like turning on a light switch, Shouray rested a glowing hand on the bare wall, which signaled the room to come to life. Floor to ceiling, large blueprints moved into view and continuously flowed, changing in color and shape.

Shouray entered the room, clearly examining the information before her, tapping her right index finger absently along her chin.

"There!" she pointed to the top right side of the wall, calling the image down and centering it to consume the majority of the space before them. "What exactly does Amelia have planned for you in the control room?"

"She said I am to protect her, and I guess you guys, while you are linked in with the ship. Making sure no one gets to you if we are under attack."

She was already nodding as she busied herself highlighting portions of the blueprint Amy eventually recognized as the control room. She noticed six glowing lights, five orange and one green.

"Is that us?" she asked innocently.

Shouray glanced up, following her gaze to the center of the image. "Yes, the orange represents Jarly heat frequencies. Humans run a little warmer, so you are the green."

"Interesting. Isn't it usually red that shows as warmer?"

"Maybe on Human sensors," Shouray shrugged, turning back to her highlighting. "Okay, so as you can see this is the outline of the control room; it's one floor, not that big. There are resting rooms here and the lavatory is here," she pointed to two doors hidden behind the five tubes. "And small weapons supplies here, and here."

"Why doesn't your team just leave when we start the attack? Get to a safe place," Amy blurted, her eyes still trying to memorize the screen glowing before her.

"If anything happens to the vessel, we will all need to be linked for repairs as soon as possible. We have to ensure there are no setbacks." Pausing, she walked over to the far side of the screen. "Amelia will connect here." The tube was twice the size of the others. "She will obviously need the most protection and need to focus. If you must talk to her, you can do the same as you did with me. Just place your lit hand along the glass and start talking, she will hear you, and will be able to communicate back. She won't be down here though. "

Amy merely nodded with each new addition, still trying to ensure she got all the possible entrances memorized, knew where not to fire, and where to hide.

After fifteen minutes had passed and further instruction from Shouray, Amy felt confident that she could secure the room and keep her assigned people safe.

"Okay, so you know where the emergency shut off controls are, and the coolant flooding system. I honestly doubt many would try and attack the command room directly. Birons hate the moist cool air; it drives them nuts, and slows them down." Shouray began to exit the room with a bounce in her step, drawing Amy out with her. "Do you have anymore questions?"

"No, I think the room is pretty secure. I know what I need to do."

"Good, and just remember, if you need anything or have any questions, I'm just a touch of a palm away," Shouray giggled at her own instruction.

"Thanks. So, how do we get out of here?" Amy's eyes drew back up to the flaming ceiling as they walked back to the seating area.

"I'll disconnect you in a minute, just close your eyes when I tell you. I won't be coming out until the invasion is over. My team can stay in here for days if needed." Shouray set herself back on the stool, as Amy made her way to the plush chair. "Amy, I just wanted to once again say how thankful I am for what you and your friends did for us last year. You ensured that we could continue our work and sacrificed your own safety to do it. You're a hero in our eyes; don't ever forget that. Once this is all over, I'd love to get to know you a bit better. Get to know all of you."

Amy blushed at the continued compliments, not able to relax as Shouray's idolized gaze practically bore into her. "Thank you, again, but we really did have a bit of a selfish motive as well. Our friends were held captive and all we really wanted was to get them back."

Nodding in agreement, "Of course, that is completely understandable. Doesn't make your triumph or status any less deserving." Amy offered her another weak smile. "Okay, well I think you're good. Please advise Amelia that the tracking sensor will be complete within the next three hours... Close your eyes, Amy."

Amy took a deep breath, breathing out, "Thank you." She squeezed her eyes tightly shut in preparation.

CHAPTER TWELVE

As the morning sun filled the guest room, Julia awoke gasping for air as she clutched at her chest, sweat soaking her every pore. Disoriented, her eyes moved around the bright room as she gained her bearings. Flopping back onto the pillow, she swiped at the tendrils of hair sticking to her forehead.

James? she thought through space.

No response made her close her eyes and repeat his name, focusing. Her next breath faltered, as her pulse accelerated. Turning her head to glance out the wide window, her gaze fell on a clear blue sky above. *Babe? Are you there? Can you hear me?*

Not knowing what possible time frame the others could be working in, she allowed herself to believe the soft white lie that he was probably still sleeping. They wouldn't order an attack when the others were tired and at a disadvantage; a couple days away would still have them feeling the pull of night on the same schedule as hers. Resigned to her conclusion, she swung her legs over the side of the bed and forced herself up and into the attached bathroom.

After a long awaited hot shower, she quickly dried herself, growing in self-disappointment when she noticed the bathroom clock marked the passing of 10:40am. She had slept in too long. Sophie would be needing her by now, probably left to lay in her crib for hours already. Julia needed to pull herself together and focus on what was to come.

Pulling the bathroom door wide open, a plume of stream preceded her as she took her first steps and let out a quick scream.

"You scared the crap out of me." Julia pulled her towel tighter around herself, chastising Abel as he leant against the open doorwell, smirking.

"Sorry," he raised his hands in surrender, taking a step further into the room. "I was just..."

"Checking on me?" Julia interrupted, " Seriously, I'm fine Abel. I don't need a babysitter."

"Actually, I was going to see if you wanted to get ready and head down to Bisbee for breakfast with John and me. Maybe walk around a bit?"

"Oh." Embarrassment crept into her cheeks as she dropped her gaze.

"I think some fresh air and new surroundings would do you some good," Abel added, turning to leave. "I'll leave and let you get ready, just let me know."

"Abel, wait." Julia closed the distance and pulled him into a tight embrace, surprising even him. "I'm sorry. I didn't mean to snap at you."

"Hey, hot stuff," Julia giggled at her nickname, "don't worry about it. Just get your stuff together and we'll leave when you're ready."

"Hot stuff? Really…" She laughed, gripping the towel encasing her wet highlighted honey-blonde hair as it threatened to tumble backwards. "You just had to say that while I'm standing here in a towel!"

With a single wink, he turned and left her to rummage through Emily's clean clothes. She needed to do some laundry soon if she was going to stay much longer; or better yet, shopping. Yes, some shopping was definitely needed.

* * *

Julia, baby. Are you there?

A sigh of relief flooded her body as Julia further relaxed into the back seat of John's BMW. Sophie was firmly seated beside her, her legs bobbing in the air above her car seat.

I'm here, James. How are things? How's Amy doing? What are you doing now?

As she continued her conversation, she watched as they passed the cars beside them, the inhabitants going about their day completely unaware of the danger and potential catastrophe to come.

Whoa! One question at a time, babe, I just woke up. We're doing fine. Amy is holding up as best as she can, but she's been quiet. Amelia took her on as a sort of apprentice, so I didn't spend much time with her yesterday.

There was a pause. Julia waited nervously for more answers, while she twisted and played with her wedding bands.

Mark and I have been training again, pretty much the same as last time. Emily has been stuck with Isobel, training and learning how to heal faster. Mark and I got into a bit of a match with Caleb and Damon yesterday; it was amazing, but intense. Needless to say, when Emily found out she tore us a new one.

Julia smirked at this, knowing full well how competitive her husband was, and the motherly role Emily still fell into when around their group.

Have you talked to her at all? She said she hasn't been able to get a hold of you. She's been a bit high strung, really worried.

The sudden guilt felt like a physical blow to Julia, as she turned and played with Sophie's soft baby fingers; her cherub-smile easing some of the tension.

Shit! No. I'm sorry, I didn't really talk to her at all yesterday, but I didn't hear anything from her either... Can you let them know everything is fine here? Soph is being a good little baby, Abel is here and John arrived yesterday, so I'm not alone.

Another minute of silence fell on the conversation before James continued. *Good, yeah, Amadeus said Abel had been advised of the situation and was on his way. I didn't know John was coming too. Say hi for me. Okay Julia, I've got to go meet the others and hear what the plan for today is. I don't even know where we are right now. I'll keep you posted. Love you.*

Be safe. I love you, too. Julia breathed in a deep sigh of relief.

Leaning forward between the two front seats, Julia interrupted John and Abel's conversations. "Um, sorry," they quieted, giving her their attention. "I was just speaking to James. Sounds like everything is on track. They've been training, and well, preparing. He's gonna keep us posted on anything that comes up, but he sounds in good spirits."

"That's great to hear," John said, smiling in the rear view mirror.

"James said hi to both of you by the way." Leaning back into her seat she continued, "I think he's actually loving it at the moment. Obviously, we're all worried about Rick, but I just know we will get him and Amadeus back. I just think all this training and action goes to James' head." She giggled at the thought.

"He's a guy, what do you expect?" Abel laughed, turning back to look out the front window as they made their way to the nearest restaurant.

* * *

Jam smeared across her full flushed cheeks, Sophie smiled, her body bouncing in her high chair as baby drool made its way to her chin, onto her soft pink shirt. Her sticky fingers smacking together with excitement, her eye trained on Abel as he blew large bubbles over the brim of his chocolate milkshake, much to Sophie's delight. Julia and John sat back and admired the jubilation and Abel's capacity for play.

Finally resting, Julia reached over with a pile of napkins. Abel grinned, cleaning the cup and table before him as Julia gently cleared the mess from Sophie's face and fingers. "There! All clean now," she commented, brushing a lone finger down Sophie's cheek. Ignoring her affection, Sophie turned to the people passing by as they neared the shop window.

"I like this area," John muttered, leaning back into his seat next to a large plate window, his gaze following the people and few cars going by. They had found a quiet café at the end of one of the main streets; its colorful brick and stone in vibrant shades was welcoming to visitors, young and old.

Nodding in agreement, Abel's focus landed on a bouncing brunette, hair pulled back high on her scalp, her short black shorts and tight tank top stealing his sight as she jogged past the window and onward up the slight incline. His eye followed her in her stride; turning in his chair he followed her rear until it was out of sight.

With a devilish grin, he turned back to his best friend. "Yes, the view is amazing," he said, his eyebrows rising in playful banter. Julia rolled her eyes, but couldn't help the laughter that escaped her lips. Shaking her head, she grinned and finished her coffee.

"So how's the fashion industry treating you these days?" Abel asked, changing the subject.

Julia's brows knit as she placed her coffee down. "Competitive as ever. After last year, when our names were everywhere, everyone wanted to know who we were, what we did. They wanted a piece of us." Both men nodded, knowing full well what associations with the Jarly meant for their privacy. "Well, as soon as people heard I was starting out with a small clothing line, you know expanding from the wedding scene, they heard about my clothes and then it all went crazy; there were orders coming from all over the world."

John looked sideways at Abel, confused, "Isn't that a good thing?"

"Yes, and no," Julia shrugged, looking down at the cooled coffee mug resting between her palms. "I guess when you're one of the Chosen Ones," she rolled her eyes and leaned back, "people have certain expectations, like my clothes had something to do with the Jarly and their abilities."

Abel leaned forward onto the table, inquiring, "So what happened?"

"I had a few big-wigs from New York, California, London, and even Tokyo contact me for designs and contracts. I did a few shows, got some praise, but honestly I think I could show up with a bunch of burlap sacks and they'd all be cheering."

"Don't say that. I know Kristine kept on about the stuff you showed her at the barbeque last summer, she loved it," John said, reaching across the table.

"Everyone is really excited about what you're doing, Julia. Now if only I could get some free stuff…" Abel tried to lighten the mood.

Julia offered them a weak smile, "I know, and I did end up signing with a company out of New York called Pristine Designs. They really did have the best options for me and they maintained that I would have more control, more of a say."

"But…"

"But, really they just threw a bunch of money my way, took my name as a labeling gimmick and now only promote one of my designs for every hundred of their own."

"Julia," John cut her off, not knowing what more to say. He knew how much time and energy she had put into her craft.

She shrugged again, her gaze distracted, following a man passing by the café window barely able to hold the numerous books he was carrying. "It's fine… I mean, I still get to design new things. I get to work from home or the little boutique they opened for me in town. I work when I want. I have no deadlines or obligations; I only have to provide two new designs every six months. I have no one to answer to in my day-to-day and at twenty-three, I could retire tomorrow without a care. I haven't had to work on anything since before the wedding; I do what I want to do everyday, so I should be thankful."

"True, but you're clearly not happy. You haven't worked in what? Two months -- you must be so bored. What about your dream of opening your own shop, downtown, with all of your own designs?"

"I still want that. One day I might do it. The contract I have with Pristine is only for five years. I don't think I will re-sign when it's done."

"And in the meantime, Pristine gets to get famous and abuse your name?"

Abel asked.

Julia bit her bottom lip and shrugged again, turning back to the table. "The price you pay to get anywhere in the industry."

"Well, I think its bullshit," John said, surprising Julia. "You shouldn't have to just lay back and let them take all the control. You should fight more for what you want."

Julia could only nod, not knowing what to say.

"What about James?" Abel asked after a moment of silence.

She cleared her throat, brightening at the prospect of changing the subject, "He's good. His construction company has just taken on five new guys. He's got contracts for the next three years. One guy, Brady, is just out of college. He finished his architectural program early and signed with Stylus right away. James says he's got a lot of potential; he's doing things that no one's seen before. I think James is excited to add a new edge to his design team."

"That's great news," John smiled and watched as Abel showed Sophie how to draw within the lines of her paper cartoon of Barbie. The page was already decorated with remnants of breakfast.

"Is Amy still at the salon?" John asked. "I haven't caught up with her or Rick in a while."

Before Julia could answer the server returned with another full jug in hand. "Coffee?" she smiled, as the three pushed their empty mugs into the center of the table. "Another milk shake?" she asked, reaching down to grip the narrow stem of the once chocolaty treat.

"Oh, no thanks," Abel smiled, reaching for his warmed mug. "The coffee is just fine."

"Let me know if there is anything else you folks need."

"Just the bill please," Julia requested, reaching over for the individual creamers, neatly piled into a pseudo-pyramid next to the condiments.

"What were we talking about?" Julia asked, dipping her spoon into the coffee. "Oh, right. No, Amy left Vivid about three months ago. She's working over on Avenida."

"Near the mall?" Abel asked.

"Yeah, just part time. I think Rick doesn't really want her to work, especially since he's taken over that second landscaping company. I think he wants Amy home and thinking about kids."

"Really?" Abel asked, somewhat surprised. "They're still so young."

"I know, but Rick comes from a big family, so I think he's just always had it in his head that he wanted to start his family at a young age."

"What does Amy think?"

"She wants kids too, though I think she'd like to do a bit more traveling before they put that plan into motion." She sipped her coffee, blowing on it to cool. "But now with all this Biron stuff coming at us, I'm sure all of our lives will be put on hold for a while."

The men couldn't disagree. As the three sat back and enjoyed the last moments of normalcy, their minds filled with concern and images of the darkness they could face tomorrow.

* * *

As the afternoon sun began to set, Sophie's head lay heavy on John's shoulder. They had spent the better part of the afternoon enjoying the famous stairs of Bisbee, Arizona, stopping at a few shops and desirable locations. Before heading back through the San Pedro Riparian National Conservation, and back into Sierra Vista. Though no one spoke of it, an uneasy heaviness filled their cores as they made their way into the darkness.

Julia had become distant and distracted midway through the day. James had alerted her that they were in the pursuit of the Biron vessel and were minutes away from battle. Moments later, contact was lost and a loneliness filled her being. She had tried to contact Emily, Amy, and even Mark, yet still no response. As the quietness grew, so did her fears.

The car remained silent as they made their way up the slight hill and neared Emily and Mark's secluded residence. Making their way down the long and winding driveway, John abruptly stopped halfway when the five shadowy outlines of men came into view. Pausing for a moment, Julia leant forward, grasping the seats in front.

Abel glanced at John, "What do you think?"

Without uttering a word John flicked on the high beams, further illuminating the strangers. The five men did not flinch or raise a hand to shield their gaze. Instead, in succession, their bodies went up in Nona's flame.

CHAPTER THIRTEEN

"I just heard from Julia, everything is fine. Abel kept Sophie preoccupied all day, and now they are both passed out and snoring on the couch," James whispered to Emily and Mark, as the three of them stood in the far corner of the training bay.

Isobel and Damon were currently announcing the unit assignments. Mark and James were assigned to two different combat teams, though they would be traveling closely together throughout the entire attack. Emily was among Mark's group as the sole medic. James' team would be accompanied by a young male healer; his long and narrow features did little to hide him within the group, as he was a clear foot taller than the others.

Eventually, those in the training bay were broken up into eight even teams. Damon, Caleb, Riley, and Isobel lead their own attack squads, with Mark and James in charge of their own; much to the dissatisfaction of many of Earth's elite. Two other teams were led by other Jarly worriers; they were well known to Caleb and his brother, but had yet to be formally introduced to the group.

When Isobel finally finished, a stone-faced Riley stepped forward. "Amelia has just announced that we'll be approaching the planet within the hour. We will send out a glider or two to take out the surface base camp. We will then begin to settle, hidden in the outer rings. Once we have a visual on their fleet we will get into formation and attack from both sides as they attempt to descend. Their controls are not as advanced as ours and will be weakened further while attempting to land."

On the wall behind the speakers, a holographic display of various vessels filled the room.

Damon continued where Riley had left off, "We believe the initial craft will be accompanied by at least seven of these ships." Damon pointed to a smaller image of a projected craft, which slowly rotated on the spot. "This is a four-man vessel, at best. Though, do keep in mind that they are fully equipped attack vessels. Much faster than the smaller fleet we will be sending out; thankfully their weapon capabilities will match ours."

"The pilots are Bazza and Tonks; your teams will man our attack fleet. Take out the basecamp, and then stay hidden in the atmosphere until we give the signal. You will maneuver and outpilot their fleet, while our gunmen will attack." With a nod from Damon, Bazza and Tonk cheered on their men and led them out of the training bay, presumably towards the ship's hanger bay.

"Mark, James," Damon waved them over. Emily followed close behind, as the now smaller group huddled closer together below the detailed hologram of the Biron ship, known to house Bates and the other traitors. "This is a general blueprint of their main ship; however, they could have manipulated it and made alterations that we are unaware of." Reaching up, Caleb manipulated the graphics to be drawn down to their head height, a fraction of the size, for close inspection.

"If no alterations have been made, there are three possible sections to house prisoners." Caleb began pointing to the visual aid as he went. "At the very base there is an open space, usually used as storage. Generally, unwanted waste. James, we're going to have your team infiltrate through here." He explained the best entrance options, possible areas for hidden attack, and where to move forward. "Mark, I want your team to enter though here," he pointed midway up the ship. "There are sleeping quarters here and rooms known for Biron barracks. Damon and I will be focusing on the weapons storage and engineering. If we can, we will cripple the ship from within."

"Sounds good," James nodded absently as he memorized the path his team would be taking.

"Isobel and Riley's team will enter above and below yours, Mark. They will facilitate escape routes and ensure all hatches are secure as we move about." Damon added.

"Once we have established control, we will likely run into each other, given the narrow parameters of the vessel. We will then begin uniting into larger groups along the way and establish the best escape route available," Isobel said.

Absently, Mark reached back and grasped Emily's left hand, threading their fingers. "Good," he said. His eyes trained on the hologram in front of him, glancing around the group. "Let's get into positions."

* * *

Minutes became hours as Rick slumped in the corner of Amadeus' jail cell. Though he tried to call out and awake his friend, no sound would pass his lips; only a heavy wheezing filed the silent space as both he and Amadeus labored for breath. The room was heavily weathered, with little more than the corrosive metal and putrid stains of previous and current victims to be seen. The air came in cold and stale, and Rick absently watched a small breeze scatter dirt across the solid floor. His own body slumped against a side wall, all but discarded, with his hands remaining bound.

Rick felt oddly energized, barely blinking despite his latest physical state. His right eye stung from added assault, the swelling ballooning out into his line of vision. His hands were scratched and scarred. Though he could still manage to muster his light, he could only concentrate enough to barely seal the seeping wet heat he felt emanating from various wounds his body was currently riddled with. He slumped, his chin resting on his chest as he scanned the remainder of his body. His clothes were damp and torn, looking more like red sponge than clothing. He noticed then that two wide metallic braces had been fastened to each of his ankles, both with small beaded green lights inoffensively flashing.

Every muscle screamed in sharp agony as he forced his arms down towards to the cuffs. The moment his fingertips touched the cold metal, a static shock surged up along his arm, across his collarbone and buried itself deep in his chest. Heaviness filled him then and he could do little more than gasp in pain as his body fell heavy to the side, his breath heaving from his lungs. As Rick's head hit the cold floor below, his eyes grew wide and watered as he tried to focus on the only person that understood his current torment.

Amadeus hung in the center of the room, his wrists bound by spiked metal, his hands a deep shade of purple from the lack of circulation. Bare-chested, his flesh was misshaped, slashed, and skewered; some metallic devices were still embedded just under the skin. He too had the metallic ankle cuffs. A sickly strain of dark amber dripped from his bare feet into a messy pool below. His head had fallen back, out of the view of Rick's gaze, his body unmoving as he continued to wheeze.

Rick's eye stayed true as he mentally screamed for Amadeus to move, to show some sign that he was still with him. At that moment, Rick had never felt so alone. A cold sensation slithered along Rick's spine, causing him to recoil and tuck in on himself. Stiffening, a tightened spot on his lower back had him arching backwards again, away from the pain, as his left hand slid around feeling for the unknown. His fingers stopped when they touched something cold and solid, something foreign and embedded. With shaky fingers he slowly caressed the corners to identify a metallic disc, roughly the span of his spread fingers, forcibly melding into his flesh just behind his right ribcage.

Panicked, he grasped at the device, trying to tear it from its mutated surroundings. In a swift tug, one corner rose out of his swollen skin more than an inch before the sound of broken flesh and stinging brought about more pain and a warm wet fluid, making it impossible to get a good grip. The energy he previously felt seemed to instantly drain from his core as his reaching arm grew heavy and his head fell back to the ground below. Resigned to his fate, Rick retrained his eyes on Amadeus, who had yet to resurface.

* * *

"Are you ready?" Amelia asked, as she continued about the control room, flicking switches as one of the larger tubes across from Shouray opened, beckoning. Amy watched as wires sprung to life, moving and making room for the next inhabitant.

Gawking at the wires, their wild movements reminded Amy of small insects and a disturbed shiver ran down her spine. "Ready as I'll ever be."

"I highly doubt you will have to deal with anything, but it gives me peace of mind knowing that you will be here to watch over us."

"Yeah, well the way I'm feeling right now, I could use a good fight. Get out some of this pent up rage." Amy rolled her shoulders as she further took in the room, strategizing, and plotting her vantage points.

Amelia smirked, nodding knowingly, as she moved over to the prepared tube. Slowly, she removed her shirt to reveal a dark lacy undergarment; a finer version of the common sports bra. Removing her pants, she stepped backwards into the tube, not batting an eye as the wires seemed to consume her figure with excitement, settling across her stomach, and wrapping around her upper thighs.

"You'll be fine. If you need me, just touch your lit hand to the casing and start talking… Good luck." For the first time in days, Amelia offered a smile that felt as genuine and encouraging as Amy had seen. Amy stepped back as the encasing consumed Amelia, and the inner tubing made it almost impossible to see inside. Within seconds, Amelia ignited her flame and the tube flickered with a steady stream of light.

Drifting towards the broad window above the extensive control panel, Amy stood mesmerized by the sheer vastness of the station before her. The control room was situated high above the center of the ship, allowing for an almost panoramic view. Formed with smooth dark materials, Amy smirked at the placement of the various windows and lights, blending almost seamlessly with the starry surroundings. Oddly shaped, she deduced the vessel was rectangular, its length easily twenty stories deep. Vast could not adequately describe the view; in contrast to the near planet they appeared to be approaching, the vessel dwarfed and obscured a third of its size.

Taking in a shaky breath, Amy examined what she could see of the planet. It was clearly orange with swirling white clouds, making it look like an orange creamsicle. Various dark flickers passed along, within the clouds, looking like rock and smoke. Upon arrival, Amy could feel the vessel decelerate, slowing enough to maneuver into the mysterious white fog. Within two minutes, the fast-paced whirling of the smoke and white cloud filled the window and any view from the control room. The vessel came to an abrupt stop and the gentle hum from Amelia's pod grew silent and focused.

Placing her hand against the glass, Amy felt the window grow colder and leant closer to hear a soft whistling of harsh winds. Glancing back at the room behind her, Amy stiffened at the eeriness of the scene, appearing alone in a dark room, now lit only by the white mist-filled window behind her, and the barely visible light from the six occupied tubes. The occasional blast of blackness, from the outside metallic cloud, filled the room with even more dread.

Preparing, Amy began busying herself by rushing down the few steps to hit the lockdown controls, swiftly sealing the room with the sound of vacuum suction. The room became airtight. Rushing back up the steps, she gathered herself and a few blunt objects in the center of the room. Sinking down, she sat up straight, her eye focusing on the door at the bottom of the steps and she ignited her flame, letting it consume her body.

CHAPTER FOURTEEN

"We're in position." Riley passed Mark a large, oversized weapon that the others already held like assault rifles. He noticed Mark's confused look, and said, "Trigger's here." He pointed to the underbelly of the gun and positioned his own gun for Mark to mimic. "Shoots like a normal gun too, though its ammunition comes from your light, so it doesn't need reloading, and the Biron's can't use it." He smirked and added, "Hold it tight to your side. It has a bit of a kickback."

Mark busied himself examining the weapon as Riley turned to Emily. "Here, attach this to your left hand." Emily delicately removed a black metallic mound from Riley's palm, looking more like jewelry than a weapon. Untangling the device, it appeared to be a four-finger chainmail glove. Mark watched curiously as Emily positioned the piece, securing it onto each finger, allowing the metallic device to fall loosely downwards, barely reaching her elbow.

Keeping her hand raised, her brows knit as she turned to Riley. "It feels really loose."

"Ignite your flame."

The instant her light engulfed her upright arm, the metal came to life, turning a glowing shade of amber, crunching audibly together, and snapping into place. Emily gasped, as her free hand reached for her other wrist, gripping it as it shook and each joint became fused. Not in any kind of pain, Emily felt overcome with a slight fear, which she knew Mark could sense as his body straightened and stiffened, his eyes raking over her face and down her arm. She felt her arm grow heavier and solid.

"What the fuck is happening?" Mark growled as he watched the show before him.

"It doesn't hurt." Emily blurted, but cringed as she did feel the final joints of her fingers temporarily lock and move of their own accord.

Gently placing his hand in the center of her back Riley moved her forward, saying, "Come with me."

Emily followed his leading hand, still mesmerized as the glowing amber suddenly ceased to reveal a smooth black finish, as if her lower arm was coated in a thick, oil-like cast with a free moving, skin-colored thumb. Mark, James, and a few prying others had followed them to a corner of the loading bay where there had been some clear demonstration of weapons usage.

Standing before a discarded pile of wooden targets, Riley ordered, "Shoot your light at the pile, using your right hand only."

Emily focused and let her light build until the top half of the nearest target all but exploded into dust. She turned back to Riley, clearly seeking his next command.

"Good, now do it again with only your left hand."

Focusing once again, she lifted her newly casted arm and focused. As her light grew and focused, the black turned back into amber before a blast obliterated three entire targets, turning them into ash.

"Whoa," James whispered, his eyes watching the remnants collect on the ground below.

Emily examined her new weapon, bending and flexing her wrist as if nothing encased it. Riley explained, "Emily, you need to be able to move swiftly and heal faster. This sleeve will enhance your abilities ten-fold without slowing you down. Interlock your fingers and press your palms together, igniting your flame when you want to remove it."

"Why don't the rest of us get those things? They look a lot more powerful than these things," James asked, lifting his own gun that matched Mark's.

"These are more localized, good for narrow fighting, and precise shots." Riley lifted his own gun, before lowering it, and gesturing towards Emily. "Though that's stronger, it's mainly used to enhance healing abilities. It's too unstable and unpredictable to be used as a main weapon. Only use it in self-defense if you absolutely have to." Glancing back up at the others, he ordered, "Get ready."

James backed up to join his assigned group, as Mark and Emily joined theirs. Separated into their teams in the bay, filled with various small vessels, Caleb stepped forward. "We will take two ships. James, your team is with us." He gestured with his head for them to move behind him. "Mark, your team will join Isobel and Riley's. We'll board at two locations, then split up to follow the plan." Taking one step back, he raised his head and voice to address the entire bay, "You have all trained well. The minute we board their ship you will need to be fast on your feet and quiet. They will be alerted to our presence within seconds, and will be equally prepared. Remember, these are warriors and they know their vessel better than anyone. Those of you without light, remember the Biron heart is center chest," he said, and absently gestured to his own torso. "They will need more than one bullet or blast to take them down, and will charge at you, given first chance. Do not let them get their arms around you, as they will easily cage and crush you."

"What about any Jarly on board?" One Israeli soldier, with a thick accent, stepped forward.

Caleb paused, glancing at his brother and over to Riley, who both nodded once while securing their weapons under their arms. Turning to face the soldier, Caleb squared his shoulders. "Anyone on that ship chose their fate; kill anyone on sight."

*   *   *

Amadeus' eyes fluttered open to stare up at his bound wrists. Old dried blood had trickled down his forearms, pooling into the curve of his inner elbows. Feeling weak, he dared not move another muscle. Eventually, the sound of a second pair of lungs drew is attention. Taking in a hard breath he managed to push he head up, allowing it to level out then quickly fall forward, needing no added support. In front of him he could see a badly beaten Rick, curled on his side, eyes wide, locking with his own.

"Amadeus," Rick croaked, still staring, unmoving.

A protective force surged through him, Amadeus felt his muscles harden and call to attention. He could see Rick was in bad shape, the clothes torn enough to reveal at least ten slashes of the electric rod. The right side of his forehead had been sealed by light, but still stayed swollen and brutalized.

"Rick, save your energy. We're going to get out of this. Just stay awake." Amadeus could barely whisper past his own pain. Not needing to examine his own body, he knew he too was in serious need of medical healing. A select spot on his lower right back throbbed and burned consistently, and he could feel the piercing pain of at least three devices within and around his abdomen.

"There's something embedded in my skin... lower back." Rick said, his dry and cracked lips barely freeing the words, as his eyes began to droop.

"I know. I believe I have been afflicted by the same device... It could be a number of things." Though Amadeus did not elaborate further, Rick could tell by Amadeus' internal struggle that he was hesitant to continue, fearful of what his explanation may mean.

Roughly fifteen minutes passed in silence as the two watched each other, helpless in their desires to heal and protect. With a loud bang, the air in the room freed up and a gush of heat entered. A door behind Amadeus had opened, revealing two Jarly, Bates, and a sneering Kavar.

"Oh how nice for us, both of our boys are awake and ready to play," Bates mocked over Kavar's shoulder, making his way around Amadeus to Rick's limp body. Crouching down, he was inches from Ricks face. "Hello friend."

"Fuck off," Rick spat out, "Get away from me you piece of shit!" he panted, his body refusing to move as his head flopped back down.

In a flash, Bates had his lit left hand like a vice around Rick's throat, choking him as Bates' right hand covered Rick's face. Bates' eyes closed as he focused and Rick appeared to go limp below him. Impeding on the view, Kavar called Amadeus' attention by jerking and twisting a metal-lic rod that was currently embedded three inches above his victim's left hipbone. The blood-curdling cry only excited Kavar, who twisted the rod further.

The only reprieve came ten minutes later when one surly Biron barged into the room, knocking the shoulder of the nearest Jarly. "Sir." His voice was deep and slow.

"What is it?" Kavar's gaze did not waver from the static light that melded with Amadeus' stomach, as he held his favorite tool in place.

"Sir, we have word that the Jarly scum are on route and may reach the base before we do."

"What?" The force of Kavar's anger had the Biron messenger cowering, taking a step back as Kavar lowered the device, turning away from Amadeus. Clearly thinking, he turned to Bates, barking, "How long?"

Bates stay crouched over Rick; his eyes were open with his third eyelid in place, his lit hands still covering Rick. "Almost done. Three minutes."

Turning back, Kavar tossed the rod across the room, bouncing and scraping across the floor until it hit the wall and settled.

"Ready my vessel and alert the others." He marched out of the room, not taking a second look. "When the Human wakes, kill Amadeus."

Shortly after, Bates got to his feet, letting his light extinguish, heading towards the door. "The rest of you stay out here. Patrol the corridor. You two stay in the room."

His order was taken in silence, and leaving those remaining, Bates left, swiftly closing the door behind him.

CHAPTER FIFTEEN

Mark and Emily took their seats - two out of the four rows of twelve - in the back of the cargo shuttle, thankfully equipped with adequate defenses. The space was filled with heavy machinery and shiny weapons. Earth's soldiers sat in silence, clearly preparing themselves for the imminent attack. Nestled in the deep seats across from them, Riley and Isobel pushed their fingers to their left ear, third eyelids falling into place, as they once did at James and Julia's wedding. Waiting patiently, Mark gripped Emily's free hand, smiling in encouragement.

Isobel drew their gaze, "Amelia has announced that we are in place and Bazza and Tonk's teams have successfully taken out the ground base. They are waiting on our flanks for the arrival of Bates' fleet."

"We're currently hovering just inside the planet's atmosphere, just outside of their radars. As soon as we get word that they are within range, we will attack," Riley added.

Silence fell then on the remaining crew as they waited. There was no known timeframe of when the fleet would arrive, but given the general information and time already sat waiting, it was estimated that they would be attacking within the hour. Forty minutes passed before a single word was uttered. Mark was about to suggest formation strategies with his team, when Isobel and Riley once again zoned out and listened.

Standing, Riley cleared his throat, "Okay, we have a go. The fleet has just come into range -- the main vessel, accompanied by five fighter ships. We will assist in their destruction, but our main focus is on the mining shuttle." Riley gripped the above railing as their ship surged forward and rattled slightly as they attempted to clear the planet's metallic rings. Once freed, their speed increased rapidly. "Get ready, we will be within fighting range in one minute."

Eight soldiers rose out of their seats and entered small rooms off of the main cargo hold. Emily looked confused until she saw one man settle into a seat in front of another control panel that clearly depicted weapons details and ammunition loads.

She caught Isobel's gaze, hearing her explanation. "Side guns... We're gonna give that fleet a run for their money." She then stood next to her protector as Emily caught a glimpse of her own left arm cast in the same smooth material.

Emily gasped and slightly jumped at the first strike against the outer hull. Mark's grip on her hand tightened in a quick squeeze, then loosened to stand and grip his gun. Following Riley's lead, those who could, engulfed themselves in their empowering flame. Within seconds the entire remaining team stood to attention and arranged themselves in formation by the exit. With each blast of return fire, the shuttle shook but remained undamaged. The noises grew immensely until the only communication could be done via shouting. The shuttle began to dip and sway, obviously outmaneuvering all ensuing attackers. Emily eventually decided that she was glad there were no windows to the outside attack, which would only add to her growing fears.

On one particular maneuver, both Isobel and Emily were taken off guard, as with a swift jerk to the right, both women lost their footing and flew back against the back row of seating before crumpling on the metal grating below. Their ship continued to move irrationally.

"Shit! Babe, you okay?" Mark rushed over, reaching for Emily's elbow, helping her to her feet as Riley did the same for Isobel.

Brushing off the nonexistent dust, Emily's cheeks grew pink with embarrassment as she kept her head down, "Yeah, I'm good."

Mark grinned down at her, wrapping his free arm around her shoulders and drawing her into his side as the shuttle continued to weave and sway. Within five minutes, the back end of the shuttle had locked onto something and the swaying ceased.

Moving to the front of the group at the rear of the vessel, along with Isobel and two other Jarly, Riley began to bark orders. "Stay with your leaders. Follow the routes we discussed. Mark, when this hatch opens and we reach the end of the tunnel, your team and Isobel's will turn right.

When you reach the end of that hall you will split up; Isobel's team goes right, you go left. Understood?"

"Understood," Mark responded. As the orders continued, Mark turned to his wife and whispered, "Stay low and behind me, you got it?" She nodded in response. "You stay with me the entire time; if someone is injured you draw them into the center of the group and heal them."

"Got it." She faced the door as a clinking noise began and an invisible seal audibly broke, affecting the airflow around them, signaling that the exit was about to be opened.

Thankfully, as the bridge-like door lowered halfway, the teams could clearly make out four heavily armored Birons, already shooting what abstract weapons they had available to them. With shared firing, by the time the shuttle door had fully opened and secured itself in place, only two Birons remained; being heavily bombarded by Earthly bullets and various blasts of light.

The entrance they had attached themselves to was very short -- only ten feet in length before it opened up into three identical looking passageways. The entire boarded vessel was colored in varying shades of black and brown; from floor to ceiling, heavily rusted metal added to its severity. It took only a few seconds for the putrid smell to hit their nostrils. Most of the soldiers continued on without batting an eye, while Emily was joined by Mark and two of the American soldiers to her left, as they clearly gagged and tried to cover the bottom of their faces.

When the last two Biron were taken out, their heavy bodies hit the ground below, loudly echoing off of the surroundings. Clearly their ranks were not being replaced, allowing the three teams to carry out their plans; they were to communicate telepathically with their bonded other, while seeking out their captured loved ones. Eventually, when Isobel and Mark's teams separated, Emily and the others found themselves practically running down darkened tunnels, barely encountering a single attacker. Each had hoped that the vessel was not as occupied as they had previously been informed.

Following the memorized map in his mind, Mark directed his team to the center of the vessel, which opened into a wide-open core. Circular in shape, the group reached a railing that opened up to view the entire ship, top to bottom. Breathing heavily, Mark ensured everyone on his team was accounted for. Before he could give his next order, gunshots and fighting were heard from below, and light flickered and blasted from many of the tunnels, drawing attention. Moments later the same came from above; firing and yelling.

Across the open expanse, Emily was the first to notice the group of Birons roughly one hundred yards away that were gathering and splitting into two groups, rushing at them from either side.

She grabbed her husband's shoulder, drawing his attention back down to their level as he continued to watch the firefight from above. "Mark, they're coming."

Her gaze followed that of the team charging to their right, nearest to them.

"Everyone stay together, go right. We need to get two levels up. Over there." He pointed to a corroded staircase halfway between them and the racing groups.

There was only enough space for two men to charge along the narrow curved path, shoulder to shoulder. Moving quickly, Mark aligned with a British soldier who rallied himself and the other men up by taunting the attackers and using a colorful array of profanity. Emily remained in the middle of the group, with four soldiers behind. In short time the bullets began to fly as the two groups collided. The Birons used their brute force to overwhelm the front runners, grabbing a man closest to the railing and lifting him into the air like he was made of feathers and tossing him over; but not before the soldier selflessly took two Biron with him.

The majority of these Biron did not have enough shielding to protect them from the barrage of bullets. Emily heard quick bursts of fire behind her and turned in time to dodge a spear that had been thrown from the second attacking group. The four soldiers bringing up the rear chose to stop, and focus their attention on that group. Within range, Emily leant against the railing, ensuring none of her team would be injured as she let off two blasts from her amplified hand, blowing away the path behind them, sending two Biron back into the others, their bodies lifeless and not intact.

"Move!" Mark ordered from behind. The right-sided team had successfully cleared a path along their route and were already making their way up to the next level.

Gaining her footing, Emily followed Mark up the steps and into another corridor. Three Biron already lay in her path, along with one Chinese soldier. Reaching down for a pulse, Mark glanced up his wife, shaking his head. Within five steps, Emily reached an open space, noting the basics of an empty bedroom with a long narrow bed and a few scattered pieces of furniture.

Opening up into a wider corridor leading to twelve short halls, Emily recognized the space from the blueprints shown to house two sleeping quarters; the space was deserted. Reaching the far end, Mark took the lead as he rounded the corner and directed the remaining group through a maze of paths, before they reached a smaller version of the revolving elevator that the group was already familiar with.

"You're not seriously suggesting we take the elevator?" Emily looked almost disgusted, turning back to Mark. "Mark, anything could happen in there; they could shut it down and we'll be sitting ducks."

"Don't you think I know that?" he burst back in frustration. "At this point in time we don't have another option. The hatch that leads to their version of a staircase is on the other side of the vessel, back the way we came."

The group held their breath as the entrance to the elevator came into view, thankfully fully functional and completely empty.

"Everyone get on, now!" Mark ordered, his rifle stiff to his chest, pointed, and prepared for anything. He was the first to enter the revolving space, quickly turning and crouching into position.

The elevator filled, the last soldier had to jump a foot up, ensuring he joined the rest of his team. Emily found herself nauseated by the slow spinning motion, her nerves getting the best of her. Choosing to focus on the back of her husband's crouched head, she attempted to steady her breathing. A flashback of him crouching in the elevator they took in the base, the year before, filled her mind; remembering the same fast-paced fear and wonder as they waited for the new entrance to be revealed. She allowed herself another moment of memory, before she stashed it away and focused on this new mission.

The remaining accompanying four completed a whispered check of their available ammo. Glancing to the fellow American to her right, Emily noted a bloody wound seeping from his left calf, slowly trickling dark crimson down the side of his forest green pants and through the rusted grating below. Her gaze followed his body, along his hard features, stopping on his face as it remained trained on the exit. Moving swiftly, still engulfed in her flame, Emily bent as she gripped the side of his leg and began to heal.

He seemed surprised by the sudden assistance, taking in a quick breath, though his eyes never left the revolving walls. When she was finished, she stood, acknowledged his courteous nod.

"Is anyone else injured?" She scanned their faces; none came forward. "Mark?" She asked the back of his head, as he had not even budged an inch.

"I'm fine," he practically growled as the first spot of light from the ensuing hallway broke into the top of the elevator, striking the far wall.

As the elevator continued to creep around to allow a full view, the two waiting Birons were taken off guard, clearly expecting any attack to come on foot through the attached hallways in front of them. Four consecutive shots sounded as the Birons buckled and fell to the grated floor below. The sounds of the bullets echoed off the siding, fueling far cries and grunts from future attackers.

Corridor after corridor, Mark began to notice the lack of bombardment. Coming to an abrupt halt, the group stilled as Mark silently communicated to his bonded Jarly, Riley.

No resistance here, these hallways are deserted. No sign of a cell-block or anything. I don't think this vessel matches the holographic design perfectly... Where are you? We can hear running and moving, but nothing attacking.

He stood in defensive mode, as two soldiers blocked Mark and Emily between them, covering both ends of the hallway. After a minute his gaze locked with his wife's.

"What's going on?" she whispered.

"I don't know. Riley isn't replying and the schematics from that hologram don't match this ship."

"What?" the previously wounded soldier added, glancing over his shoulder, "We're coming in blind?"

"Not completely, for the most part it's the same, but there are a few differences; for instance, this hallway shouldn't be here."

"Well, fuck!" The soldier turned back. "Now what?"

"Jason, relax." A second American at his side whispered, "This isn't much different than Borneo."

"You're kidding me, right? This is a little different than rebel fighters trapped on an island, in a hot ass rainforest, surrounded by American Marines and British SAS."

"Would you two shut up!" From the other end of the hall, a seemingly Swedish Viking quieted the group.

"Still nothing?" Emily pulled Mark's attention back to hers. He merely shook his head as the rushed footsteps of a raid pounded on the solid ceiling above. Near Jason's head, a large portion of the metallic siding fell from the invading vibrations, loudly hitting the grated floor at his feet, leaving the majority to crumble and slide through the grated flooring of their path.

"This piece of shit is falling apart," the second American added.

"Enough. Just keep moving." Mark squeezed past them, continuing down the narrow hallway, which gradually began to incline until the slope took a great effort on their part to continue advancing.

As voices echoed at the peak at the end of their hallway, Mark slowed his pace, ensuring their footsteps would not echo and give away their position. Choosing to release his light, Emily followed suit, to further conceal their ascent; there was no concern that they would not be able to shield themselves before any attack made contact. The voices came louder and clearer. One appeared to be barking orders, the walls muffling the actual words, and only harsh sounds cracked through the silence. Now paused at the threshold to next room, the group aligned themselves to be concealed by the obvious opening. Whoever was talking appeared to be on the other side of the wall, out of view, and all others hidden from sight.

Taking a minute to gather his thoughts, Mark glanced around the open space before him, noting possible escape routes, obstacles, and additional dangers. The person still speaking grew louder and more determined as answering noise gave away their companions. Gesturing with his hand still close to the wall, the Viking and his companion moved to the other side of the hall, keeping themselves low, shielded from the unknown. Emily leaned forwards as the entire group tried to get a better view of their opponents; however her attempts were barred by Mark's forearm bracing her back against the wall.

Silently, Mark took the single step needed to align himself with the very opening of the tunnel that lead to their barely hidden sanctuary. Raising his gun, keeping it close to his body, he was surprised when the Viking took charge and pushed past him, revealing their position; his gun began to fire, causing the others to follow and Mark and Emily to ignite their flames.

* * *

James felt confident of the route he had ordered his men down, even though barely anything matched the holographic template. Descending into the bowels of the ship, he led his obedient team through darkness and damp walled chaos. Caleb and Damon's teams had recently disengaged from his group. Accompanied by the two Scotsmen, one British, one Japanese an Israelis, and the Jarly medic, James' group surprisingly worked well together. While attempting to reach the core of the vessel, a few times they were forced to backtrack and fall back on themselves. Eventually, James regained his bearings and caught sight of a narrow, relatively well-lit tunnel that the hologram had predicted would reach the core.

"Ye sure aboot this, laddie?" Reid dubiously looked at the entrance of their tunnel, knowing full well that it would barely allow them to pass one by one, with little room to fight.

James glanced down the tunnel and then back to his group. "Yep. The map said this would lead to the center."

"Ye, well the map aint bin so accurate to date."

"True." James glanced at the others, saying, "But we don't have that many options. As I see it, we are already behind schedule and lost enough as it is. I say we go."

"I reckon we better get on with it then." The British soldier, with narrow eyes and a solid nose, jerked his chin towards the opening.

Squaring his shoulders, James entered the awkward space and took off on a steady jog. Quickly his nose was struck by yet another foul scent that made his throat burn and his eyes slightly water.

"Reid…Ye fart?" James couldn't help but smile at Al's obvious attempts to lighten the mood.

Reaching a fork in the path, James was confident that the intended path should be taken off to the right and followed onwards. As the smell began to fade and the air drew into his lungs smoothly he picked up the pace. Noting a ramp form in their path, the group proceeded with caution as the invading light grew stronger and then a new room came into sight. Reaching the very end of their tunnel, James stepped up and aligned himself with the wall, as Reid did the same across from him. The two men barely fit at the entrance. Peeking out, neither could hear anything other than the mechanical screeching and whooshing of the vessel's propulsion.

Glancing out into the belly of the beast, James noted the spacious core surrounded by barred-off hand railing at each level. With one last glance down either side of the open floor, James took a step into the open, gripping onto the railing and glancing up. They were on the very bottom floor, only a black oil-like fluid sloshed around in the space between him and the other side of the vessel. Rusted staircases and ladders connected each floor. The entire space felt like a tubular cavern. Various groups of Birons appeared oblivious to their presence, only a few floors above. It was clear they were not on high alert, travelling upwards in floors. James could see to the very top of the vessel through the grating of each level above them.

Gunfire could be heard further up, causing James to lean well past the railing boundaries to see Riley and his team three floors from the very top, rushing around the side of the ship, engulfed in flame, getting attacked from all sides. More groups were being attacked and attacking others, though James didn't recognize anyone else at that time. The sudden cascade of black slop into the pool below from three floors up had James pulling back, and then locking eyes with a near Biron, who stood frozen, taken off guard. He seemed to remember himself and call for reinforcements.

"Move boy," Reid pulled him back against the wall as three other Birons joined the other, reaching over their railing with their high-powered weapons. One missed James by a hair, as he and the others ascended the near staircase, returning fire as they went.

Now others had joined in, a second group catching wind of the attack, circling around from the other side of the vessel. Choosing to continue upwards, James' team made it up three levels before the true fight began. Taken off guard from behind, a surprisingly short and burley Biron lunged at James, almost knocking the pair of them over the railing. James was so preoccupied that he pushed back, stepping into another Biron.

Turning, James took in his next attacker. This Biron stood three foot over James, but his body stayed lean and narrow, almost forcibly bending so that his head did not hit the grating above. He thrust out his hands, grabbing James by the upper shoulders and lifting him so that their heads were at the same height. In a swift move, the Biron brought his scale-like head forward and James heard the crunch before the pain of his nose felt like it had all but shattered. The sharp distraction weakened his defenses enough to hold little resistance as James' body was further rammed up and into the grating above. He took two hits before his body was released, flying backwards and further down the corridor; the bottom of his feet knocking two members of his own team off balance.

Scrambling to their feet, the group struggled to get the upper hand while they were outnumbered three to one. The narrow row that wrapped around the interior of the core only allowed for so much room to fight. As bullets and energy blasts flew all around, the grating below bounced and creaked and the railing wobbled with each individual being thrown to and fro. Forcing as much light into his fists as he could manage, James finished with his two present attackers, clearing the view to witness the fatal blow of a jagged blade pass through Al's chest, piercing out the back side to the left of his spine. Dropping to his knees almost instantly, James lunged for him, but the Biron used the blade to guide him sideways and under the railing.

"No!" James dove for his ankles, but it was too late. Al's limp body fell, plummeting before being engulfed by the black liquid below.

Lying on the grating, his arm stretched out clutching at the air, James became overcome with rage. Rolling onto his side, he drew his arm back onto the ledge, forcing all of his power into his palm, blasting the two racing Birons nearest; their bodies all but exploded before the others. The loud boom gained enough attention to distract a couple others, giving the rest of James' team enough time to finish them off. Rising to his feet, James watched as the final Biron took a bullet above the right eye from Reid's barrel. In time to see the end of the battle, Damon and Caleb's teams emerged, reunited, from the tunnel above at the corner curve of the vessel. Soon after, they were followed by Biron forces.

James reached for Reid's near shoulder in condolences for the loss of his friend. His team regrouped, readying to assist in the battle continuing above, when the hairs on the back of James' neck stood to attention at a familiar scream; his eyes automatically drew upwards, his jaw dropping open, as he lunged once again towards the open railing.

CHAPTER SIXTEEN

Isobel's team was taken off guard by a sudden attack. Spinning around, she, along with two other Jarly, managed to block the bullets.

"Idiot!" she spat at the encroaching Viking, "Do you always shoot first, before you even see who you are attacking?"

"Jesus," Emily whispered, knowing Mark would hear well enough. The group lowered their guns immediately. The Viking even bowed his head and averted his gaze.

"Isobel, has your team found anything?" Mark stepped forward and the two groups joined.

It took a few seconds for her furious gaze to lift from the Viking before she answered. "Nothing really. We have taken out three small units, nothing overwhelming. This appears to be one of their control rooms." The others scanned the various alien devices, nothing looking familiar. "We have planted a small bomb in the engineering bay to crimple the vessel and do a little bit of internal damage. They wont be able to move and retreat. The bomb should go off within the next thirty minutes."

"Have you heard from Riley?"

"Not yet, but he rarely communicates during battle," Isobel brushed her hands nervously on her upper thighs. "Let's continue on. Have you cleared the lower levels?"

"Yes, but I'm surprised at how little resistance we have actually encountered," Emily answered, stepping forward and further into the light.

"James must not be far behind us. I think he's coming up the other side," Mark added. On cue some familiar gunshots sounded below, turning the heads of the group to the far entrance of the room, leading to the rusted barriers of the internal vessel.

Together as a large group they forced their way back out onto the narrow railing to witness the battle unfolding four stories below. Splitting her group up, Isobel ordered two of her team below to assist the others, while she pushed at Mark's shoulder, gesturing with her head for him to move forward and ascend. He immediately understood and took the lead, forcing himself up the near rickety staircase and closer to the welcoming sounds of Riley's voice hidden in the rooms above.

Three levels up, Emily froze mid-staircase, causing Isobel and the remainder of her team to practically collide with one another. In the panicked rush to reach sound footing, the others had missed the movement across the open hull, just below. Emily lowered her body further, flattening against the side of the staircase as the others moved back, against the wall, and followed her gaze.

Mark pushed past his team, crouching at the top of the stairs. "Em, what do you see?"

She didn't answer for a moment, paused, still staring down as the others nervously looking around them, clearly not happy with their current position and lack of shelter.

"There!" Emily loudly whispered, now rising to lean over the flimsy railing, glancing between Mark and Isobel as she pointed across the expanse, "Three or four levels below. Watch, can you see the movement? A large number of Birons coming in and out, carrying things... They seem completely oblivious." Her statement was reiterated by the continued battle below between James and the others.

Mark absently nodded, watching the focused Biron fill the corridor again, before vanishing out of sight. He turned to Isobel, "What do you make of this? What's down there?"

Isobel paused to think, glancing at the levels above, and then moving to lean over the railing before her, seemingly counting the number of levels below. "If my calculations are correct," her gaze returned to the growing number of Birons appearing and disappearing from across the open space, "that corridor would lead to the reserve escape vessels."

"I thought Bazza and Tonks were taking out their additional vessels?" The taller American questioned, stepping forward to speak from the railing above.

"Yes, however they might have been overcome and distracted from the final few. The outer casing of this vessel is like a camouflage. If the vessels were not in motion, it is possible they could have been mistaken for the outer shell," Isobel explained.

"How many reserve vessels are there?" Emily asked, still watching the movement below.

"Only two or three reserves at most, but they could potentially house as many as twenty Biron with added weaponry."

"We have to stop them then." Mark took the three steps to align himself with Emily as he continued to speak with Isobel, "I'll take my te…" he paused at Isobel's sudden gasp, as she turned her back to the group, her gazed turned up.

"They've found them!" she exclaimed in a rush. "They need me." Isobel turned back to her group, her eyes focusing on nothing as she clearly listened to the remainder to Riley's conversations. Eventually she smiled, focusing on Mark and Emily, "They're alive." The couple let out a held breath in unison. Isobel continued, "They're in rough shape though, I need to get to them."

"Right, go… Take the rest of your team." Mark ordered, his gaze rising to his remaining team on the platform above. "The rest of you with me. We need to shut down their escape route and cripple the vessels." Isobel and her group had already rushed around the corridor and were taking the steps up to another platform. "Emily, go with them," Mark drew back her attention with the gentle tilt of her chin to meet his gaze. "Go."

Emily smirked and whispered, "Not likely." With a quick peck to his pursed lips, Emily gripped the railing nearest and surprised the others as she ignited her flame, swinging her body over the railing, and back onto the corridor below, under the staircase. Out of Mark's reach she continued to run, gaining speed along the corridor; her destination being the Biron on the other side.

"Move!" She could hear Mark's roar behind her and the bouncing impact on the grating below as he followed in her footsteps; the others followed with loud grunts and shuffling of heavy weaponry.

In mere moments Mark was shoulder to shoulder with his errant wife as they reached the bend on the siding of the ship. Their swift movements heightened by their light drew Biron attention as many stopped and prepared themselves for battle. Only meters apart now, Mark and Emily ducked as the first wave of Biron firepower shot past them, melting the rusted metal above. Within reach, Mark let off one of Riley's signature energy waves, hitting the first two, crippling their advances as they took two others over the railing with them.

With lightning-like speed Emily lunged for the next Biron. Kicking off of the near wall, she reached for the two blades nestled into the back of her belt-line, bringing them forward and into the staggering chest of the attacker before her. With a loud grunt, he fell to his knees, revealing the armed wave of three Birons behind. Before she could react, earthly guns sounded behind her as a wave of bullet shot above her head, taking down the blockade in front. Now partially entering the wider hallway - that the Birons had continuously filled- the space allowed ample room for movement, though more Birons appeared to be returning, leaving their escape vessels to join in the fight.

Emily watched as Mark moved in swift calculated form, taking down one Biron after another. The Viking and Americans continued their fight with hand-to- hand combat, as well as blade and projectile weaponry. She was quickly pulled out of her trance as two Biron rounded on her, one taking her off guard as he wrapped his free arm around her waist, lifting her up off of her latest kill, and hurtling her back against the near wall. The impact of the shaking wall behind her vibrated throughout her body, forcing the available air from her lungs, the shock temporarily lowering her glowing field. The second Biron stepped up, weapon in hand, ready to plunge it into her upper chest. Emily forced the light back into her left palm fast enough to force her assailant back against the far wall, knocking over the Viking and a Biron already in battle.

Her gaze fell on the Biron still pressing her high into the wall, which seemed distracted, eagerly seeking his own blade with his free hand. Not giving him enough time to react, Emily reached for the bar above her head, which supported a flickering blue light. Her grip in place, she pulled herself up enough for the Biron to lose his hold on her lower half. Forcing her legs up, she pushed against the wall. With both feet planted against his chest she heaved, forcing him back and sending him toppling over the fallen bodies behind him. Uninjured, he scrambled to his feet, his attention now focused on Mark, who had his back to the others.

Taking Mark off guard, the Biron managed to get a grip on his upper body, restraining his arms as the small group of Biron in front of him gained their footing and produced their own deadly weapons. Mark struggled in the Biron's grip, but couldn't break free in time, the grip menacingly tight and restricting. Managing to back up and save himself from the first deadly slash, Mark watched from the corner of his eye as Emily surged at the group of three Birons now partially surrounding her husband. He continued to watch in awe as the impact of the force caused the two nearest the broken railing to lose space and plummet; then his gaze turned to fear as the final Biron reached out in his attempts to clutch at anything, taking Emily with him.

With the sudden slamming of Mark's head into the face of the distracted Biron behind him, the grip loosened and Mark managed to free himself and make for the open corridor. Emily's screams were his only concern as he could see the fingers of her right hand barely gripping onto the grating, keeping her from falling as well. On his hands and knees Mark reached the edge, his hands gripping his wife's dangling arm. Below, the third Biron clung to her legs and left wrist, trying to pull himself up her body. Further below, Mark noticed the first two Birons call out just before their bodies were engulfed in the thick black slop covering the lowest levels.

Mark used his light to blast at the third Biron, who successfully dodged each bolt before spinning himself around to Emily's front, sheltered by the grated corridor above, but too far extended to drop successfully to the landing below. Emily cried out in clear pain at the added weight her right hand supported and the unnatural twisting of her body and left wrist. Mark ignored the Biron below as he tried to drag Emily up and over.

"Let go of the grating," Mark grunted as he gripped her right wrist and forearm. Without hesitation she loosened her grip but shrieked as her body began to lower and Mark was extended over the edge himself. In his focus, Mark ignored the continued fighting taking place behind him. The others seemed to be holding their own, but were gradually becoming outnumbered. As Mark heaved, the third Biron made things harder as he tugged and swayed their bodies; Emily's eyes locked with her husband's in fear and great pain.

"I've got you. Hold on." Mark continued to pull, his focus absolute. "I've got you."

The fear morphed as her vision focused over his left shoulder, where a Biron stood with a face smeared with dark liquid dripping from his upper lip and chin. Emily recognized him as her wall attacker, his dark green flesh covered in a thin sheen of sweat and shredded clothing. She watched as he stepped on either side of her husband's torso, blade in hand, as Mark appeared unaware. With only seconds to react, Emily wiggled her right wrist free of Mark's grip.

"What are you doing? No. Stop!" he yelled as his grip failed and her body began to fall. "No!"

In her last moments of freedom, her right hand grew ablaze as her light shot from her open palm and into the chest of the Biron above Mark. He stood for a moment after the blast had taken affect before falling forward, his left foot grazing the back of Mark's head. The third Biron growled, pushing away from Emily as their three bodies fell.

"Emily!" Mark's face was the last thing Emily focused on as her weightless body surged to the depths below.

CHAPTER SEVENTEEN

Nearly two hours had passed since Amy had left the others and was now barricaded in the control room with Amelia and her team. The room remained dark, though the darkness did not feel as uninviting as before. Amy had moved to sit along the side of Shouray's pod, her feet extended out before her, her head resting back as her focus fell on the white-filled window. Almost in a trance, she watched various objects float by the giant screen. She angrily swiped away at the lone tear the rolled down her cheek in the moment of weakness that led her to thoughts of Rick and his current predicament.

Eager for distraction, she lazily raised her left hand, palm lit, carefully placing it at the bottom of Shouray's pod. "Shouray?" She spoke aloud, though she knew she only need think her question and it would be answered.

Amy, is everything okay? Shouray's girlish voice filled her mind. *Are you in need of my assistance?*

In that moment, Amy felt silly for disturbing her new friend. "Everything is fine. Are there any updates? Anything from the others?"

I'm sorry, I haven't been following the frequencies, but please do ask Amelia. I'm anxious to hear any updates, as well. I just need to focus on these shields for the time being.

"Of course, I'm sorry to bother you. I'll let you know as soon as I hear more." Amy felt even more foolish, distracting Shouray from such an important role.

There is nothing to apologize for... Amy, I know how lonely you must be feeling right now, but you are not alone; they will be back soon, you wait and see.

Amy could barely whisper past the lump in the throat, "Thanks."

Deciding not to interrupt Amelia just yet, Amy walked towards the white window, willing her to hear good news soon.

Ten more minutes passed without a sound, until the overhead speaker blared. Amelia's voice, though disjointed and mechanical, announced, "All levels brace for impact. Quadrants *D* through *F,* fill the corridors of housing blocks three and seven. Potential impact and boarding estimated in twenty-three seconds." Then in a fully mechanical voice unknown to Amy, the alert began to repeat.

Igniting her flame, Amy rushed for Amelia's pod. "What's happening? Are we under attack?"

I've detected two additional escape pods that have detached from the Biron vessel. One is attempting to flee, while the other is on a path straight for us. Our cloaking signals have failed... It was only a matter of time in this environment. Tonks' vessel has been hit and is currently of no use. I've ordered Bazza and his crew to pursue the escaping vessel.

With that, Amy felt the first blast hit the left side of the station, followed swiftly by a second.

Prepare yourself Amy, they are currently attacking our lower levels, but if they do breach our walls, their destination will be this control room.

Another blast shook the entirety of the control room as Amy almost lost her grip on the pod Amelia occupied.

They managed to target our weakest areas, no doubt via intel given by the traitor, Bates. I will do what I can to defend the ship and its people, but you will need to secure the room. Defend it at all costs.

"Understood," Amy nodded, knowing full well that Amelia could not see her. Stepping away, she took in the room again. Confident in its current state of hold, she filled the space atop the passageway leading to the entrance, her eyes trained on the sealed door.

* * *

Rick's head felt like it would explode; the commotion outside their cell doing little to distract from the throbbing pain. Barely able to open his swollen eyes, he watched as Amedeus' body swayed from the hook above, his bound wrists swollen and black. The two remaining guards seemed to be preparing themselves, edging towards the sealed door, listening intently.

"Amadeus," Rick could barely whisper; his mouth felt dry as if his tongue was made of sandpaper, no saliva to speak of. If not for the soft swell of his chest, begging for breath, Rick would think Amadeus was already dead. "They're coming. Just a little longer, hold on!"

"Be quiet!" One of the guards turned and took a single step towards Rick, but turned back in shock as the shielding door began to slide open, the fighting no longer held at bay.

In a blur of champagne light, Rick's gaze followed two beings as they passed through the open gap, making short work of the two surprised guards. As Amadeus' body easily lifted and was lowered off of the archaic hook, a third light slipped into the room, forcing their way to their leader. As their movements slowed, Rick recognized Riley as being one of the original two, and Isobel being the third, as they began to work on Amadeus' torn and broken body. Appearing to be an after thought, Rick watched with detached feeling as Riley spun in his crouched position, forcing himself over and practically on top of Rick.

Riley rested his palm gently on Rick's own bloody chest; the tender touch eliciting enough pain to cause a sudden coughing fit. "Hang on, buddy. We've got you." Where the palm touched his skin a tingling feeling consumed Rick, and his body began to feel numb and even heavier. In the distance he could hear Isobel shooting orders to the others. The outside hall no longer held gunshots or the groans of battle. "Rick, look at me." He tried, but his eyelids grew heavier by the second. Absently he noted two other sets of hands grabbing and reaching for him. "Rick"- he felt his body shake and his head bob - "we're going to move you. I need you to try and ignite your light one more time. Hold it together, think only of your healing." Nothing. "Rick!'

* * *

Emily closed her eyes as she continued to feel her body falling, knowing the black liquid would soon claim her. The third Biron, being much heavier, fell like a stone. A final cry was heard from below before a great wave of blackness consumed him.

Any second now! was all she could think, refusing to let her mind fill with the memories of a smiling Sophie and her love, Mark. Holding her hands flat against her chest, she squeezed her eyes ever so tightly. *Any second!*

It felt like hitting a brick wall; her eyes surged open as she gasped for air. She watched as the dead Biron she had recently slain continued past her and made an equally large black wave consume his mangled body. Her eyes scanned around, knowing she had paused only feet from the liquid surface. Her eyes widened as her body began to rise, floating upwards and to the right, until her gaze fell on James and his outstretched arm. His concentration was all consuming as he pulled her in, his face flushing at the overwhelming control. Within reach, she lurched herself forward, arms out, as Reid reached over the railing and got a hold of her, easily pulling her over the edge and onto the platform. Her grip became vice-like around Reid's neck and she held him close, silently thanking him. Feeling a soft hand on the center of her back, she turned and jumped into James' embrace, kissing his cheek as tears wetted her own.

"Thank you," she whispered over and over, hugging him fiercely, ignoring the throbbing pain emanating from her left wrist. With each word, James grip grew stronger. Emily noticed Damon and Caleb's team ascending the far side with their heads held high; they sought out Mark's team and the others.

Trying to lighten the situation, and ever the joker, James managed to make Emily laugh, "You know you're supposed to look where you're going... Hand railings are in place for a reason."

She smiled and then her eyes widened, glancing back above, remembering. "They need our help."

The remainder of James' team began to make their way up the near steps, followed by James himself, before Emily gripped his wrist, halting him. "They found them, James... They're alive."

Like Mark and Emily before him, James let out a giant sigh of relief, nodding before turning to take the remaining steps two at a time. Emily followed, nursing her swollen wrist, while attempting to heal on the move.

Rushing around the side of the building once again, Emily and the others continued up, directly below Mark and those that remained. Even from below, she could feel the rage emanating from Mark as he took on the last Biron resistance.

As the group reached the landing - Damon and the others already ahead of the group and out of sight - a loud bang was heard around them. They held onto whatever they could grip, as the entire frame of the vessel seemed to vibrate, faltering in its forward momentum. The shaking gradually lessoned until the tremors were little more than an annoyance. The dull sound of whistling air ceased; no one seemed to have previously noticed the overall loud noise from within the vessel until it came to a halt and all fell silent. Rushing further into the open corridor leading to the remaining escape pods, Emily turned a corner and ran right into a retreating Mark. If not for his quick responses, she would have tumbled backwards and down onto the grating below.

"Emily?" Mark called out in disbelief, his reddened eyes displaying the pure grief he felt only moments before. The angle that Emily had fallen had shaded much of his view; he would not have been able to see her final ascent into the blackness below, therefore he could only assume she had been consumed.

Quickly gripping the sides of his face, she pulled him in close; closing the space between them she forced her lips upon his, so forcefully so that their teeth briefly clashed. He wrapped his arms around her, keeping her close, crushing her to his chest.

"I'm here," Emily spoke between their rushed embrace. "I'm fine. I'll explain everything as soon as we get out of here." Remembering their current turmoil, they wrenched apart, turning to wait outside the entrance to the now vacant escape pod; the only one remaining.

"Two managed to get away before we could reach them. This one though..." Mark glanced inside the empty pod, "It may be weighed down with their weapons and whatever the hell they were trying to escape with, but I think we can use it to get out. Riley and the others are already on their way down."

Emily agreed. The corridor now filled with the lifeless bodies of varied Biron and few Jarly and Human victims. "James, can you use your light to push the bodies out of the way? They will need room to reach us."

Already understanding, James thrust his flaming palms out, clearing a path as he bordered the long corridor with the remnants of battle. Within minutes they were joined by the first of Riley's team. Not seen to have lost any members, he brought up the lead, with two Jarly close behind carrying Rick. Isobel's team brought up the rear with two Humans keeping Amadeus in tow.

"Rick?" James sought out his best friend.

"Not now, James," Riley chastised. "Mark, have you taken the ship?"

"Yes, Damon and Caleb have. Their teams are holding position; it's ready to go. Are there any Birons behind you?" Mark asked.

"No, I believe any remaining Biron to be cowering at their stations. We've had little resistance from their cell coming here..." By now the group had reached the mouth of the awaiting vessel. Calling backwards, "Darius, get up front and get us back to the station, now." A burly looking Jarly with tribal tattoos across the right side of his face surged passed the others, making his way to the front of the vessel; clearly, he was knowledgeable about their mechanics and control systems.

Pushing past the others, the four men gently placed Rick and Amadeus on the cold ground below. Tears burst from Emily before she could stop them, as she took in their slashed, bruised, and broken bodies. Isobel was already hard at work on her leader as something clicked within Emily, and she forcefully pushed those in her way aside to go to Rick and begin her healing. Emily fell to his right side, as Mark and James hovered near by. James gripped Rick's limp hand in both of his own, unsure of what else he could do.

With a loud bang and light shaking, their escape pod detached from the mining vessel and freed itself from the restrictive cables. The ship swayed further, causing the remaining men, Jarly and Human alike, to dig their heels in and hold on to whatever free surface they could. Mark steadied his wife as she placed both hands on Rick's chest; closing her eyes, she began to heal him.

"Sir," Darius called back, causing Riley to leave Isobel's side. On his knee beside Amadeus, Riley forced himself up and past the others towards the front of the vessel.

"Darius," Riley answered, leaning into the small cockpit.

"The station is currently under attack. Scanners show a vessel has attached itself to the outer hull of the sleeping bays. I can't tell if it has been boarded, but the outer shell has taken many hits." Darius spoke while his gaze remained on the controls before him.

"Understood. Continue as planned. Approach the top side and get us to a hatch closest to the control room; that is where they will focus their internal attack."

"Yes, sir," Darius spoke in acknowledgement.

Making his way back to the others, the group listened as Riley filled Isobel and the others in on the predicament of the station.

"When we get in, I want them taken to a secure site for medical attention. Isobel, you will lead that group. I will follow shortly behind," Riley spoke quickly.

"The medical bay on the twelfth floor has everything I need and it's relatively remote," Isobel offered, as her light continued to work on Amadeus.

"Agreed. James," Riley turned to the others, "I want you, Mark, and Emily to accompany the others down to the medical center. Emily, I assume you will be continuing to work on Rick, and will need your own protection." Turning, he pointed to the Human recruits. "You, follow them, and offer protection along the way." No one seemed to question his command and they readied themselves. Turning back to the others, he continued. "Damien, Caleb, and I will lead the others along the available corridors leading to the control room. Hopefully, we can head off the remaining others." The conversation continued into strategy, but the others lost interest as Rick pulled back their attention.

"Amy?" Rick uttered her name, his swollen eyes clearly working to open.

Emily shushed him, "Amy is just fine. She's protected in the control room on the station. She's safe."

Trying to nod, Rick continued, "Amadeus… Where is he?"

Mark gently pressed on his right shoulder. "He's right here. Isobel is working on him now... Save your strength. We're almost there."

Rick's gaze rose to the top of the escape pod, ignoring the gentle sway of the men and women surrounding him. He tried to focus on his breathing and not on the throbbing pain at the back of his head.

Three minutes later, Darius called back into the open space. "We will make contact with the upper station in two minutes. I will position us three floors above the control room; that is the closest compatible hatch."

"Understood," Riley called back. "Okay, get ready. We need to move them again." Riley turned to the two men still in dire need of medical attention. Without needing directions, the same two pairs of men stepped forward and positioned themselves to lift and carry the wounded. With another loud thud, and quick exchange of airflow, the vessel had successfully bonded with the station and Damon lunged to manually open the available side-hatch.

As the remaining party entered, they quickly recognized the state of alert that had encased the station. Sirens and flashing lights alerted others to the intruders aboard. The halls on their level were filled with frantic Jarly running in all directions, seeking shelter and protection. Those clearly trained in security remained calm and moved in an orderly fashion; seemingly aware of the invading attackers en route.

Reaching the main hall, Riley turned. "Go, now... That way. We will join you soon." Isobel led the group towards the twelfth level medical station while Riley and the brothers turned away, continuing along the opposite corridor, their light giving them added speed.

CHAPTER EIGHTEEN

The growing darkness began to interfere with Amy's nerves as the sirens sounded throughout the main station, while only silence filled the control room. After the final bombarding blows had the station being boarded, only stillness invaded the senses. Sealed off from the others, Amy couldn't remove her gaze from the airtight doorway even as the lights from the window behind her increasingly danced across the room, changing color, reflecting off of the occupied pods. Amy did notice when the color disappeared altogether. With a quick glance over her shoulder, she noticed the station was increasingly ascending out of the cloudbank as the creamsicle planet gained distance.

Confused at the loss of further cover, Amy approached Amelia's pod, hand raised as it touched the glass. "Amelia, why are we leaving the planet? Won't they all see us?" Then realization hit as she glanced back over her shoulder towards the sealed door. "Are they back?" Excitement bloomed in her chest as she awaited an answer. Nothing came. "Amelia?"

Absently watching as the clouds disappeared and the station became visible to all in the starry sky, a loud hissing sound had Amy staggering back in order for the pod to open and lift, revealing an exhausted-looking Amelia.

In a rush Amy questioned, "Amelia, what are you doing? Why did you come out? Is it over?" Then with a pause she watched her friend. "Are you okay? You look in pain and well… sick."

Raising her palm, Amelia seemed out of breath as she sluggishly stepped out of the pod after Amy had moved further back and out of the way. "I am fine, Amy." She continued to breathe heavily as she staggered to the large wall of buttons and levers under the large window, continuing to review and control.

"What's happening?" Amy managed to whisper, confused, still leaning against the now closed pod, feeling Amelia's need for space.

Rolling her shoulders and not taking her eyes off of the controls in front of her Amelia finally answered, "The others have managed to escape the mining vessel with Amadeus and Rick, and have also managed to latch on and enter the station." She paused and glanced over her shoulder after personally feeling Amy's shock and relieved emotions. The bond between the Human group and Amelia's would gradually fade as their abilities grew stronger, but in times of such heightened emotions their bond grew ever stronger. Amelia offered a small nod and grin before continuing, "It appears that the mining vessel became disabled shortly after it was invaded by our team. They are lucky they managed to find the additional escape vessels. Riley and his team are on their way here... On the heels of a number of Biron boarders."

Continuously nodding, Amy seemed to overlook the answer of immanent danger. Taking a step closer she asked, "What about Rick and Amadeus? Has Riley said anything?"

Amelia stilled herself, taking in another deep breath. Amy watched as the pink returned to her cheeks and her shoulders squared. Reaching for her discarded clothing, Amelia's eyes locked with hers. "They're in rough shape. Riley only managed to check in once. They have boarded and Isobel, Emily, and the others are rushing them to the medical bay on the twelfth floor." Reaching out, Amelia shocked her friend by softly gripping her bare upper arm, "Amy, they've been badly beaten, but nothing Isobel can't mend. It will take some time, and concentration, but they will both be okay. We just need to wait and see." Turning and stepping towards the other pods, it was as if Amelia now continued on for her own benefit. "Just wait and see," she whispered. "They're going to be okay."

Finally reaching Shouray's enclosure, Amelia raised her hand and gently touched the glass. Without speaking aloud, after a minute she stepped back, waiting. In turn, the glass before Shouray and the others began to open and lift.

"Well done," Amelia offered a hand to Shouray as she too seemed weaker, stepping out of the encasing. The remaining four - three men and one other woman - emerged, equally pale, as exhaustion filled their features and slowed their step.

"Why do you all look so sick?" As one they turned to Amy, not saying a thing. "I'm sorry, I didn't mean that, it's just… You all look like you want to be sick. You're sweating and white as a bed sheet." Turning, she spoke directly to Amelia, who seemed to have regained some of her elegant beauty and coloring. "I thought the light made you stronger."

"It does," Amelia answered as she helped guide Shouray and the others towards the small opened side room that housed their additional clothing, "but when we are in those tubes we ourselves become one with the ship. In case you didn't feel it, the hull of the station has been compromised. Our bodies take on that impact as if it wounded us ourselves." Clearly exhausted with her explanations, Amelia slashed at the air in front of her in a dismissive manor. "They'll feel better in a few minutes."

"Why did you come out?" Amy continued her questioning, regardless of the exasperation she felt from Amelia. She watched Shouray take in deep slow breaths, leaning against a free wall. "I thought the whole reason I stayed behind was to protect you while you saw to the station."

Amelia now moved around the room, constantly checking the controls and moving inanimate objects towards the door, preparing, and creating a form of blockade. "You would have done so marvelously," Amelia continued, distracted, "but now that Amadeus and the others are on board, and no outside forces are continuing their attack, our focus is now solely internal and given the numbers heading our way, you will need all the help you can get."

Finally stopping, Amelia stood at the top of the steps leading to the doorway and addressed the others as they filled the small control room, now fully clothed. "You have all performed brilliantly, but now we face an attack on this very room. Take up your positions. You know what to do." With those simple words the room began to blur with light as the team began preparing themselves for battle.

The three men were tall but lacking in muscle mass, clearly not as prepared for battle as other Jarly; one even seemed heavier set, but the conviction in each of their bodily movements spoke volumes to their knowledge and abilities. The last woman, whom Amy recognized from her brief visit to the internal mechanics of the station and Calobie, aged further than any Jarly she had met, though she still moved with grace. Her silver streaked hair and deep age lines had Amy wondering what her true age was.

"Shouray?" Amelia pulled Amy out of her internal monologue, turning to Shouray who had yet to move, though her shoulders now hunched and her gaze was on the cold grating below. "Shouray, look at me," Amelia's voice grew stronger with authority.

As her head rose, she stood straight, and her facial features grew dull and emotionless. "Yes, Ma'am?"

"Shouray, don't do this," Amelia softened, stepping towards the young Jarly as Shouray said nothing. "You did everything you could. The external environment in that atmosphere was too extreme."

"I should have done better. I could have…" Shouray seemed to explode with anger.

"Enough," Amelia placed her glowing palms on Shouray's shoulders. "Even I in your stead would have only been able to hang on for so long. I know how those systems must have been going haywire down there. You performed extraordinarily and if not for you, the station would have taken on more damage and weakened further." Amy found herself nodding in agreement, even though she felt like she was intruding and should turn away.

A soft thud sounded on the outside of the entrance door, pulling Amelia and Shouray apart; Amelia pushing past Amy and the others, returning to the step and the top of the small staircase. Again, silence filled the room. Amy became embarrassed at her own heavy breathing as new adrenalin coursed through her veins. Taking the space in the center of the room, a few meters behind Amelia, Amy and the others focused as a second thud grew louder.

Rushing down the stairwell, Amelia paused only inches from the door, waiting. Placing her left palm gently against the cold metal she closed her eyes. Slowly she grew closer, laying her ear against the door, listening; a third thud made her pull back, her hand remaining in place. A forth knock grew louder but did little to disrupt the door. Slowly turning, Amelia joined the others in the space.

"Their making noises, but I don't think they're trying to get in," she muttered aloud to no one in particular.

"Why would they do that?" one of the men spoke up, closest to the window and control panel.

Before Amelia could answer, a fifth thud hit the door with equally lacking results. Amy blurted, "A distraction?"

"There's no other way in," Shouray offered, shrugging, as she perched by her vacant pod.

"But they could create another way," Amy continued as the others either focused on her or the door. "What's around us? Below... above?" she asked with eyebrows raised suspiciously.

"There's three thick feet of solid metal on all surfaces of this control," Amelia answered.

"Then what?" She shrugged exasperated, "I dunno... Where do the air vents connect?" Amy offered her last suggestion.

Not acknowledging Amy, Amelia gestured outwards with her palms, fingers pointed, as two of the men on either side turned and disappeared behind the pods, into the adjacent rooms. The sixth blow grew louder, followed by consistent banging. Still the airtight door did not budge an inch. Amelia pushed past Amy to the clear window behind her. Looking above and below, she was clearly focused on the outer hull around the glass.

"You don't think..." Amy followed her searching gaze.

"That they could be distracting us to break through this window? Yes, it had crossed my mind," Amelia answered her unfinished question.

Amy's face grew white as she backed up, closer to the banging, now continuing behind them. "We won't be able to breathe. Won't we get sucked out or explode or something?"

Amy grew shocked as Amelia and Shouray, who was now also leaning over the control panel searching, both started to laugh and giggle.

"Don't worry, Amy," Shouray explained. "This room is still sheltered by its own environment and shield; a translucent bubble would take place of the broken glass, which is very thick. The biggest issue would be the fast rate in which the oxygen will be sucked from the room, that would be unavoidable, but we would remain standing and in one piece."

"Oh... Great," the sarcasm dripped from Amy's words as she rolled her eyes.

"Ma'am," a frantic-sounding man called from the adjacent room to the right. The others entered in time to witness the lone, heavy-set air vent, at the back of the room, violently vibrate. Taking a few steps back, they heard the man from the other room call out as well.

"Get back!" Amelia ordered as the air-vent cover shot back, hitting him and carrying his body backwards into the far wall. Amy shrieked as the arm, upper chest, and finally head of a smaller Biron passed through the casing.

Growling like a feral animal, the Biron quickly forced his way through, followed by another, as Amelia raised her hand and sent out a single blast, crippling the first and further shrinking the vent opening, hindering their entrance. Turning, she pulled Amy from the room, and helped Shouray as she dragged the unconscious Jarly out from behind the heavy vent cover. Falling into the main space, Amelia ran to the second man, now accompanied by the third Jarly male and elderly woman. The room now filled with sounds of more Birons, clearly not able to navigate the air vents quietly with their weaponry in hand. The banging on the main door grew louder and drew Amy's attention as it now grew dented and weakened.

They're coming at us from all sides! Amy thought as she now stood in the center of the control room with her arms raised.

Shouray rushed back to the main room, filled with courage and worried by its lack of commotion. Peeking in, she noticed the vent was now vacant, with no hidden Birons. Clearly choosing to retreat, or believing they were too large to force through the small mouth Amelia had created, they were gone. Shouray further bombarded the opening with her light, shrinking it further to insure no surprise attacks from behind. Using the remaining moments she could steal, she continued to block the opening with available materials, knocking over shelves and anything she could find. Satisfied with her work, she returned to the main room to assist the others, as the final blow on the entrance crimpled its resolve and caused the door to come crashing down to reveal a group of larger Birons, with very real ammunitions.

* * *

"Move," Riley ordered his team to hustle, as Caleb and Damon had just separated from his group and were now out of sight. Riley's only thought was on the Birons he knew would be bombarding the main entrance of the control room. Their corridor gave way to three hallways, two of which he had hoped the brothers could secure. Even out of sight, the stench of Biron sweat and their foul odor filled his nostrils as they grew closer. Two more corridors and they would be coming up behind those focused on the main door. Raising their guard further, Riley slowed his group; their footsteps grew silent on the solid polished floor below.

Rounding the corner, Riley took two lookout Biron off guard as his movements were concealed with a glow of his light. Not using loud weapons or blasts, which would no doubt draw more attention, Riley relied on his sharpened blades, which easily sliced through the thick armor and flesh of the slow moving Birons.

Positioning himself and the remainder of his team, which now consisted of three other Jarly warriors, even he had to admit they were outnumbered by the current view; at least thirty heavy-set Birons trained their attention on the entrance of the solid control room door. Using make shift hammers, four were currently thrusting their might into each corner of the door, which could only withstand so much. The four watched as the top right hand corner began to buckle, causing a loud whistling of trapped cold air to seep out. The Birons grew bold with excitement as the four continued to beat harder.

Just as Riley ordered his men forward, in as much stealth as they could muster, a commotion sounded in the Biron occupied tunnel off to the right - which drew many away. Riley grinned and moved forward, knowing Caleb's team had already started the fight. Shortly after, Damon's voice could be heard; rage-filled, coming from the left flanks. Finding no further need for silence, Riley and the others surged forward, attacking those Birons who had their backs turned, preoccupied in the other fights.

As the fighting continued, making their way closer to the entrance, Riley did not need to look up to know that the door had been breached and the occupants were now in equal danger. Cold air tickled his skin as the airtight room mingled its environment with the warm air of the invading hallways. Moving with ease of speed, Riley and his team used the circular tunnel walls to twist and fight, seemingly defying gravity as they showed their infinite fighting abilities. Continuing to use their blades, and occasional blasts from their own light, they took on the masses.

With equal fighting capabilities, albeit much slower movements, the Birons fought back with hatred and rage. Riley watched in disgust as two Biron soldiers managed to fatally injure one of his own, then drag him to the floor behind, as they picked and tore as his dying body. Unable to save his comrade, Riley felt a small bite of satisfaction as he kicked off the tunneled wall, blade in hand, stabbing both Birons as he managed to run and spin his body into a guided flip; his blade drew up their bodies, releasing at their shoulders. They fell where they had stood.

Turning his attention to the door, he took advantage of the lack of attack and charged through the open doorway, lunging up the short stairs, reaching for the two Biron that currently had Amy cornered and spinning one towards the open space. Kicking his leg out, Riley made contact with the surprised Biron's chest before his body flew back out into the corridor, knocking over two others as it went; as the three fell to the ground below, Caleb and another from his team were already on top of them with their own attack.

Turning back, Riley watched the last moments of the remaining Biron's light fall from his eyes as Amy gained the upper hand, spinning her body in an elegant attack; the final blow came as Amy's lit palm made contact with his large chest, forcing him back and onto a broken shard of Amelia's commanding pod. Riley turned back to a breathless Amy, nodding once in recognition and acceptance as he continued further into the room, assisting Amelia as she protected a fallen Shouray; her leg badly bleeding and clearly broken. The elderly Jarly lay dead at their side with eyes open, as the last remnant of blood trickled from her nostrils and open mouth.

Riley, accompanied by Damon and two other Jarly, forced their way through the remaining Biron resistance, re-securing the room. As the final fight quieted outside, Riley took in the sight of his surroundings. Amy lounged exhausted against the only intact glass pod, her shoulders moving as she crouched over, hands on either knee; her light fading rapidly, flicking as it went. Ignoring the other bodies, Riley reached for Amelia as she had her back to him, crouching over Shouray who was now crying out in pain. Crouching around her body, Riley placed his freed hands on top of Amelia's as they went to work healing Shouray.

"Caleb?" Damon called out to his brother as he searched around the room, moving bodies, and searching the injured. "Caleb, get in here," he called again. The lack of movement gained his attention. Turning, he focused on the door as no one came. Fear covered his features as his lightning speed rushed him from the room.

As Amy went to follow, movement came out of the corner of her eye. Turning, she watched as a hidden Biron emerged from some fallen debris, weapon at the ready, his jagged blade seeking the flesh of Riley's turned back. With a scream, her light burst from her feet, and in lighting speed that she had yet to muster, she dove for the Biron's outstretched arm. With a vice-like grip, she pulled his arm down, kicking off the wall behind him and throwing her body weight around his shoulders; she continued pushing off the wall, spinning and distorting his body awkwardly as they fell as one to the ground. Her body hit the grated floor below with a vibrating thud, with his upper body quickly landing on top of hers. Wrapping her thighs tightly around his neck, tugging his bladed arms up, she locked her knees, while releasing her left hand; she pushed against the side of his face, continuing to tug his restricted arm. The force of her light filled her newly energized muscles, forcing her hand down, easily crunching the Biron's neck and silencing his groans. In an action that took less than ten seconds, Amy had silenced a Biron soldier easily three times her size with her own bare hands.

Still clenching his limp arm, Amy turned her attention to Riley and Amelia, who remained crouching only inches away; their palms still healing Shouray, who had fallen silent. Slowly, Amy unlocked her knees and pushed away from the Biron. Freed from his body, she watched as Amelia offered a surprised grin and Riley's jaw literally dropped.

"Did you seriously just use the arm-bar wrestling move with Amelia's force of light?" His smile grew wider, seemly unaffected by the surroundings. "That's probably the coolest move I've ever seen from a female Human fighting with our light, who taught you h…" His amazement was cut off by the pained cry of Damon, still out of sight.

"Riley!" Damon called out.

A second Jarly reached the broken doorway, partially leaning in. "Sir, we need you out here."

"Go!" Amelia pushed her back into Riley's chest, dislodging his hands from Shouray's almost healed wound.

Pulling Amy to her feet, the two rushed from the control room towards the moans and cries emanating from the near hallway. Within seconds they came to a halt next to Damon, who was now crouched in front of an unrecognizable Caleb. His body twisted and broken, the fingers of his left hand and forearm charred black, swollen like ashy remains. Slash wounds of various lengths and depths covered him from face to lower torso. His lower body twisted unnaturally. If not for the severe shaking of his right hand, reaching out towards his brother, Amy would have assumed he was already dead. No Human could withstand such torment. Damon hovered over his brother, both hands possessively claiming what flesh he could find and heal.

"You four... Here, now," Riley's words filled the hall, pulling the few Jarly away from searching and moving the dead. Riley placed his hand on Amy's shoulder, pulling her out of her trance. "Go warn Amelia. We need medical specialists here now. When we have done what we can; we will need to move him." Staring down at the fallen soldier he continued, "He needs Isobel."

In a frantic rush, Amy followed his request, dashing back into the room where Amelia was helping Shouray stand, leaning against the broken control panels. "It's Caleb," Amy blurted in a breathless rush. "He's hurt bad. Real bad." Amelia left Shouray, rushing towards the hallway. Amy quickly followed after, now speaking to the back of Amelia's head. "Riley said we need to call in some medical people. He needs Isobel."

Before exiting the room completely, Amelia turned, rushing towards the last intact pod, placing her hand against the glass. Closing her eyes, dropping her head, Amy understood that Amelia was silently speaking to another, searching and calling for help. When ready, Amelia moved in a blur, exiting the room and rushing towards the others.

CHAPTER NINETEEN

"Over here," Isobel ordered the four men, carrying the now unconscious Amadeus and Rick, to place their bodies separately on two empty exam tables. The tables looked hard and cold, the metal polished to reflective perfection. As the two Humans dropped Rick onto the hard surface, his body awoke, shock and the last remaining fight left him swinging his arms and legs frantically as he tried to escape. Mark and James dove for his limbs as he kicked and screamed, his eyelids too swollen to aid him.

"Dude, calm down... It's us...Shssshhh, calm down." James grew equally panicked at seeing his best friend so afraid and tormented.

Tears wetting her cheeks, Emily stood at the top of his table, lightly brushing his hair and cheeks, trying to sooth him without words. Isobel, who had been previously preoccupied preparing Amadeus, rushed over, knocking Mark to the side as she waved a lit hand a foot over Rick's struggling body. In an instant he grew still and his head fell to the side as sleep reclaimed him.

Passing James a pair of charcoal colored scissors, Isobel spoke before returning to the second table. "Remove his clothing, leave only his undergarments... Try to straighten him out, get his arms and legs fully on the table."

In a rush, James moved the sharp blades across Rick's clothing, tearing where he could, and ignoring the additional unseen wounds as he, Emily, and Mark carefully undressed his friend. The soiled mass of material now thrown aside, Rick's wounds still bled, wept, and covered the remaining pale skin in crimson red. Carefully adjusting his body, light moans escaped Rick's lips as they tugged his arms and legs into place. Isobel returned, glancing him over before placing a lit hand on the metal surface above Rick's right shoulder; pulling back, she stepped away.

160

Within seconds the table began to transform, the hard surface gave way to a milky gel-like substance that worked its way around Rick's body like memory foam, filling in the gaps and continuing up over his legs and torso; as the foam filled in around his shoulders and up past his ears, it paused along his jaw line leaving his eyes, lips, and nostrils unclaimed. The milky substance appeared to fizzle before it transformed into a lavender colored block, solidifying around the wounded flesh.

James and the others stepped back, amazed and in awe. Isobel returned to Rick's side, swiping at the air above his body. A holographic scan of his skeletal system and organs raised, appearing a foot above his stilled self. She scanned the hologram, moving and twisting it to get a better view. Mark stepped forward from the other side of the table, equally as interested.

"What's that?" James pointed, recognizing a tile-shaped object lodged within Rick's lower back, consuming the majority of his lumbar spine. Beneath the embedded skin, purple veins connected organic to metal, organ to machine.

Isobel scanned the device, her nose wrinkling in disgust, "It's a Reviver."

She turned to the two Jarly guards hovering behind her. Signaling towards Rick, the men engulfed their bodies in flame and positioned themselves at the head and foot of his table. Using their light to control him, Rick began to turn along with the metal below him, until the purple encasing was the only thing that held Rick from crashing to the floor. Clearly there to assist Isobel, the two men stood patiently gripping the two ends with their light as she stepped up, waving her hand along the mental before her. The Humans watched, mesmerized as the apparent metal moved in a block to reveal the underside of Rick's body. The purple casing morphed the flesh below it and with another wave of her hand, the purple disappeared, revealing the large metallic object.

For a moment Isobel froze, examining the object, giving Mark the chance to step up and ask questions. "What does a Reviver do?"

Isobel, deep in thought, had Mark asking his question again; the second time she did respond. "It's a crude technology that I haven't seen in decades." She traced her lit finger along its edges, causing the unit to jump half an inch from his body, though still secure in its placement, causing the surrounding flesh to bleed and twitch. She continued, "It was originally used to nourish those that were unable to gain sustenance the conventional way…those physically ill. It was embedded into the skin and provided for the individual, just enough to keep them alive, while healing damaged organs. Later, it was manipulated to hinder an individual in sinister ways, causing them paralysis upon the flick of a switch. The machine attaches itself via synthetic veins to all major organs" – Isobel gestured up and down along her torso – "and to the spinal cord and nervous system."

"Paralysis," Emily repeated, barely a whisper, shock and fear taking over.

"Yes. Whomever these monsters are wanted Rick and Amadeus alive long enough to endure what they had planned; their bodies rejuvenating just enough to keep them lucid, while weak enough to not put up much of a fight."

With great care and concentration, Isobel's fingertips gripped two sides of the device; pulling with gentle pressure, the disc began to rise. James had to grip Mark's near shoulder; hunching, he covered his mouth, thwarting his reflexes as the metal rose slowly, dragging out thin tendrils with it. To everyone's shock, and amazement, Isobel had to raise the device a full foot above Rick's body before the veins fully detached.

"Is he going to be okay?" James asked, pulling his hand away from his face, watching as more blood pooled and filled the indentation. Where the device had lain, the skin had been perforated but not removed.

"We will know soon enough." Isobel carefully moved the device aside, placing it on a near table and instructing the guards to return Rick to his upright position. In a flash, the purple encasing solidified once again, the metal table reformed, and Rick lay facing upwards.

After Isobel had successfully found and removed Amadeus' Reviver, she returned to examine Rick's hologram.

"His stomach and liver look inflamed, but I don't see any organ damage," Mark offered.

"Yes," Isobel muttered, still reviewing and touching markers on the colorful screen.

James and Emily, knowing far less about the workings of Human anatomy, stood a few steps back, shoulder to shoulder, watching Rick's steady heartbeat.

Mark inched closer, his left hand resting under his chin, index finger brushing over his lower lip as his brows creased, focusing. "Right Fib-Tib, as well as left Humorous, oblique fractures. Acromioclavicular looks separated." Isobel nodded in agreement as he went on. Following Isobel's steps, Mark reached forward as if to grab the hologram, twisting, and moving it to get a better zoom or angle. "Sternum is cracked just above the Ziphoid. Left coastal cartilage looks damaged." As Mark continued to list the injuries, he sighed in frustration, his brows continuing to knit. "Left ribs four, five… and seven, fractured."

Isobel swiped at the air dismissingly; the hologram faded out until it disappeared altogether. Leaving the room silent, the group watched Isobel as she closed her eyes, and placed her hand on the solidified mass above Rick's chest. Pinpointed lights appeared within the lavender solid, brightest over the areas of injury. Rick's face twitched with pain as his eyes darted fiercely beneath his eyelids. Isobel stepped back and pulled away as the lights continued to work, healing the numerous injuries.

Clearly satisfied with his current state, Isobel turn back to Amadeus, who was nearby within his own lavender surroundings. Mark and the others moved closer, crowding together as they watched the Jarly work under Isobel's lead. The hologram was still in place above his body. Amadeus' injuries clearly more severe than Rick's; hardly a single bone in his upper body remained intact. Mark had seen individuals struck by vehicles with less injury. Broken bones, torn muscles, and ruptured organs riddled Amadeus' frail self. As more Jarly laid their hands to the solid mass, there seemed to be no lavender remaining. Once complete, the aiding team stepped back to reveal a fully glowing shell encasing their true Commander.

"When will you know if it's working?" Mark asked, stepping up beside Isobel.

"Soon. We should see his vital signs increase rapidly in a matter of moments. I think we found them just in time," Isobel answered. The whites of her eyes shone with flickering yellow light as they focused on the task before them.

A loud rush of commotion drew the room's attention behind them. The Jarly in the room ignited their bodily flame, focusing and preparing for what may come. Suddenly, the entrance doors burst open to reveal Damon, Riley, Amelia, and a number of Jarly in medical uniform. Seemingly floating within the circle of their group, Caleb lay, unmoving.

"Isobel," Damon called out as the group pushed forward, carefully placing Caleb on a third table.

Tearing at his brother's clothing, Damon and the others prepared him before he slammed his palm onto the table below, facilitating the white gel. In a rush, Damon ignored the others as he pulled up the hologram and pure pain covered his face; taking a step back he gasped, hunched over. The hologram revealed severe internal bleeding, organ failure. The red flashing lights within the graphics needed no explanations -- dead and/or dying materials.

Isobel rushed towards the group. "Let me through. Let me through," she pushed her way past the others. "Caleb!" The cry of his name clung in the air. Fresh tears filled her vision as she touched his naked cheek and glanced up at the visual above her. Her eyes not leaving the screen, she spoke clearly, "Out! I need room to work and focus. Anyone not vital to their recovery, please leave the room. Wait outside." Slashing at the screen, she violently moved the image around, stopping and marking off as she went. Quickly she pushed it aside and began filling his lavender pod with just as many healing lights as Amadeus'.

The occupants of the room dwindled, leaving Damon perched at the top of his brother's encasing. Emily, Mark, and James hovered silently near Rick, as Riley and Amelia waited by Amadeus' side. Isobel, now fully focused, supervised the healing of the three men, checking on lights, raising and lowering their holographic replicas to determining progress. Staying close to the wall, the others desperately tried to stay out of her way in complete silence.

Rounding the corner of the open doorway, the others looked up in time to see Amy enter, with Shouray's left arm thrown around her shoulders as she helped Shouray limp her way into the medical room, following Isobel's silent order directing them towards the vacant tables and chairs. Soon after more injured followed, further filling the room as medical staff came to their attention. Resting in a near chair, Amy released her friend. Turning, she rushed towards Emily who was already making her way to her sister. In a small clash they engulfed one another in a strong embrace. Emily squeezed her sister before pulling back, cupping her face in each hand, and searching for any signs of distress or added injury.

Pulling her hands away, Amy briefly smiled, "I'm fine," before pulling her sister into another hug. She drew in a deep breath before opening her eyes wide, focusing on the glowing lavender cocoon that she recognized to be housing her husband. Pushing her sister aside, Amy rushed to Rick's table, placing her hands on the solid barrier; she could only clearly see his swollen, bruised, and bloody face. Muffling her cries, she covered her mouth with her hand as she glanced from him to James and Mark, who remained along the wall at the top of his bed.

"He's healing quickly, Amy," James stepped forward towards her, before pulling her into his own embrace and shushing her muted cries. "He's a bit banged up and sore, but he's on the mend. It's only a matter of time... Give him some time." Amy turned her head, still holding tight to James, as she watching Rick's face occasionally twitch and move.

As Amelia stood by Amadeus, absently examining his hologram, she was approached by two Jarly. One still wore torn and blood-smeared clothing, though he did not seem injured himself. "Ma'am, we have successfully detached the Biron pods from the station, and now we can rebuild the shields around the weakened hull."

"Good. Have we heard from Bazza?" Amelia asked, giving them her full attention.

"Yes, they are staying back, following in stealth. It appears the escape vessel is approaching another Biron fleet," the second Jarly answered.

"Their location?" Riley asked.

Shaking his head before he answered, the first Jarly continued, "Destination, so far unknown. No planets or known bases nearby."

"Okay, I'm ordering a pursuit. Get us moving, but stay out of their radar range." Turning to the second Jarly, she went on, "Continue to take count of the injured, bring any remaining here." Amelia turned back to Riley, who had stepped away from the near wall and listened in on their current conversation, "Sweep the station one more time. I don't want any more surprises." He nodded, then moved from the room, barking orders as he went.

Amelia turned to the injured, scanning the room before her sight landed on Shouray, whose lone leg from hip to ankle was currently encased in the lavender solid. Within seconds Amelia was at her side. "How are you feeling?" Shouray was taken off guard, not noticing Amelia's approach.

"Much better. It's still broken," she gestured with her chin towards the glowing cast, "But it should be good as new in a few moments."

"That's wonderful to hear," Amelia hesitated before continuing. "Shouray, how long before you and your team can return to the core?"

"Ma'am?" Shouray asked, confused and clearly needing more to go on.

"We need those scanners back up and running. We need to be cloaked from the Biron sensors, close range, and if possible we need to be able to track their internal communications."

"As soon as I'm healed I can return with the others, but Amelia…" she gazed up at her leader, "our frequency cloaking all but exploded before you pulled us out of there. If it hasn't already, we will need to start over and that could take days working around the clock."

Amelia nodded. "Well, we don't have days, so what do you need?"

"More people, at least ten, but even then we can only do so much at a time. It's not going to be a quick fix," Shouray gave her honest answer.

"Understood. What about the scanners and communications?" Amelia asked, trying to ignore the growing conversation of pain and suffering around them.

"The scanners will be ready in a matter of moments. I had to shut them down to prevent damage. The internal communications… I will do what I can; if you can give me some Biron systems experts, we can sync up their systems with ours, while hopefully remaining undiscovered. We wont be able to communicate, only listen in."

Placing her hand on Shouray's shoulder, Amelia smiled, "That's all we need." Pulling back, she called Darius forward, as he was helping the injured find a place to be seen. Rushing over, Amelia continued, "Darius, listen to Shouray, organize any team and support she may need." He nodded, giving her his full attention. It did not go unmissed as a slight blush filled Shouray's cheeks and she tried to hide a flustered smile as her eyes locked with his.

"How is he?" Amelia had moved away and stood at the foot of Caleb's bed, the glow of his encasing still strong and working hard.

Isobel stood off to his left side, her focus trained on the hologram above. It took her a moment to answer, her gaze dropping to Damon who stood at his brother's head, his arms outstretched leaning on the edge of the table.

"It is okay," Damon spoke softly in encouragement.

Isobel turned back to the screen. "He is healing. The internal bleeding has been taken care of, though there is slight organ damage and scarring that will not be fixed quickly. He will be in recovery and subjected to this numerous times as his body grows stronger." She paused briefly, then spoke in a rush, "The external damage caused by the Biron blast has rendered his left hand and lower forearm too damaged to repair." Damon's head whipped up towards the screen. "Damon... Caleb will lose the use of his hand, along with the necrosis covering his left shoulder and pectoral."

"But he will live?" Damon asked.

"Yes, but his recovery will be long and painful." Isobel's response sounded cold and distant, though she felt anything but. "I'm sorry."

Damon rounded the table, pulling Isobel's attention to him as he held her upper arms. "You have saved his life. He will make it. He will come out of this because of you." Amelia watched the display before her, not moving or speaking. Damon spoke over Isobel's shoulder, "I will not leave his side until he wakes." Amelia agreed, not expecting anything else.

Turning away, leaving Damon and Isobel to continue, Amelia stepped up to Rick's table. She noticed with immense satisfaction that the lavender casing had lowered in areas that healing was no longer needed; his chest being the main focus now. She raised her palm, resting it on Amy's back as she lightly rubbed in reassurance. Amy turned, pulling from James' embrace.

"He's healing well. He shouldn't be in there for much longer."

* * *

"Amelia!" Riley called as he rounded the corner of the medical doors, dragging a wounded, but very alive, Biron behind him. Three Jarly followed.

"Over there!" she called, ordering them to the far end of the room, partially shielded from view of the injured and interested.

Throwing the Biron against the wall, he hissed and snarled, pulling himself away from his capturers. Thick dark fluid oozed from wounds across his chest and right thigh.

Riley's head tilted to the side, pure hatred emanated from his words as he spoke, "Found him cowering in the Biron quarters off of the conference room."

Amelia listened with intent, her focus on the Biron before her. "You're dying," she spoke quickly, "Answer my questions and we will give you aid."

Letting out a gargled laugh, he leant forward to spit at her feet. Riley moved forward in rage before Amelia stopped him in place. Turning to the three guards, "Lift him."

They moved forward, the Biron pulling away and struggling before she waved her lit hand, locking the muscles of his lower body, releasing his ability to struggle. Only his head remained moving, swiveling from side to side.

"Release me!" The Biron's deep voice demanded; his chin falling to his chest, watching his ridged body stand, the two Jarly at either side holding him in place.

Stepping forward, Amelia stood only inches away from the Biron himself, though he towered over her by at least a foot. Slowly and showing no fear, she asked, "Where have the others escaped to? What is Bates' role in the Biron resistance?"

The Biron didn't offer any answers, merely smirking at her inquires. Growing frustrated, Amelia raised her palm out and motioning it forward, not looking as the five-inch blade released from the grip of the third guard, soaring past her, and into the upper mass of the Birons left clavicle.

"You think this is a game, Biron!" Amelia roared, spitting her words as the Biron screamed out in pain. Her grip found the handle of the blade, tugging it sharply, it slipped from his flesh followed by more blackened liquid. The leather-like skin of his face scrunched and distorted in agony. Spinning the blade she lunged again forcing the blade lengthwise below his chin, raising it up, and gaining his attention. "Speak," she muttered through clenched teeth.

"Kavar," the weakened Biron practically snarled.

Riley stepped forward. "What did you say?" Amelia raised the blade higher, elevating his chin, reiterating the demand.

"Kavar!" The Biron barked.

"You lie. Kavar is dead." Riley inched closer, now at Amelia's side.

The Biron shook his head, the only muscles he could currently control. "No," his face scrunched once again as he fought through the growing pain, "He has returned and united us. We follow him in the fight for what belongs to us."

"And what would that be?" Amelia asked with heavy sarcasm.

Leaning his head as far forward as he could manage, the Biron paused only inches from her and roared, "Earth!" His struggle took what energy remained, as his head fell forward and his eyes closed into unconsciousness.

Stepping back in disgust, Amelia spoke to the three guards, "Take him to a holding room, heal him, and bind him. He could be of more use." Releasing her hold on his body, the Biron fell into their arms as they carried him from the room.

Riley and Amelia stood in place, turning his body into hers, whispering, "If their target is Earth, we need to warn the others."

Amelia agreed, her eyes sweeping up to his, "Call a meeting in the conference room in one hour's time. Only those of rank, as well as the Humans."

Riley remained in place as his left hand raised- lit with flickering light- to softly caress her cheek and heal a slight gash forgotten in their haste. She offered him a weak smile, tilting her face into his touch. Leaning down, he sought her lips; rising up onto her tiptoes, she offered them to him. The peck of their lips meant more to them than what a bystander would observe. Then in a flash he was gone.

CHAPTER TWENTY

"Wait here," Julia turned, reaching for the hand release, edging her car door open.

"No, wait! You need to stay here, I'll go," Abel turned, emphatic.

Julia reached over grasping his shoulder, "Abel, I'm fine now, and I can take care of myself. They clearly want to talk, and I think they need to talk to me." He tried to protest, but was distracted by the engulfing of her own flame. Her light grew strong and bright, "I've got this."

Without another word she used heightened speed to release herself from the vehicle and round to the front. With at least fifteen feet between her and the five unknown, she took a few steps forward before pausing, waiting for their next move.

After a moment of silence, a slender man to the right of center stepped forward, "Julia Pinter?" His voice was deeper than most as he spoke slowly and clearly. Taking another step forward, raising his hands in surrender, " My name is Marcel. Please hear me; you need not fear us. We have been sent by Amelia and her council."

Taking two steps closer, Julia's words came with a flood of emotion, "What's happened? Why are you here? Where's my family? Why haven't I heard from them?"

Raising his hands higher, Marcel attempted to halt her questioning, "Please, let us discuss this inside."

"You're not taking a step inside that door until you tell us exactly who you are and what you are doing here," Abel's voice rang loud and clear as he stepped up to join Julia. He settled Julia's shaking - which she had not noticed until then - by taking her hand in his and offering a light squeeze in reassurance.

"Abel Jones," a second man stepped forward, closer than Marcel. His features were illuminated by his flame and the brightness of the car's headlights. The same height as Abel himself, it did not go unnoticed that he and Marcel were clearly related, brothers perhaps. The slight difference shone through their eyes. Where Marcel's were dark, appearing to be all pupil, this man's eyes were crystal blue and with his flame enhancing their beauty, they appeared to glow. With a surprisingly Human gesture, he pushed his hand forward as if to shake Abel's. "My name is Christopher, and we, Abel, have been sent to protect you and your kind from the immanent Biron invasion."

* * *

"I see you've recovered well." Julia rounded the base of the stairs, returning from laying Sophie down for the night. She must have looked surprised by his comment as she stopped in her tracks. "News of your attack spread quickly. I'm glad you are thriving again." Marcel remained formal as he and Christopher sat across from John at the dinner table. Abel chose to stand behind John, leaning against the kitchen island as a third Jarly stood silently behind the brothers. The other two chose to remain outside, patrolling the grounds.

Offering a fleeting smile, Julia glanced at Abel before taking the seat next to John, resting her elbows on the table as she leant forward. Marcel remained focused on the two before him, while Christopher glanced between the three, his eyes falling on Abel often.

"So you're here as a protection detail," Julia said abruptly; it wasn't a question.

"Yes. When news broke of Velo's death, our council went into high alert. We have been tracking all known Biron movements in this and neighboring quadrants. With the well-known desires of many Biron renegades, increasing threats, Amelia, acting as leader in the immediate affairs, ordered our team to join you while we await for further orders," Marcel explained, before taking a sip of iced water.

"So this is all based on the assumption of an impending attack. Nothing has actually been set in motion?" John queried skeptically.

"Theoretically, yes. No formal attack plan or orders have been intercepted."

"But three fleets of Biron ships have been called into the quadrant and are in pursuit of Earth as we speak." Christopher's piercing eyes landed on John as he spoke.

John turned back to Abel, as some unknown message seemed to pass between them. Though they did not yet have the Jarly bond of communication, they didn't need it. They have been good friends long enough to know where each other's minds were headed.

"How long?" Abel stepped forward, resting his hands on the back of the chair to John's right. "How long before they could reach Earth?"

Marcel shook his head with uncertainty, not blinking, "With their current projections, they could be here within a day, perhaps two."

"What type of vessels are we talking about here? How many?" Julia asked.

There was an uncomfortable pause as the brothers looked at one another, clearly unsure of how much information to share.

"What?" John leaned forward emphasizing his full attention.

With a nasally huff Marcel clasped his hands together atop the table. "The fleets each consist of seven heavily manned, battle ready, war vessels. Fully stocked with a number of volatile Biron weapons, filled with Birons under the orders of a few who believe Earth to be theirs for the taking."

"We've seen these formations in the past, with larger planets being taken by less sophisticated artillery," Christopher added.

"So they've sent the five of you?" Abel pushed back from the chair, turning in anger as he raked his hand through his thick dark hair.

"Have they sent other teams? Alerted our governments? What is your defensive plan?" John rose from his seat, now pacing.

A soft "No" filled the room as Christopher's word stopped Abel and John in their tracks.

Julia's jaw slackened as she turned to Marcel, "What do you mean, no?" Outrage filled her breath.

"Thus far, our orders have been to join you and stay put until further information is provided. We are the only team that has been relocated at this time."

"Great," Abel muttered, "Well that's fucking fantastic." He stormed past the group and out onto the adjacent back deck, slamming the door as he went.

John turned to Julia, her eyes closed in contemplation. "I have to contact my family, are you okay?" He slightly tilted his head towards the silent brothers.

She nodded in encouragement, "I'm fine. Go phone them."

He rose from his seat, heading towards the front of the house, exiting out the front door. As the silence grew, Julia turned back to Marcel, "Have you heard from Amelia about Amadeus and Rick?"

"Yes, there has been news of their rescue." Marcel offered her a friendly smile, his eyes brimming with sympathy, as she could not hold back her tears of joy.

"They're okay? They're all safe?" she smiled through her tears.

"They are alive, though badly injured." Her smile fell as fast as it came. "They are currently under surveillance and continued medical attention. Only time will tell of their recovery."

"What about the rest of the team?" *James? Baby, are you there?*

"As far as we have been advised, only minor injuries were sustained by your immediate team. There were many lives lost among the extended Human soldiers," Christopher spoke now.

James, answer me! Nothing. *Emily?*

"Why can't I hear them anymore? I've been trying for hours." Her words broke in a painful plea.

"We have not heard from the leaders either. They could be resting or too preoccupied to answer. Please give them some more time before jumping to any conclusions. They are all exhausted and in need of sleep." Marcel's sympathy appeared genuine, as he half reached across the table.

Resolved to his recommendation, Julia stood slowly. The men watched as she made her way out onto the deck, silently. Reaching out, she laid her hand softly on the center of Abel's back. When he turned, he engulfed her in a comforting hug and they held on to each other, unmoving, as she buried her face into his t-shirt and wept.

* * *

"Kristine?" John held his cell phone to his right ear, moving to the side of the front porch, taking a seat in one of the white wicker chairs. He watched as the guard-detail walked the front borders of the property, their signifying light no longer ablaze. "Kristine, are you there?"

"Hi, yes I'm here," Kristine broke away, distracted by a woman - her mother - asking her to shut the door.

"Are the kids still with you?"

"They're just getting ready for bed; Dad's gonna take them out first thing in the morning. How is Julia doing?"

"She's good, she's fully healed, and back to herself."

"That's great. So, what are you doing now?"

"Baby, look. This is really hard to explain over the phone, but I need you to cut your visit short, pack the kids up, get on a plane and get back to Arizona as soon as you can. I'll pick you up at their airport… In fact, bring your parents too."

"What? John, what are you talking about? It's almost ten o'clock, I can't get a flight last minute, and the kids are exhausted."

"Kristine, please," John started, but she cut him off.

"No, John. Tell me what's going on, right now," Kristine ordered, anger clearly raising in her voice. "You're being ridiculous."

"Kristine, I'm here with Julia, Abel, and Sophie. Five other Jarly have shown up and believe a Biron attack force is on its way. They could be here as early as tomorrow."

"Whoa, hold up. What? What are you talking about?"

"Please baby, I don't have time to explain it all right now. I just need you to trust me on this and get moving."

"John, you're scaring me."

"You should be scared, but it's going to be okay. I need you here with me; this is about to become the most protected area in the United States and you need to get here now."

"I…I…" She stuttered, unsure of what to say.

"Don't think baby, just do it. Put Richard on the phone while you go get the kids ready. Don't tell them anything."

"Okay," she whispered. He could hear the heavy shifting of her feet as she clearly went back into the house, the heavy metal door of the bug-screen loudly smacking the frame as she entered. Finding her father, John could hear him clear his throat as he took the phone in hand.

"John." Richard's voice was always solid and to the point.

"Hello Richard, I've told Kristine to get the kids ready and for all of you to get on a plane back to Arizona tonight."

"What's all this about, John? Kristine just came in, white as a ghost, and rushed out of the room."

"Richard, I need you to trust me on this. Something big is about to happen and it's not safe for you where you are. I need you all to get on the next plane and I promise to explain everything when you get here. I need you to keep everyone calm and … Just trust me. Please, can you do that for me?" In his early seventies, Richard took care of himself both mentally and physically. Thankfully, he and John had grown close over the years and he held John in high regard.

"Okay, John. I'm going to trust you on this one and take a leap of faith. You know how much Joan hates to fly, as well. You better have a good explanation when we land."

John's relief was clearly heard thought the receiver, "Thank you, Richard. I appreciate it. Have Kristine message me the flight details when you arrive. I'll pick you all up at the airport the moment you land."

With that, they hung up and John moved on to his next conversation; a telepathic communication with his bonded Jarly, Toby.

Toby, have you heard?

It took only moment for Toby to respond. *Yes, I have just communed with my commander. I am to return to my station until further orders are commissioned. Are you with Julia Pinter now?*

Yes, but we still don't know much. Are they really here to just babysit us?

John, this is serious and you are in need of protection. Marcel and his team are among the best warriors we have, and they will stop at nothing to protect you and yours.

A wave of relief filled John as he continued. *I've contacted Kristine. She's bringing her family here now.*

Good. That's good. But I do recommend keeping this news to the few. We don't need mass hysteria to break loose before we can get a hold on the situation and know more.

Yeah, I understand that. Please, keep me informed if you hear more.
Of course. Be safe, John.

* * *

"Have we heard from the others yet?" John stepped back into the house, phone still in hand, as he noticed only Marcel and Christopher remained at the table; Abel and Julia still stood, embracing one another on the back deck.

"We are still waiting to hear from the station controlled by Amelia and her team. My council has posted various vessels around earth for the time being. We will let you know as soon as more information is provided," Marcel said, sitting still in his chair, hands folded atop the table.

John remained standing, now leaning against the kitchen island as Abel once was. "So, now what?" Christopher's brow twitched with a hint of confusion, encouraging John to continue, "Shouldn't we be doing something? Shouldn't we be out there, actively warning people or at least be doing something other than sitting here and waiting for the Birons to come knocking at our doors?"

"We understand your unease, John," Marcel leant forward in his chair, "But the best course of action at this point in time is to stay put and wait for further orders. Please believe me when I tell you that the Jarly council is working with Earth's various governments, convening as we speak, to try and avoid any catastrophic events."

Still not convinced by their answer, John folded his arms and remained silent in thought.

"Are Kristine and the kids on their way?" John was pulled out of his planning by Julia as she and Abel stepped back into the house. The cool night's air filled the room temporarily.

"Yeah, she's bringing her parents as well. They should be boarding the next plane… She's going to text me the details, then I'll have to go and pick them up in Mark's SUV. Do you know where the keys are?"

Julia walked past John - into the kitchen - to pull open one of the end kitchen draws below the phone and note pad. Swiping her hand around the heavy contents she pulled out a set of keys, turning to pass them into

John's outstretched hand. 'They had to put them all in here... Sophie kept stealing them and hiding them." Julia spoke with a smile.

"John, there is no need for a flight. I would prefer it if you would let my team retrieve your family." Marcel stood, drawing the other's attention.

"You mean with your light? That teleporting thing?" John asked.

Marcel nodded.

"Yeah, um... Thanks, but no. My family is freaked out enough as it is and my father-in-law is still just coming around to the Jarly. No offense. The flight will tire the kids out enough to keep them manageable."

"Very well. One of my team members will have to accompany you to the airport upon their arrival. I cannot allow anyone to go unguarded."

With a hesitant sigh, John began to nod his head. "Okay, thanks."

"I'll just stay here with Julia," Abel added, wanting to make sure John knew the plan.

Three hours later and John was pulling the SUV around front.

"Are you sure you don't want to go with him?" Julia asked Abel as she comforted a teary Sophie, rocking her softly near the front entrance. Her puffy red eyes barely remained open as she cradled the bottle of milk Julia pressed to her lips.

Abel smiled down, watching her every move, "She looks so much like Emily, it's kinda freaky." Julia nodded in agreement. Abel ran his hands over his face, drawing in a deep breath, "No, John will be fine. He's just gonna bring them back here anyway. I think he needed some time to figure out how he's going to explain all this mess."

Just to be sure, Abel stepped out onto the front porch when he saw the vehicle's headlights drift across the front room. In the middle of the night, the darkness filled in any and all spaces, drawing Abel's gaze to John who remained seated, waiting for Christopher's company. Strolling up to the driver's window - the gravel crunching below his feet - Abel watched as John lowered his window.

"You okay, John? Want me to come?" Abel asked, leaning down to rest his forearms on the side paneling.

"Nah, I'll be fine. Just stay here with Julia. We shouldn't be too long."

"What are you going to tell Kristine?"

"The truth… Well, as much as I can say in front of the kids and her parents. I just know Richard is going to grill me as soon as we get in the car." Like Abel, John raised his hand, rubbing the sleep from his eyes. A familiar crunch behind Abel alerted him to Christopher's approach.

"Well maybe don't say anything until you get back here. Let Marcel explain the situation. Maybe we'll have more information by then and we can stop them from worrying so much. You know how her mom gets… Maybe with him in the car too, they wont ask so many questions."

The passenger door unlatched, swinging wide, before Christopher nestled into his seat. Readying himself, he turned expectantly towards John and Abel.

"Guess we better get going," John stated as Abel grinned, leaning back out of the car's reach recognizing the awkward tone in John's voice. "See you in an hour or so," John added, before hitting the gas and driving down the driveway, leaving Abel standing in the dark, dew-filled night.

CHAPTER TWENTY-ONE

"Have you heard from Julia?" Emily nervously asked, leaning on the hard wooden table in front of her, loudly whispering to James. The pair, along with Mark, accompanied by the remaining Human teams, waited patently in the large conference room. Riley had advised them to meet the others there within the hour.

"No," James continued in whisper, "I've tried, but nothing."

"They're probably just sleeping," Mark answered their concerns.

"Aye, it mist be th' middle o' th' night back home. Dinnae worry youself aboot that now," Reid leaned forward, speaking around James.

Emily stared at him, mouth open as if she wanted to respond, but she closed it quickly, sinking back into her seat.

"Baby, they're fine. Let's just focus on this for now," Mark whispered.

In silence, the remaining Humans grew frustrated, clearly not used to waiting and wondering. Eventually the grand doors opened, revealing Amelia and Riley in the lead, followed closely by at least twelve others. Filling in the remaining chairs around the tables, the Humans leaned forward to focus on Amelia, who now took her seat at the very end.

Riley sat next to Amelia, then searched the other end of the table, stopping on Mark, "I've spoken to Isobel, Rick has regained consciousness. She and Amy are with him now. Hopefully, he will have heard some conversation while captured and can help us further."

"What about Amadeus and Caleb?" Mark asked. The absence of Damon did not go unnoticed.

"Continuing with their healing, but it will be morning before either awaken... Caleb, maybe longer," Amelia answered. After a pause she cleared her throat and acknowledged the others waiting patiently around the room, "Firstly, I want to thank each and every one of you for your continued efforts and assistance. It will not be forgotten." No comment came, but after a few smiles and nods of encouragement, Amelia chose to continue. "As you all know, we recently found an injured Biron hiding within the station. We have since healed his wounds and continue to probe him for information on the Biron attack and intentions."

"What do you know, so far?" James asked, clearly wanting to get to the point.

"It appears that a particularly brutal Biron from Amadeus' past has returned. Long believed dead, it is understood that he is the cause of the Biron attack and leads many in his own agenda."

"Which is?" Mark asked.

Amelia glanced at Riley. Understanding, he turned to the others, "In Kavar's last rise to power he led a small group in an uprising against those who sought to protect the natural rights of planets that would offer valuable resources to the Biron people… It seems Kavar has once again gained strength within his people and has set his sights on his next invasion. He would seek to ignore the Jarly and Biron high council treaty and control the rich resources available for grabs."

"Meaning?" James asked again, frustrated.

Before anyone else could speak, Emily spoke up. "Earth. Meaning he wants to invade and consume the resource we have." She looked to Amelia for confirmation, which took form in a single nod.

James shook his head, "Well, what the fuck does that mean? What now?"

Before anyone could answer, Emily turned to Amelia, "Get us back to Earth, now!" Clearly fear and concern were overcoming her.

Amelia raised her hand. "Please. Don't worry, we are returning as we speak," she watched as Emily let out a deep breath, sinking back into her chair. "I have recalled Bazza; he observed the lone escape vessel enter a cluster of stationary Biron fleet. For now they are unmoving, not even on a path for Earth. Please remember that this information was given by a captured Biron, who was clearly unstable and eager to distract us; for now, we have made contact with those of us that remain on Earth and they are warning others and preparing."

"I want my wife warned and protected," James blurted.

"Yes, we have already sent word to a nearby team, which is en route to the Claybourne's residence now," Amelia calmed him.

CHAPTER TWENTY-TWO

"Anything?" Abel asked Julia; the pair, wanting some space from the patrolling Jarly, had taken themselves off up to the spare bedroom. Abel now sat in the single chair, having removed his shoes; his sock-covered feet lay crossed at the ankle, resting on the end of the bed. Julia lay flat, playing with her wedding rings, as Sophie returned to sleep in the Pack 'n Play in the far corner of the room.

James? James? Baby, can you hear me?

Emily? Are you there? What is going on?

Julia had been trying to contact the others nonstop for the past hour.

"Nothing yet," Julia moaned.

"Hey, it's going to be okay. I'm sure they are just a bit distracted at the moment." Abel gently knocked her foot with his.

"Yeah, distracted by what? Are they is trouble? Are they DEAD? Or are they just sleeping?"

James! Answer me, right now.

As the minutes passed only more dread and fear filled Julia's body and soul.

* * *

Julia, are you there?

With a sudden gasp that woke Abel from his doze Julia sat upright, her hands supporting her body. Abel knew immediately by her distant gaze that she was no longer seeing him, but was deep in conversation.

Where have you been? Why haven't you responded?

I'm sorry, baby. A lot of stuff has happened here and I couldn't focus on this. Are you okay? James tried to placate.

Yes, I'm fine. I'm just here with Abel and Sophie. Are you okay? You sound different... How's Rick?

I'm fine; I'm just exhausted. Rick is healed; he's doing a lot better.

Good. So are you on your way home? Hope bloomed in her chest.

We are, we just had a bit of a snag when it comes to the propulsion system.

What do you mean, "Snag?"

Well, lets just say we sustained some damage and are having a bit of a hard time moving at the moment. Even in telepathic communication Julia could tell when James was hiding something.

What? James, what aren't you telling me?

It's nothing, baby. Just know that we are all okay, and as soon as we get this thing up and running we will be home in no time.

And in the meantime... James, there are Jarly here guarding us like we are prisoners.

Good! Just do what they say and stay put. I don't need to be worrying about you too.

James...

Julia, seriously... Don't worry about us; I'll make sure I check in more often. I'll let you know as soon as I hear more. Just stay put, okay?

Okay, but you better check in more often, or I will have your balls when you step through that door.

Yes, ma'am. Julia could actually hear the laughter in James' voice. *Love you, babe.*

Blinking rapidly, Julia was pulled back into the bedroom.

"So?" Abel encouraged.

"Something isn't right, but for whatever reason James didn't want to tell me. He basically said their space station has stalled and they are working to get it moving again. As soon as it does, they are heading straight back here."

"Where are they now?"

"No idea. Obviously, far enough away that they cant light-jump back here." Julia stood, stretching her legs as she stepped into the adjacent bathroom to splash water onto her face. Returning to the room she asked, "Want something to eat?"

"Julia..." Abel stood, concern evident.

"Look," Julia whispered, her gaze dropping to the Pack 'n Play, "I'm worried, but at least I know they are okay for now. There's nothing more we can do. James just said to stay put and to do whatever Marcel and his team want, and they will be back here as soon as they can. In the meantime, I need a distraction and I could really go for some coffee and something hot to eat, so are you hungry? Want some pancakes?"

Not pushing the subject further Abel agreed, gently pulling the door ajar, leaving Sophie to sleep in peace.

CHAPTER TWENTY-THREE

In the silence of night, the soft glow of healing crystals reflected off of Amy's glazed eyes; her chin resting on her folded arms atop Rick's table. His eyes still remained closed and his body remained unmoving as the colorful lights worked to heal his wounded flesh. Gradually, as the night progressed, more of his flesh revealed, slightly pink from the rapid rejuvenation, and felt warm to touch. Every now and then Amy found herself reaching out for him, needing to feel his skin against her, reminding herself that he was there and not a figment of her damaged imagination. In the lightest of caresses, Amy ran her fingers along his cheek, down his neck, tracing the lines of his body as her gaze focused on his still encased torso; the lights still glowing strong above his heart.

Sitting up from her trance, she glanced around the room. Caleb and Amadeus remained almost fully encased as Damon and Isobel stood by. Emily and the others had left over an hour ago, seeking answers and updates the meant nothing to Amy; her only focus right now was on the man she loved, laying still before her. Pacing the room, Amy drew closer to Isobel who was currently reviewing Amadeus' hologram for the hundredth time.

"How is he?" Amy whispered, glancing over Isobel's shoulder.

"Better," Isobel answered, before turning, "But he's not responding to treatment as rapidly as I had hoped." Amy only nodded, not fully understanding what that meant; her gaze falling to the encased man she considered her friend.

As Isobel raised her hand to rest it on Amy's shoulder, the touch felt like an electric shock, drawing her attention. "How are you doing?"

"Me?"

Isobel nodded in encouragement, then continued after no response, "You've been through a lot in the last short while. Not only physically, but mentally as well."

"I'm fine...Really, I am." Isobel didn't look convinced. "Okay, I'm exhausted and sore all over, but nothing a long bath and good night sleep cant fix. And before you say anything, I'm not leaving his side until we get back home."

Offering Amy a genuine smile, Isobel walked past her, her movements encouraging Amy to follow as they both returned to Rick's table, pulling up his own hologram. After a moment of review, Isobel turned to Amy who patiently waited for an update; her gaze darting between the graphics and Isobel.

"He's progressing nicely; responding to all treatment. He is almost completely healed, apart from the fractures of his ribs and damaged spleen." Turning back to the hologram, Isobel continued, "Given his rate of healing and the remaining trauma, I would estimate two maybe three more hours of healing at most."

"Good," the word was past Amy's lips before the meaning came to her, "That's good." She moved around Isobel to take up her vacated seat, and leant down to brush her fingers through Rick's hair.

Isobel took her leave, silently moving towards Caleb's encasing, continuing a previous discussion with Damon who was more animated as his brother's recovery progressed.

* * *

The feather-like touch of warm fingers along Amy's cheek startled her awake. Sitting up, alert, her eyes searched the room, now filled with Emily and the others smiling down at the table before her. Amy's gaze returned to Rick, his eyes now open wide, with a playful grin pulling at his lips.

"Rick!" Amy exclaimed, her eyes flooding with fresh tears as she lunged towards him. Her hands encased the sides of his face as their lips smacked hard into one another. Worried that she may have hurt him, she began to pull back before his strong hand came up, pulling the back of her head closer, resealing their kiss.

After a moment, and a forceful cough from James, Amy pulled back, embarrassed by their display. Her questions came in a rush as she scanned his body and noticed the lavender casing no longer remained, "How do you feel? Are you okay? Are you in any pain? Are you cold?" Then catching her breath, she turned to the others, "Where's Isobel? Can we get him some clothes or something? It's freezing in here."

Rick's voice came out in a slow scratchy whisper, "Baby, slow down. I'm okay, just a bit of a headache and I feel stiff all over. I actually feel pretty warm at the moment." His newly revealed flesh was still lightly pink.

"Isobel just checked on him and said when he is ready we can move him to your room," Emily gave some reassurance.

"We're heading home." James added, "Back to Earth. We should be there in less than a day."

"Thank fuck for that," Rick made the group laugh, then cringe as he made to sit up.

"Rick, stay still for a bit." James stepped forward, lightly pressing his friend's shoulder, encouraging him to stay down.

"Please, baby," Amy begged, her hand resting on his chest, holding him in place.

"No," his hands gripped the sides of the tables as he forced past their gentle restraints. "I can't lay here anymore; just let me sit up." They removed their hands, replacing them at his back, helping to support his rise, which still seemed to cause pain to etch into his face.

"Rick?" Amy asked, worried.

"Seriously, everyone, I feel good; a lot better than I did. Every muscle feels stiff and bruised, is all. I just need to get up and move."

Nodding, the group turned silently to Mark to offer insight. Understanding their looks, he too stepped closer to the table. "Rick, can you turn and swing your legs over the side of the table. I wanna take a look at you." Rick complied with slow and stiff movements. Amy rounded the table to remain at his side, causing Emily to step back.

The others watched as Mark checked and manipulated Rick's body, searching for pupillary response and pressing on his abdomen. "Nothing hurts?" Mark's touch was light, but focused.

Shaking his head, Rick watched the examination continue before his eyes. "No... like I said, every muscle in me feels bruised and this headache could go away any time now, but I feel good."

Stepping back, Mark crossed his arms, "Well, everything looks normal to me. Might want to work on some range of motion when your muscles and joints are up to it. But I'd give you a good bill of health. Obviously, when we get home I want to examine you more thoroughly at my office, but I think you would be safe to go and rest now."

Before the others could move, Rick took the news as a sign to push off the table and onto the solid ground below. As his bare feet hit the surface, he lost his balance, his knees bending and his upper body fell into James, who thankfully took the brunt of his weight and eased him into standing. "Dude, slow down and take it easy."

Extracting his arms from James, Rick allowed Amy to help him remain upright, resting his arm around her shoulders and pulling her into his chest. "Sorry... So unless everyone wants to see this fine specimen strut my barely-covered junk around this station... Anyone care to find me some clothes, even just some pants?" Amy giggled, shaking her head as she helped him struggle towards a near table displaying new clothing. James and Mark stood nearby, ready to assist if he became too heavy for her. In a trance, Rick slowly clothed himself in a black V-neck t-shirt and loosely fitted linen pants. Now fully covered, he rolled his eyes at James' smirk as Amy bent down to help him place his feet in the black fur-lined loafers, clearly intended for bedroom wear.

"Nice slippers, dude," James laughed, gently smacking him on the shoulder.

"Fuck off and give me your shoes."

"Sorry, man. You know as well as I do, my size fourteen's are way too big for you. You know, some guys are just... bigger," James raised his left eyebrow filled with sarcastic mirth.

"Yeah, whatever dude. I'm too tired to even go there." Turning to the others, Rick's smile faded as his gaze landed on Amadeus, whose body lay still and silent on the table behind them. Forcing his muscles to move and his legs to lead, Rick moved closer until he stood by Amadeus' side. "How is he?"

Emily stepped up, her hand resting in between Rick's shoulders as they looked down. "He's doing better." They watched the glow of lights work from Amadeus' knees to his shoulders; his lower legs and head the only flesh to be seen, "He's just going to need more time to heal, but they think he will make a full recovery."

Turning from the table, Rick spoke to the two Jarly guards now stationed near the door. "I need to speak to Amelia and Riley, right away." With a single nod, one guard left his post.

"Baby, what's wrong?" Amy returned to his side, placing her hand on his chest, eyes wide and waiting for answers.

"I remember..." He turned them both to face the others; Damon had stepped away from his brother's table to join the group. "I remember things that were said... What was done."

Within minutes, Riley and Amelia returned to the medical bay, rushing to the others.

"Rick," Riley placed his hand on Rick's free shoulder, "How you feeling, buddy?"

"I'll live. I need to talk to you about what happened."

Amelia - already nodding - motioned for the group to follow. In silence, they entered the hall. James replaced Amy as they learned Rick really wasn't up to moving rapidly. Supporting the majority of his weight, James practically carried his friend into a nearby room filled with plush comfortable seating and a wide window displaying a steady flow of moving stars.

Making themselves comfortable, Amy nestled back into a love seat with Rick as he quickly returned his arm around her shoulders, pulling her in to lay his lips to her forehead.

"Okay, Rick. Take your time and tell us whatever you can," Amelia offered, sitting in a lone seat in the corner as Riley chose to stand behind her, arms folded, face serious.

Taking a deep, shaky breath he began. Within the next forty-five minutes the group had been advised on the gruesome details of the capture and torment; pausing twice, Rick had to reassure his now distraught wife that he was in fact okay and was feeling better by the minute.

"So you saw him...You saw Kavar?" Riley asked, clearly more concerned with the parties involved than the specific events that took place.

Rick nod, "Yeah, ugly fucking dude. Half his face missing? Big grudge towards Amadeus specifically. Yep," he turned to Amelia, "so what's his story? Amadeus tried to hide it, but I could tell he was just as surprised to see him alive as you are."

"Kavar blames Amadeus for most of his life's misfortunes," Amelia began.

"Yeah, I gathered that much. Who the fuck is he?" James leant forward, resting his elbows atop his thighs as he questioned Riley and Amelia.

"When he was younger, Amadeus served as commander of a small unit of Birons that were charged with the protection of Nona and Jarly dominated land."

"This was back when civil wars sprung up almost weekly, between Jarly and Biron neighboring states," Riley added.

Amelia continued, "Over the years, Amadeus grew close to a few of his Biron comrades, which only led to added feuds of favoritism and questions of alliance. One day, he was called upon to complete a raid in a town known as Trilium, mainly populated by Biron women and children, but was also a heavily armed unit of particularly volatile scheming Biron rebels. Knowing his second in command was born in Trilium, Amadeus let him lead the assault."

"Kavar," Emily guessed, blurting with no hesitation.

Riley began nodding as the others in the room looked shocked, not having caught up to the same conclusion.

"That prick was Amadeus' second in command? He fought for the Jarly?" Rick asked, shocked.

"Trilium used to be a neutral zone where Jarly and Biron lived harmoniously with one another, aiding one another until the attacks grew stronger and closer to home. When Biron rebels threatened his home, Kavar willingly joined the Jarly resistance fighters."

"He rose through the ranks pretty quickly actually," Riley said in a sort of trance, "Before his believed death, Amadeus spoke of him as family. They were a close team."

Rick's scoff of disgust didn't go unnoticed.

"Obviously, times have changed," Amelia offered the obvious. "The night the raid took place, Amadeus split his team up into two. He led one

team to invade from the North. The Biron rebels had barricaded themselves in a nearby residence that was clearly heavily guarded. Kavar lead
his team in from the West. The mission was clearly planned and was going
perfectly until Kavar entered to find his own brother among the Biron
Rebels, along with his mother, sister, and young niece held within the confines, along with other rebel family members."

"Kavar pleaded with Amadeus to pull back, but he had no choice but
to stay the course and stick to the plan. Trying to defuse the situation,
the two teams managed to take the majority of the rebels off guard and
either kill or capture those involved; all but Kaleem, Kavar's brother and
his loyal few."

"Kavar had to have known? His own brother?" Amy asked.

"They hadn't spoken in months. Amadeus' team had been on multiple
missions, it didn't leave much time to check in with the family. They led a
pretty reclusive lifestyle when they weren't off base," Riley explained.

"Okay, so what finally happened?" James asked.

"Kaleem and three other rebels had dragged the family out into the
tunnels below the house, trying to flee. Kavar entered the tunnels after
them, while Amadeus ordered the rest of the team to take those surren-
dered into custody. When they searched the building, Amadeus found
Kaleem's plans to blow up a major village of Jarly citizens."

"The village was only six miles away, connected by the very same
tunnels Kaleem and the others were fleeing down, explosives in hand,"
Riley interrupted.

"The plan was still in play as far as Amadeus knew. Down in the tunnels,
a gunfight had broken out. Amadeus had ordered a second unit to enter
the tunnels from further down, coming up ahead of those fleeing, with
orders to kill all in sight. When Kavar got wind of the orders, he turned on
his own team and those that had joined, leaving only his terrified family,
including Kaleem, in the tunnels below.

Trying desperately to have Kaleem see reason, and unable to kill
his own brother, Kavar ultimately failed and let Kaleem escape. When
Amadeus heard of his betrayal, and the continued bomb threat, Amadeus
ordered an aerial strike, taking out the tunnels, killing Kavar's family in the
process. Kavar alone survived the explosion, which left him the disfigured

man you described before. After returning to their base, midway through the night of his recovery, Kavar escaped custody and swore revenge in the name of his family.

This was over two hundred years ago. For a few years some attempts on Amadeus' life were made in Kavar's name, but until this week it was believed he had been long dead, the wounds from that initial explosion having lodged debris that even to this day could not have been removed and would have continued to cause extreme internal suffering."

"So Kavar blames Amadeus for the death of his family, and for two hundred years he has plotted against him, and when he figured he couldn't get to him himself, he played behind the scenes, manipulating others until the opportune moment. Plotting against Earth and rising in the Biron Rebel campaign, attempting to destroy everything Amadeus holds dear?" Emily concluded, summing up the events as she worked it through her mind.

"Pretty much. I think the campaign against Earth started out as a vendetta against Amadeus, but then grew in his own desire for power," Riley finalized.

"Great, so why didn't he just kill Amadeus when he had the chance?" James asked.

Surprisingly, it was Mark that answered for them, "He's been plotting for two hundred years. Sure, he got his anger out with the brutal beating, but given his patience so far, I'd say he's going for something bigger, something that will be more heartbreaking and more of a loss than death alone. He's wants Amadeus to suffer like he did. To watch."

"And what has Amadeus been working towards for centuries, protecting?" Amy asked aloud, already knowing the answer.

"Earth," Amelia confirmed.

"And Bates thinks after all is said and done, the Biron rebels will just hand over Earth to him to do as he sees fit?" Amelia asked Rick.

"Yeah, he thinks they will reward him for his help in the attacks, by handing mankind over to him on a silver platter," Rick said.

"What a lunatic; I've been saying it for years." Riley shook his head, turning to gaze out the window, as Amelia remained stoic.

"You've known how fucked up he is and you still gave him all this power and control?" James asked to Riley's back.

"A personal dislike for someone and their thought patterns doesn't warrant mistreatment and less opportunity." Amelia inched forward in her seat, although the others didn't missed Riley's turn and rolling of the eyes. "These facts aside, Bates has always been hard working and focused. Fast learner and until this point, he has never shown any of us mistrust."

"Okay, so now what?" Emily asked.

"Now nothing," Amelia stood, surprising the group, "I expect you all to return to your quarters and get some rest. We should be in the vicinity of Earth within the next twenty-hours or so; in the meantime please take it easy. My team can handle it from here."

Making her way to the door, Riley following in her footsteps, they stopped by Mark as he said, "Wait, what about Amadeus and Caleb?"

"They're going to be healing for a while longer. You can check on them whenever you'd like, but for now we will let you know if anything else comes up." With that the Jarly left and the room fell silent.

CHAPTER TWENTY-FOUR

Amy helped Rick into their bedroom, having excused themselves from the group to rest. Rushing to the side of the bed, she pulled the plush covers back, easing him onto the bed. Pulling his shirt over his head and tossing it onto the ground, Rick kicked off his slippers and slid his body under the welcoming covers.

"Are you okay?" Amy stood beside him, not sure what to do next.

"Baby, stop worrying; I'm not going to break. Just get in here and lie down with me."

"Okay, I'm sorry." She made her way around the bed, discarding her pants as she went. "I can't help worrying about you. Isn't that what a good wife does?"

He grinned, "Well stop and get over here." Pulling back the covers on her side of the bed, she slipped in and inched her way closer until she was in his arms. "Wait." Pulling back, he tugged at the hem of her shirt, pulling it over her head and reaching around to unclasp her bra. Now bare, covered only by her panties, he pulled her close again. "I need to feel you." She kissed the soft pink skin of his chest as he made a content noise, murmuring, "Much better."

The light caress of his hand down her back eventually stilled, his breathing heavy and deep; Amy knew he had fallen into restful sleep.

* * *

"Hey, how are you feeling?" Emily surprised Rick as he sat on the couch in the communal space eating an apple. James had joined him only moments earlier.

"Good. Still sore, but I can't seem to relax."

James tried to hold back his laugh, gaining their confused glances, "Didn't seem to stop you getting your rocks off."

"What?" Rick asked, clearly amused.

"I heard you earlier. I had to start up a telepathic conversation with Julia, about her day of shopping, just for the distraction."

"I see. Well sorry, I guess we were a bit loud," Rick stated before turning back to the television.

"Well we should be there soon, I think we slept for about twelve hours." Emily was desperate to change the topic though Rick only nodded in response.

Mark came out of their bedroom then, freshly showered, and shaven. "Morning," He nodded in their general direction as he made his way towards the open kitchenette.

In a moment, the scene went from calm to chaos as a massive ripple shocked throughout the station. A siren sounded and the group lunged towards the exit.

"What about Amy?" Emily called as they rounded the door.

Rick seemed to move with renewed ease, "She's fine, she was in the bathroom; she will come find us when she is ready."

The halls filled with Jarly and Human alike. Following the general masses, the group made their way to the conference hall, running into Riley on route.

"What's going on?" James called over the growing noise of the panicked crowd.

"There was an explosion onboard," Riley yelled out, rushing toward the head of the group, forcing the Humans to run faster to keep up.

"An accident?" Emily called out.

As they entered the hall, those gathering dispersed into their comforting groups, allowing ease of conversation. The group knew something was wrong, as Riley had already begun shaking his head, "I don't think so."

"This was intentional? Meaning there is still a rebel group onboard?" Mark asked is a hushed tone.

"Most likely." Riley broke away from the group, rushing to Amelia's side as she stood at the head of the long table, listing orders to her Jarly soldiers.

As the room filled, those of rank took their place around the table. An absent bell sounded, filling the space and quieting the chatter. As the room fell silent, Emily's eyes fell on the large window beside them. What was once fleeting stars, in a blur of light, was now a solid picture of night's sky. One thing was clear, they were no longer moving.

"Please, listen carefully," Amelia spoke loud and clear for the entire hall to hear. "The shock that was felt only moment ago has been confirmed as an internal explosion. The cause of which has yet to be determined, but as of this moment, I have blocked off levels seven and eight; all entrances have been sealed until further notice. Please steer clear of those levels. While we determine the damage to the station, and find the culprit, I ask that you all remain here under the protection of our security team."

The room remained still as Amelia and her team exited into the hallway. Without asking permission, Mark and the other Humans quickly followed after them, being stopped at the door by two guards. "Sir, please remain here."

Ignoring their request, Mark pushed forward, calling out to Amelia, stopping her in her tracks. Pausing for a moment, Amelia called back, "Let them through... Only those among the chosen." With that Mark, Emily, James, and Rick passed through, the remaining Human soldiers calling out behind them as the doors to the hall closed.

Emily reached for Rick, gently gripping his long sleeve shirt, "Maybe I should go get Amy?"

"Let her rest, she's been exhausted," Rick stated, his gaze following the group ahead of them.

Moving quickly through the corridors the group came to a stop in a familiar surveillance room.

"Do you know who did this?" Mark stepped forward, asking Amelia, while his eyes remained trained on the screens in front of him.

"I hope we have managed to get them on surveillance. So far they have managed to all but cripple our propulsion system. We're sitting ducks," Amelia spat, clearly frustrated. The footage was sped up to a time just before the explosions. One of the Jarly manning the controls advised that a passcode was input into the system to gain access to the engineering room.

"Whose passcode was used?"

"Searching, Ma'am."

The room grew silent again. Inching forward, they all waited patiently as the cameras zoomed in on a slender hooded figure. Clearly male, the individual seemed to know where the cameras were located as they made their way undetected. The footage continued as they entered the passcode, slipping into the engineering room, and made their way to a number of electronic panels; stopping along the way to strategically place the solid objects he had been carrying, now known to be the explosive devices. After placing seven different objects, he returned to the open control panels and manipulated them for three consecutive minutes before rushing from the room.

"Nothing?" Amelia asked, clearly disappointed.

After a moment, Riley seemed to remember something with excitement, "What about the new camera in 7C?"

"Yes!" Amelia exclaimed, turning back to the controller and ordering that footage be reviewed.

"What new camera?" Mark asked.

"We had to install a new camera on that level after Velo's death. It was only installed yesterday, hopefully whoever he is didn't know about it."

Again, as one, they watched the suspect navigate the halls before entering a deserted elevator on the eighth floor. Slowly, as the elevator revolved, the team held their breath as the person came into view. Sliding across the screen, making no attempt to conceal himself from the new camera, the room filled with gasps and confused expressions.

"I don't understand!" James barked, "Rick?" As one, the group turned to the back of the room where Rick had followed the others in, but now only emptiness stood.

"What the fuck is going on?" James yelled, again.

"Find him, now!" Amelia roared and before the Humans could react, the room filled with Jarly flame and the hunt began.

As the room filled with silence, and the three remained, one person came barging to the front of Emily's mind, "Amy!" she cried before forcing herself out of the room.

* * *

"Amy?!" Emily called out, barging her way into the common room. "Amy!"

Forcing herself into Amy's closed bedroom, the three paused, stuck in the door-well as their stomachs dropped and Emily tried to resist the urge to throw up. Crimson red slashed on almost every surface of the room. Both night tables all but destroyed, broken glass, and furniture filled the space before them.

"Amy, where are you?" Emily feared the worst. A running shower called their attention as they entered the bathroom. More blood spilled across the cold, white-tiled floors, the glass mirror shattered; the glass entrance to the shower revealed a full steady stream, but no Amy.

"So much blood." Emily returned to the bedroom, rounding the room to the large walk in closet. "Amy?"

Pulling at the hanging clothes, she separated them, revealing the space behind.

"Emily!" James pushed past her to a large wooden cupboard at the end of the closet; its handles clearly bound by the cord of a nightgown. In a rush he twisted and yanked it free, unbinding the doors, which fell open at the last turn. In a heavy thud, Amy fell forward, taking James off guard, falling to the ground beneath her.

"Amy!" Emily pulled her away, frantically. Clothed only in Rick's previously discarded t-shirt and her panties, Amy lay unconscious and white as a ghost, her body sustaining many injuries, but nothing compared to the brutality leaving her face all but unrecognizable. Darkened red splotches covered her skin, as she slowly took in air.

"Mark... Mark, help me!" Emily laid her sister flat on the carpet below as she attempted to heal her. Mark and James placed their lit hands on Amy's cold flesh, but nothing seemed to be working.

"Isobel. We need Isobel and one of those tables," Mark spoke quickly, forcibly moving Emily aside so that he could raise Amy into his arms and rush from the room.

* * *

"What happened?" Isobel exclaimed, rushing from Amadeus' table to join them mid-stride, "Here, lay her here." Emily wept, gripping tight to Amy's lax hand.

"Emily, let go!" Mark had to ease her free, placing Amy's hand onto the metal table so Isobel could start the process of healing. As before, the white gel rose to solidify into a lavender case; only Amy's eyes and lips remaining free.

As Isobel raised the hologram, examining her patient, she spoke to the others, "What the hell happened?"

"Rick," Emily whispered, her eyes scanning the graphics, watching as lights flashed throughout Amy's cocoon.

"It's not Rick," James said adamantly. Emily turned to him, pure hatred and anger oozing from every pore. Grabbing her elbow harshly, he pulled her further away from the table. "Emily, it's not him... Jesus, you know better than anyone that Rick would die before laying a hand on her."

Isobel stood confused, as Mark took a moment to explain, "Physically we believe Rick is responsible for these injuries, but obviously something has happened." Gesturing to his sister-in-law, he said, "He would never willingly do this. He's not acting like himself."

Her brows knitting, Isobel turned back to the graphics, deep in thought. "When did you last see them together?"

"Right before bed. They were fine. They went to bed together when the rest of us called it a night." Slowly Emily had drifted back to the table; now she gripped at the free metal edge. "They were smiling, happy..."

"My god," Isobel's eyes widened as if a distant thought had resurfaced. Spinning around, her gaze turned to Amadeus, almost fully healed with little-to-no lavender covering his bare skin; he still lay unconscious.

"What?" Emily asked, as James and Mark stepped forward, "What is it?"

Turning back to the others, she moved around the table in a rush, as she placed the healing lights in the solid mass surrounding Amy. "Where is he now?"

"They're out looking for him," James muttered.

"I need you to find him, now. Bring him to me. I need to be sure..." The last words seemed to be for herself rather than the others in the room, ending in a whisper.

"Sure of what?" Emily stopped Isobel mid-stride, reaching out to place a hand on her forearm.

"I think I know what has happened, but I can't know for sure and it's too detailed to explain it now." Turning to James and Mark, she pleaded, "Please... You need to find him and bring him to me before anyone else gets hurt."

Without a word, James turned on his heels and rushed from the room.

"Go," Emily turned to Mark. "He might need your help... I'll be here."

As Emily turned in a trance towards Amy, Mark stepped forward, pressing his lips to her temple before stepping away and running after James.

CHAPTER TWENTY-FIVE

"Okay, so how do you want to do this?" Mark said, stepping up to James as they marched along the hallways, "Riley thinks he is hiding somewhere on the lower level, near that energy thing…"

"Calobie," James answered. Pausing, he turned to Mark, hands raised, gesturing as he went, "Okay, I think once we have him in our sights we need to split up and surprise him. I'll take him from the front and you come in from the back."

"Alright… James, how far do you want to take this? Something tells me he's not going to come quietly."

Running his hands through his blonde curls, James thought, "Okay, look, I don't know what is going on right now, but one thing I do know is whoever that is, it's not our Rick." Mark only nodded, allowing James to continue, "I say we try and take him by surprise, knock his ass out, and drag him back to Isobel where we can restrain him and figure this all out."

"Good. Yeah, fine. Something tells me we need to get him before the Jarly get their hands on him."

They continued on their way, until one particular tunnel grew bright with Jarly light, followed by screams of anger and grunts of fighting. Without looking at one another, they quickened their pace, rushing around a corner to be met by a railing and light coming from an open space below. Both careening over the railing, they witness the horrific show below. A group of four Jarly soldiers, with two in reserve, had Rick surrounded; he was backed into a corner of mechanical design. As they grew nearer, Rick's face contoured with anger as blood trickled from his right temple, across his brow and down to his chin, clearly hindering his vision. One tall, dark-skinned Jarly stepped forwards, his arms raised as if to lunge. In a flash Rick gripped his forearms, forcing his body and head forward, head-butting the soldier. He then spun him around, arms encasing his head and neck, dragging him back in a chokehold.

"Get back or I shall kill him," an unrecognizable version of Rick's voice filled the void.

"Let him go, Rick," Mark called from above, drawing Rick's attention long enough to have the remaining others dive on the two.

Rushing down from their post, James and Mark hit the landing as bodies moved in a blur of light and power. Bodies fell like rag dolls as Rick fought back with all his might; one by one he overcame the others.

"Rick, enough!" James screamed as a younger Jarly was thrown into his path, dropping before his feet, unconscious. Now alone, with a single Jarly who had sustained a brutal blast to his upper chest, the three once again cornered Rick.

Reaching for the Jarly to his left, Mark placed his lit hand on the man's shoulder, not removing his gaze from the heaving mess that was Rick as a sinister grin spread across his face.

"Go," Mark encouraged, "find Riley and the others."

Unsure of what to do, the Jarly stood taller, his gaze drifting from Rick to the two Humans.

"We said go!" James ordered more forcefully.

Slowly, as if to not surprise a wild beast, the Jarly began to back up before reaching up and holding his own chest as he made his way out of sight.

"What the fuck is going on?" James spoke loud and clear, his light still ablaze.

Rick remained silent, pacing back and forward like a caged animal.

"Rick?" Mark called, unsure.

Rick turned to stare at them, his face now sullied with blood and oozing wounds as he spat.

"Rick, you need to calm the fuck down right now and come with us so we can heal you and figure this out." James took a step forward, but stopped at the onset of heavy laughter emanating from Rick's throat.

"You're pathetic," Rick muttered.

Confused, James took another step forward, with Mark edging closer from the opposite side.

"Stop!" The shout came from behind. The three turned to see a row of Jarly led by Amelia and Riley. "James… Mark, step aside. We will take over from here."

"What are you going to do?" Mark called back; he and James stood unmoving.

"That is not your concern. Please move."

"The hell it's not our concern… He's family," James called back. "We want to know he won't be harmed anymore until we figure this all out."

"James, move!" Riley called back, striding forward with his shoulder held high in warrior mode.

"He will not be harmed if he comes willingly," Amelia spoke softly at Riley's side.

"Isobel wants him," Mark spoke, already preparing to move aside, reaching for James' forearm to lead him out of their path.

"We know," Amelia spoke with a softness that invoked sympathy for them, but also power and control.

Turning to Rick, whose eyes flared, backing up into his corner further; a semi-circle formed around him with Mark and James at the right far side.

Tilting his head examining those around him, Rick focused on Amelia as she stepped forward, Riley remaining close behind.

Spitting before her feet, he took a deep breath. "Amelia," he nodded in mock respect.

Taking a step closer, she tilted her head in much the same way. The right side of her lip raised in a sharp grin. "Bates."

CHAPTER TWENTY-SIX

Contrary to John's hopes, the front door swung open to reveal the whirl-wind that was Erik and Tess. Laughter and excitement filled the house in the early morning hours as they sought out their favorite adopted uncle.

"Abel!" Erik cheered, pushing his sister aside so that he could lunge into Abel's waiting arms.

"Hey, buddy. How was the flight?" Abel genuinely asked as he helped Tess get situated on his lap, as well. The three filled the small armchair in the family room.

"Good. But Tess cried most of the way."

"Did not!" She shoved her brother's shoulder.

"Did too!" Erik was emphatic, turning back to Abel, "She was being such a baby. Crying because she wanted to sleep and was tired."

"I did not," Tess huffed, but then cuddled up onto Abel, resting a cheek onto his chest.

"I didn't cry. I was an adult, Uncle Abe. I stayed up the whole night, and helped Gramma with her seatbelt and held her hand when the plane took off."

"Good job, Erik. That was very adult of you," Abel smirked as Kristine and Joan hugged Julia, who had been waiting in the kitchen preparing a fresh pot of coffee. John drew his attention to the front door with a grunt, as he, Richard, and Christopher brought in the oversized luggage.

Finally returning to the living room, Richard approached Abel, hand raised, not expecting him to stand with the two children on his lap. "Abel, good to see you, son."

Shaking his hand, Abel smiled, "Likewise, Richard... Good flight?"

"As good as could be expected at short notice."

Erik had dislodged himself from the chair, rushing to the kitchen to hug Julia, before raiding the pantry for food. Easing a sleeping Tess into the chair, Abel managed to stand, throwing a blanket over her, before stepping up to greet Kristine and Joan into tight hugs. It did not go unnoticed that Christopher bypassed the rest of the group and stepped out onto the back deck, joining Marcel and his team in a private meeting.

"Joan, dear, why don't you go lay down?" Richard offered.

"Oh, yes, please feel free to take any of the rooms upstairs. There are also two bedrooms in the basement... You all must be exhausted," Julia stated as she passed Kristine a cup of coffee.

"I think I might just do that. John, can you carry Tess; she and I can take a nap in one of the guest rooms downstairs." John reached for his sleeping daughter, the movement jostling her awake for only a moment before she lay her cheek on his shoulder and fell back into slumber.

"Erik, you too. Go with Gramma and Tess," Kristine spoke, pulling out one of the kitchen chairs as Erik stepped out of the pantry with a large bag of chips in hand.

"Mom, I'm not tired," Erik whined.

Before he could open the bag, Richard gently pulled it out of his grasp, "Go on son. Do as your mother says."

"But, Grampa!" Erik remained still-footed.

"Now, Erik," John called from the top of the basement stairs. Joan was already halfway down the steps. Stomping his feet and mumbling to himself, Erik reluctantly did as he was told.

As if waiting for a meeting, the remaining adults took their place around the large dining room table. John returned, and wanting to leave two seats available for the Jarly he pulled the second swiveling stool away from the kitchen island to join Abel, sitting behind Kristine and Julia. Waiting patiently, eventually Marcel and Christopher broke from their team, leaving the remaining three to continue their watch.

Taking their pre-offered seats, they sat silently for a moment, scanning the room and calculating their approach.

"Well, spit it out young man," Richard took the lead, turning to Marcel at his left, making Abel chuckle.

"Um, Richard," Abel tried to hide his amusement, "Given what we know of the Jarly, I'm pretty sure Marcel and Christopher are old enough to be your great-great- grandfathers."

A simple grin acknowledged Abel's theory as Marcel turned to Richard.

"Richard, as Abel has pointed out, I am Marcel. You have already met my brother Christopher."

"Nice to meet you. Now, tell me why I had to drag my family into this stifling heat in the middle of the night."

Richard had one thing right; as the sun had begun to rise, so did the temperature. Not even 9:00am and the sun had already burnt off the morning moisture; a smoky mirage of heat could be seen in any direction.

"Firstly, how much do you know about the recent events that have taken place?" Marcel asked Richard, but his eyes drifted to John for the answer.

"They pretty much know everything about our friends, the Biron attack on the station, and what happened to Amadeus and Rick."

"I see, well then you will understand that there are a number of Biron entities that are not as interested in keeping the peace among the Jarly and Human alliances. In the last three days, those of us within this galaxy were called upon to return to the planet, on a defensive order. It appears these Biron rebels have united and are in pursuit of Earth as we speak."

"So they're coming here? How long?" Kristine asked as John gently gripped her shoulder.

"It could be days, but… more likely, hours," Christopher answered.

"Okay, so when they get here, what happens?" Julia joined in.

"Our stations have been positioned around this planet, roughly twenty at this moment. Not large vessels, but they will stand in the way of any Biron attack. Six others patrol the general system."

"How many Biron ships do you know of?" John asked, reaching past Kristine when he noticed a coffee waiting for him on the table.

"Our latest count is twelve and growing," Marcel answered, matter-of-factly.

"Well, that's something at least." The group looked confused, so Kristine continued, "Twelve against twenty- six, plus we have some fighter pilots and weapons." Her words were animated, more for herself than anyone else.

"Yes, for now the odds do seem to be in our favor, however we cannot offer any additional vessels at this time. If their numbers grow rapidly..." Marcel stopped, turning to his brother.

"If their numbers grow we will not be able to hold them off indefinitely. Their vessels, though smaller in numbers, are war machines equipped for battle and filled with soldiers," Christopher added, turning back to Richard who remained silent for the moment.

"Well," Richard spoke up, "At any given time Humans are ready to blow themselves to smithereens with our own technology. Maybe this time we can put our issues aside and turn those weapons on the real enemy."

"For all our sakes', I hope it doesn't come to that," Abel spoke, before sipping his coffee.

"How can we prepare? What can we do?" Kristine asked before turning and reaching a hand up to John, "John... The kids."

"Babe, right now this is probably the safest place for them," he turned to Marcel for encouragement.

"Yes, Kristine. Unfortunately, if Earth were to be attacked, there is nowhere that your children could hide that would be any better than the protected confines of this house. Not even our vessels would be safer. "

"So, what do we do? Have you heard from the others?" Abel asked.

"For now, we continue to wait. I have heard from my station; Amelia and the others are approximately half a day's journey from Pluto. As I am sure you have heard," Marcel turned to Julia, "their vessel has sustained some internal damage that will need time to repair. As of this moment, they are unable to move closer. My council has dispatched one of our closer vessels to retrieve your friends and help with any repairs. They should intercept within two hours."

"Good," Julia smiled with encouragement, but it was short lived. "Wait, you say they're still half a day away from Pluto, meaning even if they meet up with this other ship and head back, the Birons could already be here, or worse, attack their ship before they even get here?"

"That is one of our concerns also, but at this point, we do not have any other option. As I said, Nona cannot afford to dispatch further vessels. This is their only option," Marcel explained, as Julia's mouth remain opened in shock. "We can only pray that the Biron fleet approached from another system, or are delayed."

"Delayed! Really…that's your great plan?" Julia pushed away from the table, turning to leave the room. Abel reached for her arm, but she pulled it free, not making further eye contact. "I'm going to check on Sophie." Julia left the room.

"I'm sorry that this upsets her, but this is all the information we have to go off of at this time."

"It's fine. She's been through a lot already… We're all high strung at the moment," Abel replied.

CHAPTER TWENTY-SEVEN

Emily sat at the stool her sister once occupied, resting at the side of Amy's table; her eyes red and swollen from warm tears. It had been hours since Mark and James had left them. Isobel had been called away, so now Emily sat alone with Amy, and Caleb. Damon had advised of his departure only moments before, though he said he would not be long. In the initial assessment, Isobel had concluded that the large amount of blood found on Amy's body and in their bedroom could not have been hers alone. Emily felt slightly better knowing that Amy did manage to fight back; getting her pound of flesh, so to speak.

Isobel did, however, conclude that Amy has sustained a broken wrist, bruised internal organs, dislocated shoulder, and three broken ribs. Adding to that, she had a rather deep gash along her right thigh, left cheek, and various slashes along her torso that had accounted for a large portion of the blood loss. On the whole, Isobel claimed that Amy would heal rather rapidly from the attack and would be out of her encasing before morning.

As the lights continued to flicker and flare, Emily was momentarily distracted by a light moan emanating from across the room.

"Amadeus!" She pushed her stool aside, leaping up and over to the man now regaining consciousness. "Amadeus, can you hear me?"

Isobel, he's waking up!...Amadeus is waking up!

I'll be right there.

"Amadeus?" Emily whispered again. To her delight he began to rock his head - left and right - as he tried to open his eyes, his forehead scrunching as he returned. His dark eyes opened, blinking rapidly to focus on the woman hovering above him.

"Emily," His voice broke into a whisper.

"Oh Amadeus, it's so good to see you awake and talking. Are you okay? Are you in any pain?"

"I am fine, though these tables do not lend to comfort. Can you please help me sit up?" He gripped the sides of his table as he used what strength he could to force himself forward.

"Umm, wait," she gently laid her hand on his shoulder, "maybe we should wait for Isobel before we start moving?"

"Truly, I am well," he pushed past her weak restrain. Abandoning her concern she helped him up into a seated position before helping him turn, letting his legs dangle over the side. "Thank you," he offered her a weak smile before turning to the next table. "Is that Amy?" he asked with concern, "Oh, I am truly sorry, Emily. Biron attack? Was she injured in the rescue?"

Stepping back, sadness filled her features as she stepped closer to her sister. "Not the rescue. No."

Amadeus was clearly confused, so Emily felt the need to add, "We're trying to figure out what happened. But, so far all we know is that something has happened to Rick ever since he was healed."

"Rick did this?"

She only offered a single nod in a sad confession.

Before more words could be exchanged, a blur of light filled the room and within seconds a tearful, yet smiling Isobel stood before her leader. "Amadeus," she slightly lowered her head in acknowledgment.

His returning smile was warm and heartfelt. "Isobel."

Gently, and with more affection than Emily was used to seeing between the two, Isobel raised her right hand and trailed it down Amadeus' upper arm, "You're feeling well?" she asked, her eyes following his body; no scars or visible injury in sight.

"I am well and looking forward to an update. Where is Amelia?" Pushing off from his table, Amadeus walked with confidence towards the clothing table at the end of the room as he covered himself in fabric.

"She is with Riley and the others." Stepping forward, Isobel spoke softly, "Sir." She gestured with her head towards the far table where Caleb still lay healing.

Amadeus' eyes grew wide as he rushed to Caleb's side. Without needing Isobel's assistance, he pulled up the hologram to reveal the damage done. "His left hand?"

"It had to be removed due to a Biron blast. He's also lost a large portion of muscle mass in his left shoulder and breast tissues," Isobel reiterated what was clearly displayed above them. "He is healing well, and will wake, I hope, soon."

"Damon?"

"Has been at Caleb's side since the incident occurred." Turning to Amadeus she explained, "Sir, the station was invaded as Amelia suspected. We were able to contain the majority of the carnage, while they attempted to gain access to the control room. We have healed all others that were injured. You will be debriefed on those of us that were lost."

"Commander," a familiar voice sounded at the entrance of the room, gaining attention of all those nearest.

"Amelia." A visible sigh of relief released from Amadeus, "How are you?" Joining each other at the center of the room, Amelia embraced Amadeus in a tight hold as Riley and Mark entered the room behind them.

"Sir," Riley nodded in welcome, reaching his hand out, patting Amadeus on the near shoulder.

"I am happy to see you are all well," Amadeus, though formal, filled the room with his sincerity.

Ignoring the others, Emily ran into Mark's embrace. "Where have you been? Did they find him?"

Mark kissed her lips in calming reassurance, before explaining that Rick had been captured and was being held until they could figure this all out.

"Where's James?"

"He's staying with Rick."

"I want to see him. I want some answers," Emily spoke adamantly.

Stepping back, Mark gripped her shoulders. "Emily, you need to know that it wasn't Rick that did this to Amy."

"What? Then who was it?"

"Bates."

"I don't understand… How did he get on board?"

"It's hard to explain baby, but somehow Bates is inside Rick. Baby, he's controlling Rick."

* * *

"Let me out of here!" Rick's fist pounded on the cell wall of a thick clear glass. He watched the two Jarly standing, arms folded, near the lone door. The room was as basic as could be, fairly large, the walls and floor were of gunmetal grey. The room was divided by the clear, glass-like solid; on Rick's side, only a metallic bench with a blanket held any comfort.

"Seriously, what the fuck is going on? Talk to me, God damn it!" His breath fogged the glass in front of him as the guards remain silent and as still as statues. "Fuck!"

James! James, where are you?... Amy? Baby, are you there?

Minutes passed as Rick slumped to the ground, his back to the metal siding, as his head, shoulder, and left leg rested against the glass. With a whoosh the door opened, revealing James.

Rick jumped to his feet, "About fucking time, get me out of here!" Rick stepped back expectantly.

James stepped closer to the glass; now only inches away he spoke calmly, "Rick? Is that you?"

"No shit, Sherlock! Of course it's me. What is going on, dude?"

"Hold on, I'll explain in a minute, but tell me… what's the last thing you remember?" Now both men stood only inches apart with the glass barely obscuring their view.

"Seriously?" He stepped back, running his hands though his hair as he spoke, "We were all hanging out watching movies, it was like ten-thirty, and Amy and I went to bed. We got into bed and basically as soon as my head hit the pillow I was out like a light." Now pacing around the room, he continued, "Next thing I know, I woke up on the metal bed, in a sweat, practically blinded by this bright fucking room." Turning to speak over James' shoulder, he yelled, "Seriously, can we turn down the lights in here? I can barely see straight!"

"That's it?" James asked, thinking.

"Yeah, James. So tell me what I'm doing in here? One good thing is I do feel like myself again, not so sore, ya know."

"Rick, go sit down." James moved over to the other side of the glass, encouraging Rick to follow, facing the bed.

"James, cut the shit and tell me what happened? ... And where are Amy and the others?"

"Rick, sit the fuck down and I'll explain everything that I can. Amelia and the others will be here soon to explain more."

With a huff of frustration, Rick sat on the edge of the bed, elbows resting on his knees. Jutting out his chin and opening his hands wide he looked expectantly at James as if to say *Well... get on with it!*

After another moment, "Okay, so something happened. I did something?" Rick asked. James remained silent, causing Rick to raise his head. "James, where is my wife?"

"She's in the medical bay at the moment," James practically whispered.

"WHAT!" A wave of sickness overcame Rick as he launched to his feet, smacking his hands on the glass before James. "Take me to her, James. Now!"

"I can't do that, Rick. Please, just calm down for a minute. She's going to be okay."

"James, I swear to God, if you don't tell me what the fuck happened..."

"Bates took control of your body," James blurted, not knowing how else to begin.

"What are you talking about?" Rick spat.

"Bates, somehow... He managed to take over your body and...Dude, he killed some people and blew the fuck out of the ship's engine. We're stranded while they work to fix it and Kavar and those fuckers are getting closer to Earth by the minute."

"How... I don't understand," Rick asked, resting his forehead against the cold glass, looking down.

"That's what we're trying to figure out. Amadeus just woke up so we're hoping he can offer some answers, but in the meantime buddy, you have to stay in there. For your safety as much as anyone else's."

"What did I do to Amy?" Rick closed his eyes, not sure he wanted to know the answer.

"Rick, it wasn't you."

"Just answer me!"

"Honestly, dude. I don't think you want to know. Just know that she is healing nicely and will be back to her normal self in no time." With that, Rick broke down, real tears filled his eyes, and he surprised James by rearing back and slamming his fist against the glass. Spinning around, he slid down to the floor below; knees bent up, he rested his head on his forearms.

Mimicking his position, James lowered his back to the glass, just off to the side. Back to back with Rick, he continued, "Look, Amy knows it wasn't you. She knows you would never willingly hurt her."

"Doesn't change the fact that she was hurt enough to be in the medical bay. Hurt by my hands." James could barely hear the whispers that Rick spoke.

Another whoosh filled the room as the door opened. Remaining seated, James watched as Amelia and Riley entered the room, followed by Isobel, and finally Amadeus.

"It's him. He's Rick, again," James uttered.

Standing along the length of the glass, the Jarly waited.

"Rick, please stand and face us," Amelia spoke up.

Together, both James and Rick stood. Rick turned to face his old friends.

"Amadeus, I'm glad you're awake. You look good. I...I...I don't know what to tell you. I'm so sorry for what I've done," Rick's shoulders hunched in pure defeat.

"Rick, please don't feel so remorseful. You had no control over what was done to you. What was done to us..." Amadeus spoke clearly, "The only reason you must remain in this room is for our continued protection."

"You think he could take over again?" Fear now filled Rick's expression as he glanced around the room.

"Unfortunately, I do."

"Well, what the fuck do we do?" James asked.

Ignoring James, Amadeus stepped closer to the glass, focused solely on Rick, whose attention was faltering. "Rick, do you remember when we were in that last room? You were beaten and laying on the floor and Bates continued to taunt you."

Rick nodded, "I'm surprised you remember it. I thought you were dying."

"I was. We both were. This is something that we will both have to deal with for the rest of our lives." Amadeus cleared his throat, continuing, "Although, my memory is still a bit hazy; when Bates hovered over you, did he place his lit hand over your face? Did he hold it there for a pro-longed amount of time?"

"Yeah, that's all he seemed to do when he wasn't torturing us. It just added to my headache though, nothing more," Rick recalled.

James watched as the other three looked concerned, glancing at one another. "Okay, what does that mean?" James once again tried to gain some answers.

"There is something among the Jarly known as Vincosha," Isobel started, then turned to Amelia for approval before continuing. "Vincosha, is an abuse of our given light. It's seen as blasphemy; even the strongest among us fear it."

"Okay, so it's pretty safe to say Bates did this Vinco-whatever to Rick. So what is it?"

"Vincosha is a bonding of our light. Not in the same sense as what we first did with you and your team, but an all-consuming bond," Amadeus now offered further explanation.

"Meaning?"

"Meaning, Bates has used his light on Rick, bonding his own light with Rick's energy and mind. In doing so, he consumed Rick's own light and can now manipulate it whenever he sees fit."

Riley finally spoke up from the back of the room.

"So Bates can just flick a switch, I go bye-bye, and he takes over?" Rick asked, mortified.

"Yes."

"Shit!" James yelled out in frustration, raking both hands through his hair. "How do we stop it? How do we get him out?"

"There is only one way to break a Vincosha bond," Amelia placed her hand against the glass of Rick's cell as the two Humans waited for her to continue. Taking a deep breath she turned to James, "We have to kill Bates."

CHAPTER TWENTY-EIGHT

"How's she doing?" James asked, startling Emily and Mark as they waited at Amy's side.

"A lot better. She's healing nicely, no permanent damage," Mark answered.

"How's Rick?" Emily spoke softly.

James pulled another chair up and sat at the end of Amy's table. The room remained dark as they spoke over the flickering lights. "He's been better. Amadeus and the others are trying to coach him through this Vincosha bullshit. He needs to try and stay awake, keep his mind focused, and stay alert; apparently, it's a lot harder for Bates to get control then. All he can think and ask about is Amy, but they won't let him leave the cell. I'm here because I told him I'd check up on her. Jesus, he is miserable."

"Of course he is. Maybe I should go talk to him... reassure him?" Emily offered, taking a step down from her stool.

"Yeah, maybe in a little bit. Let him work with them for a while longer. He really does need to focus."

"So what is their plan? Are we going after Bates now? How do we find him?" Mark asked, turning completely towards James.

"I don't know. They are going to call another meeting pretty soon here to decide. Either way, when I get my hands on Bates, I'm going to kill him myself."

"Well, I for one will be by your side." Surprising the whispering group, they turned to see Riley entering the room. Shortly after, Damon returned as well, offering them a single nod before returning to his brother's side.

"How is he?" James asked.

"He'll be okay, as long as he can remain in control. We have some tools to combat the affects, but as soon as Bates regains control there is no telling when Rick will return. And if he returns without our knowledge and hears that we are on his pursuit, things could get worse," Riley answered, standing across the table from Mark and Emily, his eyes cast down on Amy.

"How can they get worse?" Emily innocently asked.

"Well, once he figures out he can't get out of that cell, and we won't be divulging any more information, he will start digging through Rick's mind, painfully I might add, until he finds some useful information or at the very least, until he figures out that Rick is no longer any use to him."

"Then what?" James asked.

"Then Bates, using the bond to control Rick's body, will manipulate it, using his abilities against himself until Rick's body is destroyed."

Before more questions could be asked, Riley's eyes glazed over, followed by his third eyelid before his attention returned to the group, "Amadeus has called a meeting in his private quarters. We need to go now."

The group made to move, but stopped when Emily hesitated.

"Don't worry. Amy will be fine. Damon will be remaining here."

Damon stepped forward, "I shall watch over her."

"Okay. Thanks." Stepping away, Emily continued, "Can you please come and find me if something changes?"

"Of course," Damon bowed his head, and then returned to his brother.

* * *

Amadeus sat waiting at the end of a smaller table, almost a replica of the one in the large conference room. With more than enough seats for the group, everyone settled in comfortably before continuing.

Amadeus' room was darkly lit with red walls and dark wood paneling. There was something oddly intimidating and equally exciting about the room.

"Thank you, all, for coming so quickly."

"We're glad to see you back to your normal self," Mark smiled, as he sipped from the glass before him, surprised by the lack of water and hint of a wine-like taste.

"Thank you, Mark. I am feeling much better, though I have not yet fully recovered." Amadeus rested his hand atop his chest, as if to rub out an internal ache. "I am sorry to hear about the horrific events surrounding Amy's attack." He had turned to Emily, who took a long gulp from her own glass.

"She'll be okay. She knows it wasn't him," Emily reiterated.

"So what's the plan then? Are we going after Bates and Kavar?" James wanted to expedite the conversation, growing tired of the awkward tension.

"No," Amelia began.

"No?" James interrupted.

"For now, we have a vessel that has come to offer assistance and return you and your team back to Earth. Riley will lead a team of our soldiers in pursuit of Kavar and..."

"Screw that! I'm going with you," James turned to Riley, ignoring Amelia once again.

"James, please let us take care of this," Amadeus tried to calm the angered blonde.

"No," James stood, now pacing his side of the table, "Rick's like a brother to me. I wont go home to sit and wait for him to either be overcome by that asshole, or rot in that cell while you guys figure out what you are doing."

"James, please sit down," Amadeus spoke calmly, but his voice gained attention.

Like a petulant child, James returned to his seat, but not before his final say of, "I'm going with you," directed solely to Riley who sat across from him, smirking devilishly.

During their exchange, Emily and Mark watched as a conversation commenced between Amelia and Amadeus. You could clearly see the frustration in her eyes, before she lightly bowed her head in a silent agreement.

Turning back to the group, Amelia addressed James. "Alright, you and Mark" - she turned her head in Mark's direction before turning back - " may join Riley and his team, but only if you strictly abide by his orders, and Emily and Julia consent." James' triumphant smile dropped at the mention of her second demand.

"Babe?" Mark turned to Emily, who was already grinning at James' internal dilemma.

Turning to her husband, pausing with surprise, she said, "Do you want to go?"

"I think if James is going, I need to join him… I owe it to Rick."

Taking a moment to let her eyes fall upon his features, she thought for a minute. "Okay, if you think you can help, but I want Riley's reassurance that you will be of use, and you won't just be a distraction?" The majority of her statement had been directed to Riley, his gaze holding hers as she spoke.

"Emily, I cant say that their presence won't be a distraction, but it's nothing we haven't all dealt with before; nothing my team isn't prepared for. If they want to come and can obey my command," he paused, turning to James for emphasis, "then they are more than welcome. They are both great fighters…Strong and faster that even I would have expected. Plus, Mark still has traces of my own light and training specific to my own style."

Satisfied with his response, although apprehensive, Emily offered one last nod to Amadeus.

"Very well then," Amelia gave the order.

Over the course of an hour a plan was hatched. Once rescued from their standstill, they were to return to Earth together, where the women would remain, along with Rick, Amelia, and a handful of foot soldiers. Rick was to remain detained in the custody of the Jarly, monitored, and controlled. Even with the news of Amy's continued healing, Rick was a broken man, tortured and vulnerable with his only focus being staying in control of his body. He would be kept at Emily and Mark's residence until Bates had be found and killed.

Meanwhile, Amelia would take charge of Earth's defenses. In small teams, Amelia would command the few using their light to transport to those areas of importance and those most at risk. With their telepathic ability she could offer advice and guidance, even from afar. To the great unease of Amelia and the others in the room, Amadeus announced that he would be joining Riley and the others in their pursuit of Bates, and more evidently, Kavar.

"Sir," one rather short female Jarly stepped up to Amadeus' shoulder. Among the Human race, this particular Jarly would appear of South American decent, all but her eyes, the lightest of blue - almost silver - in their coloring. "We have been alerted to an incoming vessel."

"Biron?" Amadeus asked with hesitation.

"Unclear, Sir. Our sensors were further damaged in the blast. There does not appear to be any hostile movements or hesitation in their approach. From the size and shape, it would appear to be under Jarly control."

"Thank you, Jesi."

With that, the small Jarly left in a rush.

Standing abruptly, Amadeus had the others at their feet. "We need to be prepared for another attack, but more likely this will be our rescue." Turning to Amelia, "You know what to do." In a flash of light he was gone, leaving the others standing still in confusion.

Moving around the table, Amelia barked orders to those that remained. "Riley, take Mark and James. Convene with your team and advise on what we already know. I will meet you in the training bay with additional intel in twenty minutes." Before added questions could be asked, Riley reached across the table, grasping Mark and James each by the arm, and with another flash they were gone.

"Emily, take my hand," Amelia reached out. Within seconds they - accompanied by Isobel - had returned to the medical bay. "I want you to stay here. When Amy awakes, help her dress, and be prepared to move quickly." Their presence had alerted Damon to move, now within earshot. "How is Caleb?" Amelia turned, not seeing his physical approach, but feeling his presence behind her.

"He is well. He woke briefly, moments ago, but now he returns to rest," Damon spoke calmly, emphasized by the frantic movements and orders Amelia presented.

"Good. You've heard the alert?" she asked.

He nodded.

"Stay here with Emily and Isobel. Let Caleb rest as long as possible." Turning to Isobel, "Has his new limb been tested?"

"New limb?" Emily blatantly asked, clearly confused.

"Yes, it has been fitted successfully. It will take some rehabilitation and training, but he will fight again," Isobel answered, ignoring Emily.

Allowing the three to continue their conversation and too curious to ignore the subject, Emily inched away, before turning and edging closer to Caleb's sleeping form. As she reached the edge of his table, her jaw dropped in awe of what lay before her. Now seemingly healed, though pink, fresh skin evident in some areas, Emily focused on his left hand. Only hours before, a healed stump below the elbow accompanied by extensive deep inlaid scarring up onto his shoulder and left pectoral muscle, now lay filled with a flesh-like material. Although pale in comparison to the rest of his body, the new hand lay lifelike with fingernails and freckles.

"It's our version of a prosthesis," Isobel whispered at her side, not wanting to startle her.

"It's amazing. It looks so real," Emily reached forward, gently brushing a finger along the top edge where his old skin met new. "It feels real too," she lightly pressed down, feeling warm skin and muscle.

"For the most part, it will act and appear as if real, though any real strength and control will have to be assisted by our light," Isobel explained.

Emily gasped, pulling her hand back as only the prosthetic portion of Caleb's arm went up in flames. Her eyes darted to his face, meeting with his wide-eyed gaze. A hint of a smile played on his lips.

"Sorry, I didn't mean to wake you," she stepped back.

"It is alright, Emily." Caleb sat up in a fluid motion, placing his lit arm onto the table to balance himself. He swung his legs over the side, ignoring prying eyes. Caleb examined his new limb, opening and closing his fist, while twisting his arm.

"How do you feel?" Isobel stepped closer, occupying Emily's previous space.

"Good." He continued to examine his new body, "I feel good." In a show that caused Emily to even avert her eyes, feeling a voyeur, Caleb reached out with his new hand, cradling the back of Isobel's head before pulling her in closely, crushing their lips together. She rested her palms on the top of his bare thighs as his right hand brushed along her cheek.

Taking another step back, Emily averted her gaze further until she locked eyes with Damon. In a very rare form, he stood with his arms folded, a wide smile spreading across his face as his eyes locked knowingly with Emily's. In an obvious play for attention, Damon turned back to the two before him and clearing his throat rather loudly. Separating fractionally, they lay their foreheads together.

"Brother," Caleb spoke clearly, his eyes still locked with his love's.

"Emily?" A small whisper from a soft voice sounded behind them. In a rush that left her dizzy, Emily spun on her heels and returned to Amy's table where she found her sister blinking rapidly and looking confused.

"Amy, thank God! Are you okay?" Emily reluctantly helped her to sit, tugging town the hem of her t-shirt as she sat only in her panties.

Isobel moved closer, placing a lit hand on Amy's shoulder. "Amy, how do you feel? Does anything still hurt?" Isobel gently moved Amy's limbs, checking for further injuries and any slowed function. She had her gaze into the light, adjusting her eyelids as she asked more questions.

"I'm fine. I'm fine," Amy muttered, still seemingly confused. Turning to her sister she asked, "What happened?" Then after another moment her eyes went wide, "Where's Rick?"

"He's fine. Don't panic. Amy, what is the last thing you remember?" Isobel answered, calling her attention back. In the moments that had passed, Damon and Caleb had stepped up behind them. Now clothed, Caleb looked relatively well, though the dark circles under his eyes and light hollowing in his cheeks told a different story. The brothers now stood in similar clothing, both with arms folded.

"I... I woke up in the middle of the night. Rick was sat up on the other side of the bed, his back to me..." Tears filled her eyes, her head cast down as she tried to remember. "When I reached across to touch him, he went stiff and stood up... He wouldn't answer me, just went into the bathroom. After a while, I went to go check on him and he just sprung at me." Her tears overflowed, rushing to her chin as she locked eyes with Emily. "He attacked me, Em. He did things..." Amy's face contorted with pain as she gripped at the flesh on her sister's arms.

"Okay, Amy listen to me," Emily reached forward, cupping her sister's face and consuming her attention. "It wasn't Rick," she shook her head in emphasis.

"What do you mean? "

"It was Bates. When Rick was being tortured, Bates did something... something terrible to him. He bonded himself to Rick so that he can take over his body and control him. Rick had no idea what he was doing. It was like he was asleep while Bates took control."

"Bates... Bates is in Rick?" Amy asked, even more confused.

"Yes. Rick is back with us now... It seems like he can remain in control as long as he stays awake. As long as he can focus and keep his mind strong," Emily rubbed her thumb across Amy's warm cheek. "Amy... I'm so sorry. We didn't know."

"Oh, Emily..." Amy surged into her sister as they held tight to one another. Emily kept repeating, "I'm sorry."

"Emily, Amy... There was no possible way for you to have known," Isobel said, stepping forward to rub her hand gently between Emily's hunched shoulders.

"That is correct. Unfortunately, this could not have been foreseen or avoided," Caleb added for emphasis.

Pulling back from her sister, sniffling unattractively, Amy wiped the bottom of her nose with the back of her hand, "Caleb! You're awake. Uh... How do you feel?" she asked, continuing to clear the wetness from her face.

"I am well, Amy. As you are," Caleb offered her a sympathetic smile.

"Your hand?" Amy asked, pushing off of the table as Emily helped her add layers of warm clothing.

Once again, Caleb held out his hand, now unlit as he moved and rotated it before her. "It will do, for now," he smirked, gaining the first small smile from Amy.

The room filled with light as Amelia returned. A face-splitting smile took hold of her as she hugged Caleb and praised his recovery, and then turned to do the same with Amy.

"You both look well," Amelia said, then continued as if she had just remembered something important, "The approaching vessel is in fact one of ours. We are readying our teams and preparing to leave. Are they okay to leave the bay?"

"Yes, though I would like them both to remain close to me for observation," Isobel answered.

"Of course."

Amelia went to continue, but Amy interrupted, "I want to see him... I want to see Rick."

Offering unsure glances to the group, Amelia paused on Emily who nodded with encouragement. "Very well, but Amy, you need to know that it is still not safe. He will have to remain where he is for the time being."

"I get that. I... I just need to see him for myself."

Taking her hand and Emily's, Amelia spoke to the others, "Gather what is needed and meet on level 10 in fifteen minutes."

Within moments the three women stood behind a heavy metal door.

Confused, Amy glanced up and down the hallway they were currently occupying, "Where..."

"Rick is behind this door. If you would like, we will give you a few moments of privacy before we need to prepare to move."

"You okay?" Emily asked, "Want me to go in with you?"

"No. I want to see him alone..." Amy answered too quickly, before turning to face her sister, "Just a couple minutes then you can both come in."

Without words uttered, the door slid open as two Jarly guards exited the room, approaching Amelia; it was clear her orders for them to leave the room were given silently.

Amy stood in the spot, staring at the open doorwell just to her right. Taking a deep breath, she moved with hesitation towards it before taking a step forward and into the brightly lit room. At first her sight needed time to adjust. As she grew closer to the glass barricade before her, her gaze searched the other side of the partition until it fell on Rick, who lay partially on the metallic table, his nearest arm over the side with his foot planted on the ground. His forearm covered his face. With calculated movements, Amy moved closer until she stood directly across from the bed, only inches from the glass.

"Rick," she whispered. Slowly lowering his arm, he didn't move his head to face her, though his brows creased, as if he wasn't sure he had truly heard her. "Rick," she spoke louder now.

Cranking his head to the side, he turned and looked up at his wife who stood so delicately before him. In a flash of movement he rushed towards the glass, his eyes wide, pressing his palms against the clear boundary. The rapid movement startled Amy, and though she hated herself for it, she cowered slightly, taking a step back. Real concern, followed by pain, washed over Rick.

"Amy," Rick spoke, clearing his throat as his eyes filled with sorrow.

Taking a breath and squaring her shoulders, Amy took another step forward, closing the distance between them, placing her hands where his were waiting on the glass. "Rick, are you okay?"

"Forget about me. Are you okay?"

"I'm fine," Amy said mechanically.

"You're not fine, you're practically shaking," Rick closed his eyes, scrunching them shut and lay his forehead against the glass. He continued in a whisper, "You're afraid of me."

"No... no, I'm not. I'm just... confused," Amy answered, shaking her head.

"I can see it on your face. You're afraid."

"Not of you," she stated emphatically, "I'm scared about what's going on and I'm worried about you."

Opening his eyes, he didn't meet her gaze as his eyes raked over her skin. "Tell me what I did."

"No."

Rick pulled away, surprised, stepping back until his legs met the metal bed and he took a seat. Resting his elbows on his knees, he bent forward, running his hands through his hair.

"It was bad," he muttered, more to himself than her. After a moment they locked eyes, "Baby, I need to know."

"No, you don't. And even if you did... I cant, not right now. But I know it wasn't you!" Amy answered, still standing with her hands pressed firmly against the glass. "Just know that I am standing here because I am okay. I am your wife and I love you. That's all that matters."

Rick was already shaking his head, "I'm so sorry, baby. You have to know, I would never...."

"Of course, I know that. Please, don't do this to yourself. It wasn't you. You just need to focus and stay strong so he can't come back."

"He won't!"

With that, Emily and Amelia entered the room, followed by the two guards; one held what appeared to be metal shackles.

"Rick, we need to get ready to move," Amelia spoke as she neared the glass.

"Move where?" Rick asked while getting to his feet. If anyone were to see him now, it would seem that he had aged ten years, with the dark exhaustion growing under his eyes, his skin pale, and his eyes glazed.

"Another Jarly vessel has docked with the station. We are in preparation to move a select few onto that ship and continue our journey back to Earth. The others will remain and repair what they can."

"Shouldn't I stay here then?" Rick genuinely asked, while Amy and Emily both blurted, 'No!' in response.

"No, Rick you are coming with us. Though heavily controlled, we have every intention on getting you back home."

"What about Bates and Kavar?"

"Amadeus and Riley have assembled teams, including Mark and James, to hunt them down. Once we have returned to Earth, they will part ways."

"No, please. I need to go with them, I need to help..." Rick stated.

"I am sorry Rick, but you will be little help to them in your current state." Amelia nodded to one guard who placed a lit hand onto the glass between them. With a crunching noise - much like cracking glass - an unseen line formed in the center of the glass. As both parties stepped back, the bottom and top portions retracted into the floor and ceiling, leaving only open space.

Seeming to take a breath of fresh air, Rick stepped forward, towards Amy. "Can I hold you for a moment?" he whispered.

Tears rushing to her eyes as she closed the space between them, crashing into his chest, her arms gripped at his back tightly as he buried his face into her hair. Amy felt movement behind her and with a 'click' she felt something cold around his wrists where they remained behind her. Pulling back, their eyes met before he leant down and offered her a sweet kiss, raising his now shackled hands over her head and stepping back. They both examined the metallic restraints, with only two inches between each hand, his fingers curled inwards by a thin casing only leaving his thumbs moveable.

"I am truly sorry for these," Amelia gestured her head towards the metal.

"It's necessary. I know that," Rick mumbled.

"They will prevent you from igniting your flame, further hindering Bates' ability to take hold."

Rick only nodded in understanding. Amy brushed an errant tear away from her cheek, "How long does he have to be like this?"

"Only until we get back to Earth, at which point they will be replaced by these," Amelia raised her hand with two plain metallic wristbands, nothing extraordinary about them. "These will also prevent the use of light, and can only be removed by someone utilizing light. Once we have returned to the Claybourne residence, I believe supervision by guard will be more then enough."

With that, the group fell silent again; Amelia turned with Emily and Amy on her heels. Rick slowly stepped out of the room followed, closely by the two guards. Navigating the corridors with ease, Amy kept glancing back over her shoulder at Rick, who offered her a weak smile in encouragement, gently pushing her to continue. At last they met with a larger group, who appeared to be moving supplies in and out of the new vessel. Upon their arrival, Mark and James headed to greet them.

"Hey, dude," James patted Rick's shoulder, "You in handcuffs... Now that brings back memories," he tried to joke, feeling triumphant when Rick smirked and shook his head.

"Not funny, James," Rick stated, though he couldn't help but smile.

"Okay, well we're all pretty much set to go. Are you ready?" Riley stepped up behind them, now having changed into darker clothing with weapons tightly attached to the leather-like grips around his waist and upper thighs.

"Yep, ready as we'll ever be," Rick answered for the others, stepping forward toward the narrow corridor that led to the entrance.

CHAPTER TWENTY-NINE

Julia, can you hear me? We're on our way home now. Shouldn't be much longer... Julia?

Those remaining of Earth's soldiers occupied their own quarters. Emily sat in the much smaller common room allotted to her family and Rick's guards. Her hands rested on a small table as she picked at her cuticles and gazed out the near window. Turning away from the starry view, she watched Amy and Rick nestle together on a plush loveseat. Amy lay once again within the confines of his arms, her head in the crook of his shoulder, as they gazed at one another while whispering. Mark and James sat in two single chairs across the room, deep in discussion, no doubt about their next battle.

Leaning forward onto her elbows, Emily covered her face with her hands and rubbed at her eyes with concern and frustration. *Julia, please answer me. Is everything okay?*

"Em, you okay?" Rick spoke from the loveseat.

It did not go unnoticed that he was concerned about her, while he himself lay in shackles.

Taking an audible breath, she dropped her hands and turned to now four sets of eyes, "I'm fine... Just tired." She offered them an unconvincing smile.

Mark stood, stretching before moving to stand behind Emily, where he laid his hands on her shoulders and began to massage her stiff neck. "We're almost home."

"I know," she said rolling her head before letting it drop forward, enjoying his strong hands. "James, have you talked to Julia?" she asked; her eyes closed and her chin resting on her chest.

"No, but last I heard it was late there. I'm pretty sure they're asleep now. John's family has pretty much taken over the basement," James answered, the second half sounding almost sympathetic.

"That's more than fine. At least we know they'll be safe with us," Mark added, working on the knot in Emily's left shoulder.

"Sophie will be with me in my bed, Amy and Julia can share the guest room. We'll find somewhere for Rick, Abel, and the others to go."

"I'll be with Rick," Amy stated as if it were obvious.

"Baby, you need to rest some more. I'm sure the guards will want me in the living room or somewhere where they can keep an eye on me," Rick explained, speaking calmly, but with authority.

"No. I don't care. We've spent too much time apart. I'm not letting you out of my sight." Amy reached up, kissing the side of his mouth, "Maybe Julia can sleep with Emily and Sophie... Your bed is huge, anyway. Rick and I will just take the spare room."

Emily's head whipped up then, desperate to say something, but as her mouth hung open, no words could come. She looked sadly at Rick. He knew what she wanted to say.

"Amy, listen to me. I think it's best we aren't alone together until we get Bates out of my head. I'd never forgive myself if..."

"Stop," she said dismissively. "Okay, I get it... Don't worry, we'll figure something out."

* * *

"Look at this," Emily exclaimed with excitement. The others joined Emily at the wide window. Looking slightly upwards, they watched Pluto come into their sights. The vast globe grew larger as they continued on by, the planet appearing harsh with red-grey swirls across the surface. From their vantage point it looked like a desolate wasteland, speckled with rock formations and dark spots of debris. They remained watching, mesmerized, though it did not take long for them to pass on by, their eyes following the rock until it was out of sight.

"That was amazing. You realize we're probably some of few Humans that have ever seen this view," James smiled, his eyes still on the starry space, searching for any hidden secrets and sights unknown.

As the time passed, the group grew more exited at the prospect of getting home; easily forgotten in the moment that they passed through

Saturn's rings, and grew even more enamored by the sheer size and pull of Jupiter. It was just when Jupiter fell out of sight that the team felt the slowing of the engines, until they came to yet another stand still. Confused, they knew better than to go wandering.

"What's happening?" Mark stepped out of their common room to speak to one of the guards that had been replaced four hours before, after the previous had stood for twelve hours without uttering a single word.

"There seems to be a problem approaching Earth; nothing for you to be concerned with at this time. We will let you know when we hear more," the man spoke, pushing open the door in his way of telling Mark to return to his confines.

Not satisfied, Mark huffed upon returning.

"What's going on?" Emily asked, stepping away from the glass wall; her arms crossed tightly atop her chest.

"He won't tell me anything. Let me talk to Riley," Mark answered quickly, before clearly retreating to his own thoughts. *Riley, what's happened? Why have we stopped?*

Mark, stay where you are. We've just been alerted to a Biron fleet heading our way. This ship has little to no defenses, and would be no match for these types of vessels. We're going to try and use Jupiter's size to conceal us, Riley responded quickly.

Then what? They're still heading towards Earth aren't they? Won't they know we are following them?

There was a long pause before Mark got a response.

Once they are in range of Earth, they will come in contact with the Jarly vessels sent to Earth's aid. Hopefully, they won't pay much attention to us.

Okay... Wait, is Bates on one of those ships?

Yeah, I am pretty sure he is. Mark smiled at Riley's tone; even through silent speak he could hear Riley's excitement.

Well, that's something at least. If we can keep them occupied, we might be able to board before they can get halfway across the galaxy.

Fingers crossed. I'll come see you all when I know more.

* * *

"Dude, go to sleep," Rick muttered from his own seat. Amy lay asleep within the embrace of his arms. Emily slept in a tight ball on Mark's lap; the pair fast asleep. James stood, leaning next to the window, his eyes watching the stars around them. Two additional hours had passed as their vessel lay dormant.

James turned to look over his shoulder at Rick, who stared back, "No. If you're awake I'm gonna stay awake."

"Yeah, but I have no choice. Plus they gave me those adrenalin shots... I couldn't sleep even if I wanted to."

"You look like shit though," James smirked.

"Thanks... Then again, you would too if you had been tortured for days, then in the brief hours of rest, wake to find your body went on a killing spree, attacked the ones you loved, and then were told you basically couldn't fall asleep again or you could go on to do worse or die altogether," Rick said with heavy sarcasm, but it didn't stop James' smirk from falling rapidly, as his face went stiff. "Ah, come on dude, I'm just screwing with you. Just go get some sleep. You're exhausted and you have to get off this ship just to go kick some more ass anyway. You need rest."

"I'm fine," was all James said as he turned and took a seat at the table, his gaze still holding Rick's.

With great effort, Rick eased Amy out of his arms, laying her down on the couch as he made his way to the table, taking a seat across from his best friend. "So what's Riley and Amadeus' plan then?" Rick asked as his right thumb absently scratched at his left cuff.

"Well, it all depends on if Kavar and Bates are together, which Amadeus thinks they will be... Riley's not so sure," James reached for the pitcher of water in the center of the table, pouring two glasses and easing the second glass between Rick's clasped hands. "I don't know why they didn't just put those bracelet things on you now," James wondered aloud.

"I get it. I wouldn't risk it either. This is their second ship... Probably the last chance we are getting back to Earth anytime soon, so if this is needed for the time being, so be it." Rick gestured with his bound wrists.

"Yeah, still fucking sucks."

"Tell me about it! So distract me and tell me about how you plan to kill them."

GLIMPSE INTO THE DARKNESS **231**

"Right… Well, once we board their ship and Amadeus has taken his team after Kavar, Riley is gonna have us stay together in an attack formation. There will be about eight of us together. He thinks Bates will be held up somewhere, surrounded by Biron. Doesn't surprise me. From what I've heard he sounds like a pussy to me." James took a large swig of his drink before continuing, "Trouble is, Bates is a Jarly, meaning not only is he trained with his light, but he can teleport all over the ship. So we need to get a hold of him and get another pair of those bracelets on him so then we can take him down as if he was Human. Even then, he knows how to fight."

"What's to stop him from jumping to another ship or down to Earth?" Rick questions.

"Well apparently when they were jumping us from Earth to the station, that's pretty much the limit to their transporting, safely. We're hoping to get them far enough from Earth and the other ships before we board so he really has nowhere else to go. Then again, if the ship is as big as the station he could be jumping nonstop; that's why we have to tire him out and get those stupid bracelets on him before he can run. One good thing is Bates is proud as fuck…" Rick scoffed in a mock laugh, remembering Bates' banter with him while they were held captive. "He's cocky and he loves to get the last word in, and who better to get him frustrated enough to stick around?" James mock-smiled, tilted his head, and opened his arms.

"Okay, so you get him cornered and take him down," Rick ran through the plan in his mind.

"Yeah, we corner him, weaken him, and take him down."

"Then I'm gonna be free?" Rick asked, a hint of nerves overcoming him. "Dude, I have to be honest, I'm kinda nervous. We are linked and all…"

"No, Rick, don't… Don't worry, don't stress about this. Yes, you are linked, but in light only. They've told us plenty of times…He goes down, you get your life back."

Rick leaned back in his chair, still not seeming convinced. They both sat in silence for a while, deep in thought.

After a minute, Rick surprised James with what he said next. "Do you ever regret it?" he said, barely whispering, then continued when James raised his left eyebrow, questioningly. "Regret agreeing to the whole Jarly unveiling."

It took a moment for James to speak but when he did, Rick was just as surprised. "Yes, I do. More so now, than in the beginning." Leaning back, James linked his hands together before pulling his arms back behind his head as he spoke out to the room, "At first it was exciting. Like we were an elite team chosen for this mission to save the world, ya know?" Rick completely understood. "I mean, not only did we save our friends, but we also got to be the first to see and experience things we wouldn't even dream of. I know we probably would have hooked up anyway, but the whole rescue and events leading up to it made me fall in love with Julia. Hard and fast," James smiled, remembering the few happy moments they had together before and after the rescue in Sierra Vista, but then his smile began to fade. "But then all this shit happened. We were in the limelight for months, interrogated by our own government accusing us of treason, being hounded by reporters and paparazzi. Then they just disappeared on us for weeks, right after the wedding and then... Well the conference, Velo's murder, Julia got hurt, you got taken and tortured, now look where we are." He spread his arms wide again. "You're in shackles, one nap away from being taken over by a sadistic fucking alien. Amy and Julia are both pretty shell-shocked at this point. Emily and Mark have been away from their kid for days, only to come back to a house full of people they barely know and Jarly dictating their lives. So yeah, when I'm alone long enough to deal with all the bullshit, then I do regret it."

"Then again, if it wasn't us then it probably would have been another group. Or if we didn't do what we did and the Jarly did have to pull back, we'd probably all be enslaved by the Birons by now anyway," Rick added.

"Yep," James cracked his knuckles, "I just try and think of the good stuff... The benefits of being united with the Jarly and the fact that we do have options in defending the Human race, even if for only a little while longer."

* * *

Wait. That's all James and the others could do now. They had begun moving three hours ago and still only stars filled their nearest window.

"Seriously, there has to be some news by now," Mark stood from the couch, returning to pace the length of the room. *Riley, come on! We are going insane in this box of a room.*

Minutes passed with no response, then those in the room stood abruptly; even Rick, with his hands still uncomfortably bound in front of him. The dark circles beneath his eyes grew larger as the red in his eyes grew stronger; staying awake was taking its toll, as his body stood sluggishly, half leaning into Amy for support.

Amelia, Riley, and Isobel stood at the threshold of the room.

"Rick, how are you feeling?" Isobel stepped forward with a large glass of thick green liquid. Rick scrunched his nose, recognizing the foul tasting fluid that prolonged wakefulness. Reaching for the glass he raised it to his lips and took in a long gulp, attempting to finish the glass in a single pull.

"Like I could sleep for a week," he answered, gasping for air as he brushed the remnant off of his lips with the back of his right hand, "I feel like I've been awake for a month."

Nodding knowingly, Isobel stepped back, placing the empty glass in the nearby sink. "That's the bond. Granted you have been awake now going on forty hours, but the bond makes it worse. The pull from Bates' light to take over grows stronger with every attempt at control."

"Bates must know by now that we are aware and are purposefully trying to keep you awake. He will continue to try to take over," Riley added, stepping further into the room and sitting almost casually onto the armrest of the nearest sofa. Signaling for the others to take a seat, the room fell silent as the others found a place to rest.

"I don't know how much longer I can stay with it. I can almost feel him pulling me back in," Rick admitted, returning to the loveseat with Amy at his side.

"Unfortunately, that glass was the last safe dose I can give you in such a short time frame," Isobel spoke up, concern bunching her eyebrows.

"Then what? What does that mean, what if Bates takes over again?" Amy asked, now frantic, glancing from Jarly to Jarly.

"We hold out as long as we can, but when the time comes I would rec-ommend a medically monitored status," Isobel offered, her gaze focusing on Rick.

"What does that mean?"

"You're talking about a medically induced coma?" Mark asked, leaning slightly forward, while Emily occupied his lap in one of the single chairs.

"Yes," Amelia answered, matter-of-factly.

"No!" Amy spat with outrange. "You're not going to-"

"I'll do it," Rick stated to the room, ignoring his wife's concern.

"What? No, absolutely not." Amy turned, confused, towards her husband, "Rick, you're not…"

"Baby, I don't want to hurt you or anyone else. If Bates does manage to take over-"

"He won't!" Amy began, her eyes pleading.

"Amy, there's a chance that if Bates took control and found himself locked up, unable to do any more harm, that he will just turn on Rick and do more self-damage. He can't do that if Rick's body is out of it, can he?" James asked Isobel, leaning forward in the other single seat.

"No. As long as we can monitor Rick and get him all set up while he is still Rick, we can control the level of sleep and ensure he stays under. Then when we have taken care of Bates, we can simply revive Rick without complication."

"What if Bates takes over before you can get me under?" Rick asked.

"We will still have to get your body out; it will take more medica-tion and sedative to ensure he stays under, but it will be manageable." Isobel advised.

"If we sedate his body, right after Bates takes control, could that make the real Bates weaker?" Mark suggested, ignoring the disgusted looks he gained from Amy and his wife.

"That could be the case, but I would highly recommend not testing that theory at this time," Riley surprised the others by fielding their question.

"Okay, so we wait until I can't fight it anymore or we get to Mark and Emily's," Rick started, turning to Amy to reassure her. "Then do it."

"Rick, what if you don't wake up?" Amy's face reddened and her lips trembled.

"Amy, I'm not going anywhere. You can stay right there with me. In fact, it will probably be one of the best sleeps in my life," he offered her a smile, raising his hands awkwardly to wipe his thumb below her eyes, drying them before reaching his arms back over her head and pulling her into a tight hold, settling them back into the cushioned seat. "James, if that prick takes over before we can do this, it will be your chance to finally knock me on my ass," Rick joked, and the room laughed; but as their eyes locked, a sincere message passed.

I mean it dude, if I lay a hand on anyone else, I'll never forgive myself.

James blinked, trying to hide his surprise at the sudden internal conversation. *I know. Don't worry, I've got your back.* James smiled for the others to see, but a part of him was more worried than anyone.

You do it and you do it fast. Get the job done, no matter what that might mean.

* * *

Amelia sat on the couch, resting her side into Riley; her arm across his thigh.

"We are within sight of Earth now," Amelia began to explain. "We've slowed our decent, given the present state of affairs."

"What's that supposed to mean?" Emily asked, clinging to Mark.

CHAPTER THIRTY

As night fell in Arizona the silence grew. Julia had fallen into silence as she gently rocked in one of the white-wicker chairs atop the front porch; the sun had set less than thirty minutes before. The red rock in the distant landscape grew darker, until it was all but lost in the blackness. With Abel and John at her sides, in their own seats, the three enjoyed the perks of Emily and Mark's remote hillside home. Lush greenery, artfully placed bordering the red gravel path, surrounded the home; the group relaxed into their seats.

Pulling a blanket around her shoulders, Julia watched John gaze back into the house, watching the rest of his family stay together, watching a movie in the living room as if it were any other day. He smiled as the family laughed at one of Adam Sandler's comical performances.

"How are they?" Julia whispered, pulling back John's attention.

He sighed, "Better than I thought they would be. We're not telling the kids just yet. I don't think Joan understands the magnitude of it all. Richard, is strong… I can tell he is worried, but he's not the type of guy to let it all fall apart when faced with a problem."

"And Kristine?"

"Kristine is terrified. I think she's keeping up appearances for the kids, but she is beyond scared… I know we're all scared, but she never took on the light training. I think the whole concept of these aliens and everything… it's been hard for her to get excited about. I think she knew something like this was coming, even before I told her about the recent stuff." With nothing more to contribute, silence once again filled the air as the three turned back to the night's sky.

"Have you heard any more from James?" Abel asked.

236

"No, just what I told you about the Jarly ship finally reaching them and that they were on their way back, again. I think they basically switched ships and the other team stayed behind to fix the big station. I think the majority of the people stayed behind too. Only our people, Amelia and her team, and a few other soldiers are heading our way. To be honest, I wouldn't blame them if the rest wanted to fix the ship just to hightail it out of here. That was a couple hours ago though; he should be checking in soon, I think they just needed to get some rest."

"What is it?" John asked, recognizing the added concern darkening Julia's eyes.

Hesitating at first, she looked between John and Abel, and then down at her hands as her fingers twisted in her lap. "I think something is really wrong. I don't know what and James wont tell me more, but I just feel like something has happened. Plus he hasn't mentioned Amy or the others; usually she would be the first wanting an update."

Reaching over, Abel took hold of her hand, squeezing it tight, "I'm sure they are all okay. They're been through a hell of a lot in the last little while. They all must be exhausted, and now they know what they are coming back to. I'm sure they are just as worried and distracted."

"Yeah," John added, "just give them some time to focus on whatever they are doing. They will be back before you know it and everything will be fine."

They smiled at her, encouraging her to do the same.

* * *

Jostled awake by the sounds of wild dogs, Julia jumped, still occupying the front porch. Both Abel and John still remained in their own seat, now covered in blankets and breathing heavy in their sleep. Glancing back into the living room, the room was deserted, the television turned off, and only the dim light from the kitchen illuminated the furniture. Turning back to the external surroundings, only the light from the porch lamp offered any direction.

Careful not to wake the others, Julia raised from her seat, rubbing the kink out of her neck as she crept along the porch until she reached the front steps and made her way down onto the gravel below. A flicker of glowing light drew her attention to the right, where she noticed all five of the Jarly standing still, engrossed in discussion. Gaining on them, Marcel and Christopher noticed her approach.

"Julia, I recommend you return to the house," Marcel stepped forward.

"What? Why?" Julia stopped mid-step, confused.

With a sympathetic smile, Marcel stepped closer, raising his hands to rest on her shoulders. Her eyes grew with concern before he turned her to look back toward the house and into the night sky. With an audible inhale Julia's gaze drew upwards into the night sky, where the darkness of night and small twinkling of starlight had been replaced by dozens of mechanical lights, obscuring the view. A dreadful feeling burrowed into the pit of her stomach as her eyes jumped from one light to the next; it seemed as though hundreds of lights had appeared, not close enough to make out an outline of any ship or vessel, Julia recognized the similar lights from the night of the rescue, one year before. Then, Amelia had raised her lit hand in welcome, but this unveiling was not joyous or familiar. The yellow Jarly lights were clearly outnumbered by the green glow of unfamiliar forms.

"Julia," Marcel whispered over her right shoulder, "they're here."

A SNEAK PEEK AT BOOK THREE

CHAPTER ONE

"Abel, John, wake up!" Julia rushed up the steps of the wooden porch, her feet slapping with every step.

"What? What is it?" John asked. Still half asleep, he stood, pulling his blanket aside.

"They're here."

"Who's here?" Abel asked, looking around the driveway as if someone had just pulled up in a car.

"The Birons," Julia exclaimed, talking so fast that she almost walked into the front door, before pushing it open in frustration.

"What?" Abel and John exclaimed. Now fully awake, they rushed down the creaking steps and onto the front path, kicking gravel as they went. Their heads were held high as they ran further out of the blocking view of the house, and then they both stopped, eyes frozen on the lights above. Swiveling their heads in amazement they took in the night sky, almost completely overcome with twinkling colors of all shapes and sizes. They watched as the duplicate of shooting stars moved into position with a flash of an ominous light.

"We need all of you back into the house," Marcel approached with heavy feet. His shoulders somehow appeared broader as his jaw clenched. It was clear he was trained in battle and his body was on autopilot.

"What are they doing?" John asked, ignoring Marcel's request as he and Abel remained looking up.

With a huff, Marcel stopped, following their gaze as he stood stiffly, folding his arms across his chest. "They haven't offered any communication yet. They appear to be strategically aligning themselves around Earth... Waiting."

"Waiting for what?" Abel looked at Marcel then.

240

With an almost indecipherable shrug of his shoulders Marcel continued to look up. "Biding their time as more of their fleet arrive, waiting for the Humans or Jarly to attack first. They're clearly in no rush, and they are already outnumbering the Jarly vessels two to one." The group was surprised when three fighter pilot jets flew over above with a loud hiss. "I guess your military fleet is getting prepared," Marcel commented as they watched the small fleet move off and into the distance.

"Cool!" Erik surprised the others, now standing at the base of the porch, his eyes on the night sky watching the lights grow.

"Erik! Back in the house, now." John panicked, rushing towards his son.

"Awe, come on Dad...I wanna see," Erik batted away at his father's attempts to gently push his back up the steps.

"John?" Kristine pushed open the heavy screen door, which had cooled the house in the dead of night, but offered no shield to the outside brightness emanating from above. Stepping out further onto the porch, Kristine's hand went to her mouth, covering a gasp of shock, as a fearful cry escaped her lips. Her eyes grew wider and she craned her neck.

"Sweetheart, everything is fine. Can you take him?" John gripped his arm around his son's waist, hoisting him up to the top step. "Kristine?" John spoke softly, waiting on the bottom step, "Baby, go back inside. Keep everyone inside."

Seeming to regain her senses, Kristine placed both hands on Erik's shoulders and steered him into the house. "But, Mom! I wanna see... I wanna stay with Dad," Erik continued to complain, while John stepped up to the house, closing the door and shutting exterior screen from the outside, returning to the group.

"What can we do?" John asked, stepping up to Marcel and the others.

"Nothing, for now. But we can't very well patrol the grounds and worry about the rest of you, so please return to the house and stay inside until we hear more," Marcel asked with just enough frustration in his tone to get their feet moving.

* * *

James, are you on your way home? Where are you now? Julia looked out of the kitchen window with concern; the lights in the sky had faded as the sun rose, concealing what she knew still lay waiting just beyond their grasp.

Yes, baby, I'm here. Are you okay? Clear concern echoed James' words.

Oh, thank God.

Julia, are you okay? Are the Jarly still with you guys?

Julia had to pause to really consider his question. Was she okay?

Julia?!

Yes... Yes, we're fine, for now! When are you coming back? Have you seen what's out there? Babe, there are hundreds of lights. Just hovering there, I don't think Marcel and his team know what they should be doing... I'm scared, James. I want you to come home. I need you to be here, already.

James replied with an internal huff, frustrated that his girl needed him, and admittedly, he needed her.

I know, baby. And we're doing everything we can to get back there. We're so close, but we're also on the other side of the Biron and Jarly wall. We can't move any closer without causing a reaction. They're trying to calculate the best way to get us back home. I promise baby, we'll be there as soon as we can.

I know you will. After another brief pause, Julia continued her probing. *James, where are Amy and Rick? Why haven't I heard from either one of them, are they okay?*

His hesitation was evident. Julia couldn't be sure, but she thought she heard an agonized moan in response. He almost pleaded with her to let it go, until they could discuss everything in person. So much had happened in such a short amount of time.

James, don't do this, don't shut me out. I know something has happened... I have a right to know if my friends are okay.

Julia, they're both fine, Okay? A lot has happened, and yes, there are things that we will have to discuss, but I'm not going to try and explain that right now. Just know they are both alive, breathing, exhausted, and a bit shell-shocked, so just give them their time.

Surprising even herself, Julia gasped as the single tear that brimmed over her right eye, fast-paced trickling down to her chin. She squeezed them both shut, taking a shuddering breath that even James sensed.

Okay...

Baby, we will be with you soon. His words came fast and sympathetic. *I love you.*

With that, he was gone, and her concern only increased as she felt a rumble as another group of American fighter pilots passed across the early morning sky. Her gaze followed, craning her neck as she watched them pass over the city center and turn left, as one.

"Julia?" She turned in time to see Kristine enter the kitchen, surprised to witness Joan already seated at the dinner table behind her, blowing at the steam emanating from the teacup she held before her.

"Are you okay, dear?" Joan noticed Julia's confused expression as she lowered the mug.

Clearing her throat, she hummed her reassurance as she took a seat at the table, watching Kristine make her way around the kitchen, opening doors and cupboards as she went.

"Can I get you something?" Julia asked, leaning on the table with both hands, lifting once again from her seat.

"I'm fine. Sit back down. Just looking for a spoon?" Kristine asked, her eyes still probing the kitchen.

"That one," Julia pointed to the drawer embedded beneath the island top. "The right side."

"Thanks."

Ten minutes passed in silence before Abel walked in, his hair damp and glistening in a stylish mess, his cheeks flushed, his clothes clinging to his hard chest, clearly having dressed in a hurry after his shower. He moved smoothly towards Julia, Sophie clinging to him, with her left hand raised to tighten her grip around the neck of his t-shirt, her faced buried in his neck.

"I heard her crying," he said by way of explanation, as he reached down, easing her grip as he placed her into Julia's open arms.

"Oh, sorry. I should have been listening more closely." Julia grew concerned, looking down at her goddaughter, whose eyes were watery, her cheeks red and wet. Though Sophie no longer cried, it was clear she was unhappy as she now clung into Julia's embrace, the fast pace of her pacifier indicating her discomfort and hunger. "Are you hungry, baby girl?" Julia brushed her hand gently down Sophie's cheek, as the child nestled her face below Julia's chin.

Making to stand, Abel held out his hand to stop her, "Stay put, I'll get her breakfast ready."

"Thanks." Julia offered him a brief smile as she gently kissed Sophie's crown, rocking them both back and forth.

Knowing his was around the kitchen, Abel made short work of preparing a bottle of formula for Sophie. Light giggles drew his attention back to the table behind; a wide smile pulled at his cheeks as he watched Joan reach across the table, gently tickling Sophie's bare feet. Where she clung to Julia, she raised up, a smile forming around the soother, as she tried to pull her feet away. An eventual squeal from Sophie had the room laughing together.

"Mom!" an angry cry from Tess in the basement pulled the group's attention. Children could be heard fighting from below, before a tearful scream filled the air. "MOM!"

Kristine slouched in her seat before rolling her eyes and getting to her feet. "They're the best at that age," she jutted her chin towards Sophie before offering the others a weak smile.

"Here we go." Abel paced towards Julia with enthusiasm, watching as Julia turned Sophie in her embrace for a feeding, and as Sophie's little hand came up to her face, eyes locked on her bottle as she gripped the pacifier, dislodging it from her lips and dropping it wherever she saw fit, her mouth open wide, tongue already moving, waiting for her meal.

Placing the nipple to her lips, Sophie pulled it in, her eyes closing contently as little hums of appreciation could be heard with each breath. Gripping the side of the bottle with her right hand, absently her left raised up until it tangled in Julia's soft hair, her fingers playing with it, comforted with the feel. Unable to raise her head, Julia grinned widely, her gaze reaching Abel's as he smiled and took a seat in Kristine's vacated chair.

* * *

"Have you heard any more?" John asked Marcel, as he and Abel exited the house, onto the attached upper deck. The others had remained inside, waiting patently, while trying to distract one another.

"Not yet. How is your family?" Marcel turned at their approach, his gaze previously on the sky beyond.

"They're hanging in there. We haven't told the kids anything... Erik thinks these are all Jarly," – John pointed to the late afternoon sky where the growing lights grew brighter and more persistence - "Joan is oblivious, as well. I think Richard would like to keep it that way. She has a way of overreacting..."

"Though, I don't think any reaction to that would be an overreaction," Abel added, his eyes briefly pointing upwards for emphasis.

"Good, it is best to keep them preoccupied for the time being," Marcel responded, ignoring Abel's comment.

"What is your plan to secure the house?" John asked.

Not surprised by the question, Marcel began to detail the protective strategy surrounding the premises, surprising both men at the level of security being placed on their lives. Over the course of the night, two other teams had been recruited to the area, and now a group of seventeen Jarly men and women patrolled the near area.

"Surely, we should be alerting others in the area to join us? More Humans could use this level of protection." Christopher was already shaking his head at Abel's comment, approaching the others. "We've seen the news, the world is already in panic mode. You can't really hide a giant fleet of warships hovering over every major city. And worse, the Jarly are getting the blame for all of this. People are scared. You need to make some kind of announcement to the general public, you need to reassure the Humans that you are on their side."

"Our orders stand as is. We are allowing the Human governments to make decisions based on the wellbeing of their people. When your governments are ready, I am sure an announcement will be made, and I too pray that many Jarly representatives will be invited to speak on behalf of our people as well." Christopher paused, his gaze focusing on the above. "We do not intentionally wish to add to the fear, but for now, those of you that reside in this house are our top priority," Christopher explained.

"Thankfully, the Claybourne residence is well hidden, secluded from the town in the pursuit of added privacy. This wooded space" – Marcel gestured to the large trees that acted as a backdrop to the house, bordering the back yard – "provides much needed shelter and exclusivity."

The sun had only moments before it would inevitably set over the horizon.

"As soon as the sun goes down, the lights are going to get brighter and people will go ballistic; there will be mass hysteria in the streets if an explanation is not given soon," John said.

As if on queue, a familiar siren tore through the night's sky. Emanating from the city center, the terrifying call of an air-raid siren drew the attention of those outside.

"Remain inside. Stay with your loved ones," Marcel barked back at the shock-stilled John and Abel, as he and his brother ignited their flames and lunged for the deck railing. Without hesitation, they raised themselves up and over the edge. Surprised, John and Abel glanced and each other before rushing after them, reaching the railing, they looked down in time to see the two figures land gracefully on their feet below, the fifteen-feet drop doing little to distract them as they sprinted towards a grouping of lights in the distance.

* * *

"What's going on? What do we do?" Kristine all but collided with John as he rushed inside, feeling rather ridiculous as he turned to lock the deck door. He offered a knowing glance at Abel, as they made their way around the wide glass windows, lowering blinds and pulling curtains into place, further disrupting any view in, or out.

Pulling Kristine into his side, he cradled her head to his chest, speaking into her hair. "We're fine at the moment. Just keep the kids downstairs… away from the windows. There hasn't been an announcement made yet. I think this is just to ensure everyone stays inside and doesn't try anything stupid."

"What could anyone possibly do?" Julia asked, entering the kitchen.

Abel shrugged, "You never know. People become surprisingly resourceful when they are afraid."

Heavy footsteps could be heard nearing the front of the house. At least three pairs of shoes marched along the creaking porch. The small group stiffened; given the continued siren blasting in the distance, their thoughts were distracted. Richard entered the kitchen from the right side, through the open door, having been in the basement.

The front door swung open to reveal Marcel. Letting himself in, he closed the door. "When I leave, I want you to lock this." He gestured to the heavy door, before making his way to the group. "I have news... Amelia and her team are preparing to travel back. They will only have a short amount of time as the Birons are distracted. They should be with you within the next ten minutes." Looking around the floor plan, he seemed to be assessing the house, though he had been inside many times. Nodding as he made mental notes, he said aloud, "The structural integrity of this house is good. I suggest you all take shelter in the basement, remain away from any walls or doors, and keep the noise down." Marcel began to back away, shifting towards the front of the house.

"Are they releasing ground troops? Do you think we'll be attacked directly?" John asked, clearly concerned.

"Not as of yet, I am simply advising on the situation. Unfortunately, a Biron vessel appears to have picked up on our communications, and has settled in the airspace above. They have made no move, just yet, but they have clearly noted the large number of Jarly surrounding this residence; it will be all the more intriguing to them."

"Fantastic," Abel blurted with heavy sarcasm. "So what was one of the most secure places in the United States, now has a big neon sign staying, *We Are Here!?*" Abel gestured with his right hand raised, as if emphasizing each word on a banner.

Marcel's mouth opened, but closed quickly, choosing to ignore the comment. "Just stay inside," he said with a bite of finality as he turned and pushed past the threshold closing the door.

ABOUT THE AUTHOR

Lauren Somerton

Writing stories has always come easily for Lauren Somerton. Born in Southern England, Lauren grew up in Calgary, Alberta, Canada, where her education included subjects in cultural studies and ancient history. This led to a Bachelors Degree in Anthropology, where her continued studies spurred a love of mythology and conspiracy theories, both of which come through strongly in her writing. Encouraged by her parents to read exten-

sively and coax her creativity through writing, Lauren has used her vivid imagination and quest for answers to bring us a fascinating science fiction adventure filled with conspiracy and intrigue, along with stimulating technical and combat detail. Lauren truly enjoys telling stories, relishing in the idea that people always want to be surprised and excited, captivated and distracted.